WE
ARE THE
BEASTS

ALSO BY GIGI GRIFFIS

FOR ADULTS

The Empress

FOR YOUNG ADULTS

The Wicked Unseen

GIGI GRIFFIS

WE
ARE THE
BEASTS

DELACORTE PRESS

Text copyright © 2024 by Gigi Griffis
Jacket art copyright © 2024 by Jorge Mascarenhas

All rights reserved. Published in the United States by Delacorte Press, an imprint of Random House Children's Books, a division of Penguin Random House LLC, New York.

Delacorte Press is a registered trademark and the colophon is a trademark of Penguin Random House LLC.

GetUnderlined.com

Educators and librarians, for a variety of teaching tools, visit us at RHTeachersLibrarians.com

Library of Congress Cataloging-in-Publication Data is available upon request.
ISBN 978-0-593-70772-2 (trade) — ISBN 978-0-593-70773-9 (lib. bdg.) — ISBN 978-0-593-70774-6 (ebook)

The text of this book is set in 11.3-point Warnock Pro Light.

Editor: Alison Romig
Cover Designer: Trisha Previte
Interior Designer: Cathy Bobak
Copy Editor: Colleen Fellingham
Managing Editor: Tamar Schwartz
Production Manager: CJ Han

Printed in the United States of America
10 9 8 7 6 5 4 3 2 1
First Edition

For the feral girls. Always bite back.

1765

1

THIS LAMB IS GOING TO BE THE DEATH OF ME.

I don't mean that figuratively. He's been hell-bent on dying ever since he was born. Running headfirst into bramblebushes so deep that we both come out looking like we lost a knife fight. Catapulting himself into deep pools with steep sides he can't climb out of. And now: off the cliff. Like he thinks he can fly.

It's only luck that catches him on a small outcropping with a crooked tree. Fifteen feet down the cliff. And this time he's really ruined me because have I mentioned that I hate heights? Not mentally, not on purpose—but hate in the way that I can't help. Where my body goes all funny and turns to stone.

"Poor baby." Clara's voice is breathless, and her deep-brown eyes are already brimming with tears, like the little softy she is. A tear collects in her black lashes, bounces off in a blink to trace a path down rich-brown skin.

"Poor devil, more like," I mutter. "Merde."

I shake my shoulders, trying to stave off the rubbery feeling of looking over the cliff edge. And then, before the fear can paralyze me fully, I'm on my knees, backward, pale hands clenched around a tree root, and over the edge.

My heart is thunder, and my mind the static of a building storm. The thoughts come, unbidden: I see myself crash to the sharp rocks below. Break my back. Crack my head like an egg. My limbs twist outward like a spider's, dark shadows over gray stone. Dead before I turn seventeen.

I clench the root and my first handhold, tense my whole body. Not today, Satan. I'm not going to freeze on this climb. I'm not going to lose this goddamn lamb. I'm certainly not going to die and leave Clara and Mémé with the whole burden of life on their own. They saved me once. What kind of repayment would that be?

The lamb is screaming as I ease myself onto the next foothold, and I wish he'd stop. If there's anything that makes this worse, it's the sound of his fear scraping against my own.

I ease to the next handhold. Another. Another. And then I'm there, the cursed lamb trying to clamber up my leg and almost throwing himself to his death. I grab him by the front leg and smush him between myself and the rough stone.

"Fool." I scowl at him, easing myself more steadily onto the outcropping, propping one foot against the crooked tree.

"BLEAAAA," he answers, and that better be lamb language for *Thank you, goddess.*

I glance up. How am I going to get out of this? Climbing all the way back up looks pretty impossible. Below me, the cliff gets smoother, so descending isn't an option. Maybe I could somehow unlace my dress and throw it up to Clara and she could hoist me . . .

"Clara!" I shout, realizing the simpler solution. "Take off your dress and throw me the end!"

"Joséphine." Clara's voice has an edge of incredulous laughter above me, and I glance up. She's lying on her stomach at the edge of the cliff, one hand around a root, the other holding a sturdy-looking branch down toward me.

"Oh." Trust Clara to already have solved the problem while I was spinning out about whether one of us should get undressed.

She raises an eyebrow. "Did you seriously just suggest I take off my dress?"

"I'm kind of in crisis."

She shakes her head.

"All right, grab hold."

Clara has moved to brace her feet around the roots of the tree above and is reaching the branch as far toward me as she can. Still, there are a few feet I'll have to climb on my own before she can help. With a screaming, frantic lamb in my arms.

Merde, I didn't think this through.

I reach behind my back and loosen the ties on my dress (I guess I wasn't completely wrong to consider dresses as a solution to our problems), then shove the squirming, muddy, screamy lamb down the front and tighten the ties as much as I can.

"BLEAAAA!" he screams, and it echoes in my ears even after he finishes.

"Sacré Dieu, if you move an inch, I will throw you down this cliff myself," I mutter, rubbing slow circles into his head to calm him.

"BLEA." He's quieter this time. Good.

Here goes nothing. I white-knuckle into the nearest handholds and ease off the ledge. Up. A few inches. A few more.

"BLEAAA."

"You, shut it."

Clara giggles, a release of energy more than mirth, but I focus on the wall, the fool lamb trembling against me. This is the most ridiculous rescue in all of history; I'm sure of it.

And then my left handhold gives, and I feel my body tilting to the right.

No. NO. NO, GODDAMN IT. This is not how I'm going to go. Egg-cracked, broken-backed on the rocks below, my brain flashes the images at me, and I growl—a guttural sound, a wild thing hell-bent on survival.

I tense every muscle, pushing the fool lamb and myself back toward the cliff and ending up with my face smashed against rock, my left hand scrabbling for another crack in the wall.

Safe.

Safe, I tell myself. My brain responds with a swooping feeling, the image of me and the fool lamb smashed on the rocks together.

"You can do this." Clara's voice is steady above me. "You're almost to the branch. You're so close."

I take a beat. Steady my heart, then go. Left foot. Right. Left hand. Right. And then I'm halfway up the cliff, and the branch hovers just overhead.

"Good. Now grab the branch with one arm, and I'll pull you as far as I can; then you'll need to grab the wall again while I sit up and get a better bracing position." Clara, so gentle and seemingly breakable in day-to-day life, is steady in a crisis. Calm and calculated. So many steps ahead of how we're going to pull this off. The thought calms me. I might make it out of this fool lamb's death trap yet.

I wrap my left hand around the branch, feel it pull taut.

"On three," Clara says. "One, two, *three*."

I let go of the wall, press my right hand against the lamb in the front of my bodice, hold tight to the branch with my left, and push upward with my toes. And Clara—stronger than she looks—hefts me up several feet.

"Grab the wall." Her voice is strained with effort, and I do as I'm told, finding new footholds, new handholds.

"All right. I'm on the wall." I let go of the branch, feel it pull away from my hand as Clara sits up above me, braces herself in a seated position instead of on her belly, and then lowers the branch to me again.

"This time grab as tight as you can and hold on for dear life," she says. "I'm going to pull you up as fast as I can. A burst of energy."

I nod, even though she probably can't see me. My brain sends the worst image yet: Us failing. Me pulling Clara down with me to our deaths.

My breathing is staccato. My heart a drum.

I grab the rough bark, clutch tight.

"NOW!" I shout.

"BLEAAAAA!" the lamb screams.

7

Now: she pulls.

Now: my face scrapes across sharp cliff.

Now: the lamb is slipping, and I press my arm against him.

"AUGHHHHHH!" Clara shrieks. A cry of pure determination. The scream of a survivor. A savior.

And then I'm at the cliff edge, my foot catching a stone, pushing me up and over the edge. Rolling away from the drop-off, rolling toward safety.

Clara falls backward as I release the branch, and we collapse into a pile mere feet from the edge of the cliff.

Our more well-behaved sheep edge toward us, curious, as we both devolve into a cacophony of tears and giggles and hiccups. In this moment, we're either the world's worst shepherdesses—or the world's best. I wrap my arms around her, pressing the now-struggling lamb in between us.

"If you think I'm letting you out of this dress, you have another think coming," I scold him as he kicks me, knocking my head covering off and releasing unruly red curls into the wind.

"Nom de Dieu," Clara murmurs, the swear more like a prayer in her mouth. "If you ever do that again, I will kill you myself."

"And God won't blame you." I roll onto my back and press my hands over my mouth, cold fingers on warm lips, and breathe out long and loud. *I almost just died.* I'm even more aware of it now that I'm on solid ground. How utterly foolish it was to go over that cliff. Though what choice did I have? These sheep are everything. The only thing standing between us and starvation. Without their wool to sell, we have nothing except our foraging skills to keep us alive. And those wouldn't be enough, not with the harsh winter that's inevitably coming, the snowdrifts taller than a man, the ice strangling out every green thing worth eating, strangling us, too, if we let it.

I'd do it again. I know that. I'd risk my life a thousand times for Clara and Mémé—who saved me and raised me when winter took my own family seven years ago. I'd give anything for them, people with nothing who gave me everything.

I roll over beside Clara and reach for her hand, squeeze it, white skin against brown. The early morning air is chilled, but her skin is hot where it presses against mine. Sweat-glazed from our brush with death.

I sit up and pull her up with me, take her in. She's mud-drenched front and back from lying on the cliff, her hands scraped as raw as my own. That mud down her front was for me. Tears rise to my eyes.

"So, you want to tell me what you were thinking with the whole 'take off your dress' idea?" she asks, laughing a little as she uses her thumbs to wipe tears from the corners of my eyes.

Instead of answering, I wrap her in a hug, and neither of us lets go for a long time.

Once we've done our best to wipe off the worst of the mud and my dress is re-laced sans lamb, we continue our normal loop with the sheep, guiding them away from the cliff (for*ever*) and into the gentle slope of a wildflower field at the edge of thick forest. No rest for a shepherdess in Gévaudan, even after a brush with death. There's no possibility of retreating to the safety of home, the warm comfort of a blanket on a straw mattress. The sheep must eat, and so we must continue.

As we walk, my heart smooths back into a normal rhythm, the familiarity of birch bark and yellow wildflowers like a balm. The sheep love it here, where it's heavy with dandelions and ryegrasses. And even though the forest is dark and foreboding, I've rarely had to fend off a wolf.

"We should probably move them away from the trees." Clara fractures the silence. "There was another attack just last week—only a few miles from here."

Ah, yes. Lambs falling from cliffs and nudging us over the edge of starvation aren't the only danger this year. Wolves aren't the only predators lurking in our forests. For the past year, shepherdesses in the region have been disappearing along the edges of dark-wood forests and plunging canyons. Most reappear in pieces. A leg, an arm, a skull sucked dry.

None have been here in the village, but the rest of Gévaudan is full of horror stories, and we all know the evil could come for us here in Mende any day now.

We call the culprit *the beast* because nobody knows what it is. Even those who've seen it. It's a wolf but not a wolf, they say. Larger, deadlier, with fire in its eyes, murder in its heart. Some believe it's a flesh-and-blood creature. Others, a devil conjured from the pits of hell. Still others, a human trick—trained by man to kill or conjured by a witch to do her bidding.

I shiver, even though the sun is up now.

"From the stories I've heard, it won't matter how close we are to the trees," I answer after a beat. "It prefers hunting in the open areas. In fact"—I try to lighten the mood with a grin—"perhaps we'd be safer taking them in to graze on willows in the forest."

"Or maybe a wolf would take the lamb you just risked your life for."

I glance at the lamb, now happily munching a dandelion patch, already forgetting his ordeal. If the beast did show up, that particular baby would probably march right up to it like it was his long-lost mother and invite it to eat him in a single bite.

"A wolf I can handle," I answer, brandishing the short staff I carry with a sharp knife tied tight to its end—a homemade pike. We all have them around here. If you're not careless, they're usually enough to convince a wolf that your sheep aren't his supper. The beast, though. The beast is something else—something more interested in girls (and the occasional boy) than lambs, something not easily dissuaded by staffs and knives. And since peasants aren't allowed to carry guns, if the beast comes, there's nothing to do but run.

"I'd really like it if we could move away from the wood." Clara tries a new angle on her request, and this one gets me. She's saved my life enough times that I owe her when she asks for a favor. Even if I disagree that it'll make a difference.

I click my tongue and start to walk away from the tree line, my sheep following in their usual chaotic formation. Clara's sheep cluster tighter and walk closer to her as she follows.

"Did you hear about Geneviève?" Clara asks, her shoulders dropping with relief as we shy away from the wood, step by step.

"That she's gone—or something else?" The fool lamb has taken an interest in the forest, and I nudge him onward with my shin, shaking my head.

"The girls in the village are saying she ran away—maybe to

Paris. She always did glamorize the idea of a city." Clara's voice is lighter, hopeful, and something about that creates a pinching sensation in my chest. Is Clara thinking of *leaving*?

I frown. "Or the beast got her. You know that's more likely."

Clara furrows her brow at me. "That's a dark interpretation."

"Or a realistic one." I shrug, trying to look casual and feeling anything but. The idea of Clara leaving pinches harder in my chest, and I try not to think about it.

"Well, *I* like to think she got away. That she's in Paris now, finding her way."

"You didn't even like her," I say. A rare thing that I get to accuse Clara of, since she tends to grant people the benefit of the doubt. But Geneviève was impatient with Mémé one too many times, and Clara has given her the cold shoulder ever since.

"I never said I don't like her." Clara stops walking.

"You didn't have to. She might not know it, but *I* can tell when you hate someone."

"*Hate* is a strong word." She pauses. "Besides, then her going to Paris would be a good thing in two ways. Someone got out, *and* I never have to see her again."

I'd normally enjoy Clara admitting that she doesn't want to see someone again, but I'm stuck on the words *someone got out* and how uncomfortably close they are to *I want out.* So I just grunt in a way that I hope ends this horrible conversation and redirect my focus onto the sheep spread out around us, the sunrise colors lighting up the trees, shifting them from dark to dusky to orange and pink.

We're not far from the forest—I can still see the individual knots on the trees—when I see the miracle beside a lonely, twisted tree ahead, so far from the rest of its fellows. The sight uncinches that place in my chest, and I breathe the cold, clean morning air as I watch.

Butterflies.

Hundreds of them, their wings shimmering, flitting, flickering. They're orange and red, sunset and rose. Heart-shaped wings beat gently in the warming morning air. Like a promise that even after one of the scariest mornings of my life, things will be all right. There's still beauty in the world.

"Clara," I breathe. "Look."

They're so perfect, so mesmerizing—magic, miracle—that I don't notice the shape of them until I step too close and they all take to the sky at once: an excitement of orange red against the blue-gold heavens.

But.

But.

My mind pauses, trips over itself, pauses again. The red is wrong, its wrongness like a cold sweat, a splinter just under the skin. Something I can't quite reach.

It's the red. Something about the red.

Not the red of perfectly traced shapes on a wing—symmetrical arcs, circles, lines. It's a red of chaotic drips and splashes. Like the butterflies have been dipped in paint, doused in a spilled bowl of stew.

No. Not paint. Not soup.

Blood.

The butterflies have been dipped in *blood.* Have dipped themselves in it.

Clara realizes what we're looking at just as I do and falls to her knees beside me, muddy hand over mouth. My hand flies up to my own. Time slows, and my vision narrows until what's below the butterflies is all I can see.

It's a body: blood-soaked, still as a stone.

Boy-shaped.

A boy our age.

The butterflies are draped across and flying away from a corpse.

The beast.

The beast.

The beast was here.

2

OH LA VACHE, *THE BEAST WAS HERE*. AND HERE SO RECENTLY. The body still warm when I reach out to touch his arm, to make sure I'm not seeing things. Clara is even more practical, her fingers feeling for a pulse in his neck. Neither of us is rewarded. This boy is dead. We should have already been certain: there's too much blood for any other conclusion.

The ground around him is a wreckage, too. Weeds torn up at the roots, flowers shredded, smashed, flung at every angle. The butterflies take flight not only from a corpse but from a battlefield. A place where this boy must have fought tooth and nail for his life.

I picture his fingernails raking through the deep-black dirt. His arms thrown upward in vain to protect the paper-thin skin of his throat. The kicking, twisting, screaming mess that not a single one of us must have heard this far out.

My throat is so tight that I'm shocked that any air is getting through. I glance at the trees that I was so nonchalantly walking past only minutes ago, a thousand shades of green and gold, shadow and light. A dozen scents of pine and fern and dew-soaked dirt. Is that a movement between the trunks? The flash of animal eyes? Or just a trick of the light?

"We need to get help." Clara is the first to speak.

I look at her, somber. "What could they do now?"

"Search the forest for it. Enough men could take it down. They just haven't been able to find it yet. It could be nearby." Her breathing is too fast, and I reach out and squeeze her shoulder.

"You're right. Go. I'll stay with the sheep. Go get help." The unspoken part: If the beast comes back, I'd rather it be me here than Clara. I'd rather this time I save her instead of the other way around.

She would hesitate if she knew I was thinking that way, but her heart is with the boy on the ground. *She probably knows him,* I realize with a twist in my chest. Clara knows everyone in the village. He'll be more than a boy to her—more than the nameless tragedy he is to me. He'll be a name, a family, a story, a list of ailments she's treated, secrets she's kept. Clara is something of an amateur healer, and everyone in the village has come to her at one time or another. She's such a good listener that they all bring their wishes alongside their wounds. Fears alongside fevers.

"Go," I say again. Because going is helping, and she'll need to help.

She reaches out to squeeze my hand, a line of worry creasing deeper between her eyebrows, and then she turns and starts to run back along the path toward the village. Her sheep, confused, try to follow at first, but I manage to get their attention and direct them back to the dandelions. My own lamb, keeping up his bastardry for the day, takes that as his cue to wander toward the trees. Oh là là, tell me I wasn't predicting the future when I said this little idiot was going to march up to the beast and call it Mama.

"Get back here, you," I call out, my voice as tight as my body as I march toward the tree line and sweep him up with one arm.

The forest stretches before me, all soft and golden in the morning light. The exact type of place you wouldn't expect to die. The exact type of place I *might* die.

My heart skips a beat.

If this *was* the beast, the boy is still so intact. No missing leg. No missing head—the beast's signature move. Did we interrupt the evil thing's meal? Is it crouched just a few feet away? Is it—

A movement snags on the edge of my vision. I squeeze the lamb involuntarily, and he screams in protest. Is that the noise I'll make when it—

No.

My mind catches up with my eyes. The movement is something small. Eyes flash at me through a bush, but they're not a predator's. Too wide, too afraid.

I blink. Blink again. It's—*a child.* A skinny girl, maybe seven years old, ghostly pale, big-eyed and bony-kneed, dark brown hair almost blending into the tree trunk she's pressed up against. She's tucked between the twisted roots of a large tree, mostly hidden behind the dense scrub at its base, ferns the size of her whole torso.

I unfreeze and step toward her, shifting the lamb to one hip and offering my hand, palm up. "You can come out now. It's gone."

I don't *know* that. But I do know that hiding won't help when the thing hunting you is a predator. At least, not the predators I know best: wolves. They'd sniff you out even if you looked exactly like a tree yourself.

She doesn't move.

I step closer. "Really, it's all right. You're all right."

Her eyes dart to the lamb in my arms, who is thrashing like a fish in an attempt to get down and escape me.

I change tactics. "I'm glad you're here. I could use some help with these sheep while we wait for my friend Clara to get back."

"Clara," she repeats, the word just above a whisper.

"Yes, Clara. She's coming back."

She stands, shaky, and takes my hand, easing herself over the brush one leg at a time, her brown skirt catching on the sharp twigs and having to be pulled free.

"Did you see what happened?" I ask, still holding her hand.

She only looks at me.

"Are you all right?" I try again.

Silence.

She probably saw it all; she's probably in shock. I've heard Clara diagnose that before for people who couldn't speak or respond normally. I imagine any of us would be speechless if we witnessed what I suspect this little girl did. If I'm right that she's

18

around seven or eight, she's old enough that she probably works in the fields, herding livestock, but even if she's been unlucky enough to witness a wolf attack in the year or two she's been working, I doubt if she's seen someone die. The wolves rarely take us out. The usual worst-case scenario for a wolf attack is that they take the sheep. That's another kind of death, starvation, but not one with a wolf at your throat. Not the kind that strikes most of us silent.

Or perhaps she doesn't work the fields at all. Most children do, but some help their parents with weaving, lace making, candle making, or charcoal burning from a young age.

It doesn't really matter, though. Even a lace maker or weaver knows death well. Gévaudan isn't a safe place—wolves, disease, cold, famine, the fists of an angry father or brother—pick your poison. Since France lost the seven-year war, even the little bit of money that used to flow in from the cities has slowed to a trickle. We're all two inches from death, at best.

I shake my shoulders to dislodge the grim thoughts. This kind of death is something else. The brutality of it has stolen something from her—more than the usual amount of death theft.

"Here, let me look at you." I kneel and examine her for wounds. Not that I'd know what to do if I found a serious one, other than point at it when Clara gets back. But I can pretend to be comforting until then, I guess. Other than a few scratches from the bushes, though, she seems to be physically fine.

She's lucky the beast didn't drag her off. She's a third of the size of the boy, and the beast is known for taking little girls. I wonder if he sacrificed himself for her, and the thought settles heavy in my throat. Did the boy save her life?

Another question rubs uncomfortably at me, one the whole village has been asking for months: Why is the beast taking children at all? Sheep are easier prey than shepherds. And yet we haven't lost a single one. No lambs dragged into darkness. No ewes silenced at the end of a set of fangs. When the sheep lose their lives, it's to the wolves. Whatever this creature is, it's stalking *us*. Not them.

No wonder at least half the village thinks it is the devil himself. God's punishment for our sins, for our lust, the priest says.

The girl is looking into the distance now, toward the path Clara and I arrived on, and I follow her gaze. Clara! She's running back across the field with half a dozen men following. Relief warms across my skin. There are no stories of the beast attacking groups of adults. We're safe now; sheer numbers make it certain.

But as the tension unknots across my muscles, it seems to ripple *into* the girl's. She goes stiff, her hand squeezing mine so hard it hurts.

"Nom de Dieu, what—" I start to say, but then she's letting go and jumping back through the bush, where she nearly disappears.

I stand, frozen, my mind racing to catch up. She's an animal hunted, all fear and survival instinct. A deer startled. A rabbit disappearing into the brush at the snap of a twig. But that fear didn't come from being alone with me in the field, waiting for an unknown predator. She'd been calming, accepting help. Until—

Until she saw the men running toward us.

Her sense of danger infects me, my muscles bunching again, ready to run. There is something wrong here that isn't about the beast. My own wild-thing instincts tell me so in no uncertain terms. If a little girl would rather face the dangerous woods than the men running toward us, *what have they done*?

I make the split-second decision to let her hide and pretend she isn't there. My feet carry me away from her hiding place, point me and the men toward the dead body, now fully visible since the butterflies have faded into the sunrise.

The boy looks smaller without them, less substantial. He's my age, and I'm sure I've seen him around, though I don't know him. That bodes well for him, since the only boys I make a point to recognize are the ones I consider a danger. The trouble-makers, prank-pullers, the ones who've put their hands on me, the ones I think might put their hands on Clara.

This boy isn't on that list. Isn't on any list now, I suppose, with his soul someplace far off, no longer bothering itself with any of us.

I force myself not to look over my shoulder and check the woods for the girl. Force myself not to give her away. Is that why she's hiding? Is one of these men on *her* list? Having put his hands on her or someone she loves?

My thoughts turn—involuntarily—to the former priest, a man who read Mass in a quiet voice and preferred his own company in between services. The most terrifying example of men in this town putting hands on someone.

It was a plague year, a cursed year. Some unknown illness

rippling through us all and snuffing out every fifth soul. Everyone lost someone that year. Even those usually best fed and best cared for. And when the illness pushed the daughter of the richest man in town to death's threshold, the men decided enough was enough. It wasn't an illness; it was a curse. It wasn't a coincidence; it was a *witch*.

The *priest* was a witch.

That was why he kept to himself. It was why he preached in a quiet voice (because what witch could speak God's name loudly?). The men came for him in the night, an angry, roiling mob. They burned him in his own firepit, held his head down in his own water bucket. Insisted that he lift the curse, that he unbewitch the bewitched. He couldn't, and he ran. Haunted and hunted and whimpering into the night. Most let him go, but three men went after him, insisting the curse would never lift unless they severed the last thread of life from his body.

They returned blood-drenched and self-satisfied. And anyone who didn't know what our men were capable of before knew then. Which is exactly how they like it. Worse, because the girl survived, their belief in the justice of their actions runs even deeper. He *must* have been the witch. They must have lifted the curse. How else could you explain that Eugénie lived?

I try to ignore these thoughts as I watch the group approach now—not the same men who killed our priest and replaced him with his fire-and-brimstone counterpart, but somehow capable of scaring a little girl back into the woods where a beast might await her. My fists clench and unclench at my sides. My right eye twitches, readying for a fight.

Clara reaches me first and throws herself into my arms. I hug back, fierce. The feathery halo of hair around her cap tickles my ear, and my loose auburn curls press between our shoulders. Then there are five men standing around us, their faces echoing back my own worry and fury and fear as they stand and stoop around the corpse. I feel suddenly exposed and reach for the cap my lamb dislodged, fitting it back over my hair as best I can.

"Pascal." The first man to speak says the name in a gasp, then turns to stare at another man. Pascal's father or uncle or some other relation, I gather based on the look the first man is giving him.

The second man swallows, then stoops to touch the boy's forehead, close his eyes with two fingers. He stands abruptly, turns away. Like it's too painful for him to look.

"The beast," he says, staring into the trees. "The beast has expanded its territory."

It's an odd thing to start with when your son or nephew or cousin is lying there feeding the soil with his blood. Not a guttural scream but a steady proclamation. His face is calm, and I wonder if the look he's wearing now is the one my father wore. When Mother was dead and my brother was dead and I wasn't dead yet, but he walked into the forest and never came back.

I shove the thought away. Now is not the time to dwell on past death when future death stares out from the woods. Not the time to pick at the scab of my father's hurt when something—someone—else dangerous stands in this circle.

Which man is the girl afraid of? All of them? Some? Just one? I chance a glance toward her hiding spot, but she's too well hidden and I can't make her out. I hope she didn't leave, take herself farther into the woods. I hope I didn't lose her. Didn't force her to save herself the way I had to.

Even as I think it, I realize that my hope is wrong. I *do* hope she went deeper into the woods, because now the men are moving away from the body. Clenching fists and setting jaws, spreading out, looking into the trees.

"Jacques, I'm sorry." One man grasps the boy's father-brother-cousin-uncle by the shoulder as the others draw closer to forest, scanning the ground for animal prints, the trees for broken branches. A trail to follow. A path to the wild thing.

For an eternity, we stand there, watching them as they move through the field, along the tree line. No one cries out, so the girl must still be well hidden. Or perhaps she did go deeper in.

And then they return with a proclamation. "We should take the body back to the village."

"What?" Clara's voice is a shiver. "What about the beast? Won't you follow it? Find it?"

"We don't know where it's gone," one of the men says, motioning toward the trees. "Can't follow what hasn't left a trace."

Hasn't left a trace. Something about those words tightens around my heart like a fist. A big animal like that should have. Scraped off bark where the trees grow so close together. Left heavy footprints in morning mud. Dripped blood onto moss and root and thick, black soil. *Hasn't left a trace* makes it sound as if the beast is ghost or devil instead of flesh and blood. Something invincible, unfightable, unknowable.

Though I suppose you could say that of any mysterious

24

being. Until someone puts a bullet or a spear through it, until it's lying dead before us, how can we prove what it is? Those who've seen the beast say it's like nothing else they've ever witnessed. Its chest is as wide as a horse's, body sturdy, muscled. Its hair the color of dried blood with a black stripe like charcoal down its back. Fire in its eyes. A voice like a man's. The tales grow more fanciful as they go. It's a witch, a shape-shifter, devil, werewolf. God's punishment for France losing the seven-year war with England. Skull cleaner, child stealer, horseman of the apocalypse.

The men take the body and leave us with the sheep. But my fear doesn't recede with them. They're one threat, gone and leaving me free to go back to the little girl. But another threat lingers, invisible. I feel suddenly, unbearably raw and vulnerable, my uneven heartbeat a beacon calling the evil toward us.

"We should go," Clara says.

I put a hand on her shoulder, even though every part of me wants to run. "Wait."

I wait until the men have disappeared in the distance, then lead her to the woods.

To the child.

To a different danger.

To a mystery.

3

THE GIRL WON'T COME OUT.

I don't blame her. The last time she stepped over the brambles and held my hand, the thing she was afraid of materialized—one or more of those men. It must feel safer to tuck herself into the tree, pretend she could melt into the bark, live inside its sturdiness.

Clara tries to coax her out, and when she won't come, Clara steps over the bushes and sinks into the tree's roots with her, wrapping her arms around the child's skinny frame. I never would have thought to do that, but I can see the relief drop the girl's shoulders, tear off the blank mask over her emotions. Her eyes fill with tears, and her little body shudders with a loud, unsteady breath.

Clara motions with her eyes for me to join them, and I clamber over the bushes and sink to the ground on the other side of the girl, each of us a wall between her and the forest. Tree behind her, Clara at her left, me on her right, and bushes in front. My fool lamb doesn't like being left out and bleats angrily at us from the other side of the bushes until I reach over and lift him into the girl's lap. She wraps her arms around him and tucks his head under her chin. And he must have some small amount of sense because he calms at the touch.

It's like swaddling a baby, except we're swaddling the girl with people and lambs and plants. Surrounding her, pressing up against her. The comfort of it isn't lost on the girl, whose sobs grow louder and then quieter again as she presses her face into Clara's shoulder, still clutching the lamb.

We wait the same way we'd wait out a drenching rainstorm, letting roar become trickle, sobs become sniffles. This was the storm that was blocking her voice. I know because when she's done sobbing, she whispers the truth we've been waiting for.

"I couldn't save him." Her every word is a broken, ruined thing.

Clara kisses the top of her head, leaves space for her to go on.

"Papa killed Pascal." This time the words are so faint it's hard to hear. The fear in them is stretched out, thin.

I open my mouth to ask which one was Papa, but Clara shakes her head the tiniest amount. Then she presses a cheek to the little girl's hair, and the girl goes on.

"I wasn't supposed to follow them. Don't tell anyone. I was supposed to stay home."

"We won't tell anyone," Clara reassures her. "Do you want to tell us what happened?"

"Papa was angry at Pascal. I don't know why. I heard them

yelling early this morning, and Pascal slammed the door. We're not allowed to slam the door. Then Papa went after him, and I was scared about what might happen, so I followed them. But Papa was so angry, I didn't want him to know I was there, so I was really quiet."

Her next pause stretches long, the only noise the sound of our sheep grazing lazily just outside the patch of bushes, the sharp alarm trill of a bird far in the distance.

"What will he do to me?" Her voice is barely a whisper again, her fear palpable, cold, and dark, draped over us all.

Nom de Dieu, I might tear that man's eyes out with my bare hands. There are enough things to be afraid of in this world without adding your own father to the mix. And yet somehow fathers keep on competing for the lead role in the theater of our terrors. I clench and unclench my fist.

"You know who her father is?" Clara's voice is a whisper. When I shake my head, she adds, "He's one of the 'go back where you came from' men."

Nom de Dieu again. Of course it's one of them—the men who tell anyone with a bronze complexion that they don't belong here. Probably the same man who went door to door asking everyone to stop cooking such "strong-smelling" food.

Clara presses her cheek to the girl's head again and gives me a significant look. I know what it means, and I agree: we have to help this girl.

But how? This is a small village. If we take her home with us, her father will know by the end of the day. The nearest village is a day's walk away, and she'd be found easily there, too. And it's not like she can just stay here in the pine-scented, dew-damp roots, a nice little supper for the beast whenever it does wander this way.

"After he hit Pascal, he left," she whispers into the long silence. "He left, and he came back with the knives."

My stomach clenches around the words. *Came back with knives.* She doesn't have to go on. I know immediately what she's saying: He killed Pascal in a fit of anger. And then he came back to make it look like the beast had done it. The actual death was too tidy. A bashed head, a broken neck, something bloodless and human. He had to make it look like something animal. Not only is this man a killer—he's something worse. The kind of man who could come back and desecrate his child's body to cover up his guilt.

There was so much blood, and all of it had been a trick.

Well, two can play at that game. Or, in this case, three.

I put my hands on the child's shoulders and hold her gaze. "Do you want us to take you away?"

Hope sparks there, deep in the dark brown irises, tucked into upraised eyebrows, shivering through a small gasp.

"Yes."

Clara raises an eyebrow at me from behind the girl's head, but I don't break eye contact.

"I already know you're good at hiding. Can you keep secrets?"
She nods.

"Tell me your name."

"Charlotte."

"Charlotte," I say, moving my hands from her shoulders to her hands and squeezing all my conviction into them. "I need your dress. We're going to fake your death."

4

I TEAR INTO HER DRESS WITH MY PIKE—SLASH HALF THE skirt into uneven pieces and hand the rest back to Charlotte. Then, leaving them at the forest's edge, I return to the scene of her father's crime, where I drench the fabric in blood and mud, smashing it between the ground and my hand. Blood stains my fingers. The dirt rubs raw against my palms.

The violence is satisfying, purposeful. The sounds of tearing, the feel of cold earth under my knuckles. I curse Charlotte's father with every breath, every rip, every touch of pooled blood against my skin. I wish him pain. I wish him *terror.* The kind of terror that comes for you when you know you are about to die, when there is nothing else you can do, because your life has been taken out of your hands. *Powerless* terror. The kind that takes something from you permanently.

The same terror Pascal must have known in his last moments.

The same Charlotte is still gripped by, the skin of her hand pulled taut as she clings to Clara's arm for dear life at the edge of my vision.

The same terror I knew when I was her age, though for a different reason. I can feel it now, creeping back in, with a power even the warnings about the beast haven't had over me. The fear wraps tight around my heart, my lungs, as if it'll crush them.

I can feel it coming for me: death. As it came for my family in the grips of a fever that swept through the village those years ago at the height of winter. All of us too weak to move, to boil water, to feed ourselves, to feed the sheep. The snowdrifts were too high for anyone to think of checking on us, to even know they needed to.

Now, tears burn at my eyes as I drag cloth through blood. The fear—the anger—build like a scream in my throat. It's unfair. Unfair. *Unfair.* For us to be in such powerless danger.

Then, I watched my brother die first, saw his soul blink from body into sky. A wisp, a vapor, rising through ice-cold air. Or perhaps that was the fever. An illusion. I'll never know. There's no one else alive to confirm or deny it.

Did Charlotte see the same thing? Her brother rise like vapor into the sky. Gone, gone, *gone.* Never again to tell her a story, sing her a song, save her from the big, bad wolf.

Then, my own fever sizzled even as ice formed under the eaves of our little stone house. I didn't see my mother's last breath. I must have been sleeping. But when I woke, my father had enough strength to sit up, to gather his things.

He kissed me on the forehead before he left. A strange

kindness when he was leaving me to die. When he was taking the last of the food, the thickest coat, the warmest gloves.

I managed to pull myself up on the windowsill and push the heavy flap aside to watch as he disappeared into the trees, pointed his feet away from the village. The thick snow covered his footprints almost instantly, leaving no trace behind.

He wasn't coming back. I could feel the finality of it in my bones as I fell back into feverish dreams.

When I woke, I knew that I was going to die. And my last wish was to *see Clara*. She was the one I wanted to comfort me, the one who'd comforted me so many times before. Over skinned knees, cruel boys, lambs lost to illness. I needed to say goodbye to her. I needed her to hold my hand—hold my heart—as I went.

I dug through a snowdrift outside the window, dragged myself through the ice. Strangely comforting against my fever as it crept around my clothes, finding its way into the tiniest openings between cloth and sheep's wool and skin even as I immediately started to shiver.

I shiver again now, so fully transported back to that moment that it's like I'm in two places at once. Summer and winter. A hand-carved tunnel through snow and a field of wildflowers destroyed by a struggle, a few butterflies returning to drink the blood.

Then, it was a miracle I didn't lose a limb to frostbite. A miracle that Mémé and Clara brought me back from the brink of death. They spent days upon days coaxing broth down my throat, wrapping themselves around me as the nightmares clutched cold fingers around my neck. Mémé used to sing to me when I'd wake up crying. Sing and sing and sing until I could breathe again, sleep again. An old lullaby in an unfamiliar language. To this day, the cheerful notes of Amharic soothe my soul.

Now, I am clawing for another miracle, my fists clenched tight around fabric as I march toward the trees and leave an intentional trail. Scraps of fabric by the forest edge, as if a struggle happened here. A piece strategically snagged on a low branch, another on a thorny bush. I cut myself on the bush by mistake and rub my own blood against bark and leaves without missing a step. Just like that day, I move without thinking. A creature of pure need. Single focus. Then: to see Clara one more time. Now: to save Charlotte.

Like I wish my father had saved me.

When I return to Clara and Charlotte, the latter is in what's left of her dress and the scarf Clara always carries because the weather here can snap to cold in a second, even in summer, and she's always been the practical one. The three of us would be quite the sight if there was anyone here to see. Clara still streaked with mud from rescuing me as I went after the fool lamb just hours ago. Me, similarly mud-covered and with knuckles blood- and dirt-caked. Charlotte with a half-torn skirt and tear-shiny cheeks. All of us flanked by a gaggle of chaotic sheep.

"We have to get her home before anyone else comes out here." Clara runs a hand reassuringly through Charlotte's hair.

I nod, though my stomach sinks in a new way. *Home* is a one-room stone house. Hearth, straw mattress, three people, twenty-five sheep. There's nowhere to hide a child. Not for long.

For the first time in this frantic, panicked mess, I pause and really think about what comes next. *How* are we going to keep her away from her monster of a father? How will we hide her? How will we feed her? What happens when these last dregs of summer turn to autumn, then winter? How will we keep another girl safe, alive? I bite my lip as the questions unfold, each more daunting than the last.

Clara leads us home, taking the long way, the quiet way—all thick ferns and ankle-twisting rocks. The path where we're less likely to meet anyone. Though perhaps the path more likely to take us into the jaws of the beast. These are the kinds of choices we will make now, I realize. Perhaps the ones we've always made. Face the monsters we know or risk the ones we don't.

We're all quiet, lost in our own thoughts as we lead the sheep along thinly trampled paths through the fields, giving the gorge that almost took my lamb this morning a wide berth. My thoughts return to the question of where to hide Charlotte. There is a better answer than our tiny house at the edge of the village, but I hate that answer. Every part of my body rebels against the possibility. The place that scares me so much more than this village, the forest beyond it, the sharp drop-off of the gorges just north of us.

My house. The place where I lost it all.

It's a wreck more than a house now. A place ruined. Never claimed by me or anyone else because the village believes the same thing I know deep in my marrow: it's cursed. The farthest house from the safety of the village. The place you can't get to in a blizzard, a hailstorm. A place where no one can hear you scream.

It's also a place that no one would look for a missing little girl. Especially one who seems to have been taken by the beast.

She would be safe there, from him. The monster we know. But by taking her there we'd make her vulnerable to so much more. A house derelict, not well protected from the elements. Her own childhood inexperience. The nightmares that I know better than anyone are coming for her. Perhaps have already come for her for many years. Because a man who could kill his son is also a man who has hit them before, isn't he? How much terror does she already live in?

And, of course, the beast. The wild thing that's stalking little girls. That never takes a sheep when there's a shepherdess to be found. She wouldn't stand a chance against it.

It's a terrible idea, taking her there. But then, so is taking her home. I can picture that outcome clearly, too. Give it one day, two perhaps, and someone will notice her. They'll glimpse her through the window, stop by for a medical consult with Clara and see the girl as plain as day with nowhere to hide. Even if we ban consults from the house, Mémé could have one of her bad days, when her mind can't hold on to things, and she'll bring someone by. And the moment one person knows where Charlotte is, the whole village of Mende will.

Mende is strange like that. Full of secrets and yet unable to keep a single one.

Then Charlotte's father will come—and what would he do to us? Would he only take her, or would he hurt us? Kill us? Would he—

My mind refuses to shape the words, but it sends me the

images, just like on the cliff. Charlotte bruised and bleeding. The man's hand around my throat. Clara's body splayed in Pascal's place, a casualty of our rash decision. Bruised throats and broken arms. Blades and balled fists.

Blood, *so much blood.*

I'm so lost in the horror of it that I startle when Charlotte slips her tiny hand into mine, pulls me forcefully back to the present. Out of the horrors of the past and the ones my mind is ever busy conjuring for the future.

My heart gasps as if it has come up for air after too long underwater. It stutters back into the now and sends my consciousness crashing back into my body, feeling the realness of the moment. The light tap of my feet against earth. The tickle of a breeze on my face. The warm certainty of the little fingers pressing into mine.

Her hand in mine is such a small gesture—and yet I want to cry. Because right now we are *safe.* Charlotte is alive, far from her father's reach. We have, at the very least, bought her time. Bought ourselves time, to come up with a plan.

And this little girl isn't alone. Not like I was. I marvel at that. Because I didn't leave her behind. I, the abandoned, deserted, the one left to her fate—*I* am helping her. Even though I don't know how. Unlike me, Charlotte won't have to save herself. There's something about that that's like a blanket, warming my heart.

Her hand in mine tells me that she believes that I—that we—can save her. Believes we're strong enough. Trusts us not to leave her.

As my heart settles into a more normal rhythm, as we follow

the sheep path closer to the village, I know that I won't let her down. *Can't.* Like when my godforsaken lamb slipped off the cliff, I've gone over without thinking. Now I cannot let her fall. And just like with the lamb, Clara is here, too, probably saving both of us.

The tears build until one escapes the corner of my eye, arcing downward to linger on my cheekbone. I squeeze Charlotte's hand, my silent promise.

I may not know how to save her, but *I will find the way.* Just like I found the way up the cliff. Just like I carved through ice with my own fingernails. I will not force her to save herself or die trying.

I will save this little girl if it is the last thing I do.

5

SOMEHOW WE MAKE IT HOME WITHOUT BEING SEEN. ALONG the knife-thin sheep trail, between trees draped in growing daylight, through the cluster of houses at the edge of this slice of forest and into the small stone house we call our own.

I'm relieved as I slump against the door and Clara draws the shutters. But something tugs at the edges of that relief, and it takes only a few moments to know what it is: our little cluster of houses is *too* quiet. This time of day, the shepherds are out with their sheep, like us, but not the weavers, the candle makers, the wool spinners. Normally there's *someone* here. A flutter of life. A toddler screeching in joy or disgust. Someone singing while they scrub dirt from a hearth. French songs and Ethiopian ones, because this particular little cluster of houses is inhabited mostly by a pocket of French Ethiopians. People whose parents, grandparents, great-grandparents somehow found their way to this tiny, middle-of-nowhere slice of forests, gorges, and fields.

Today, there are no voices, no children playing. Only birdsong and the rustle of leaves in the wind.

Has everyone gone to the village center? Have they already heard about Pascal? Or is there something else that's driven our neighbors away? Something toothier, wickeder.

I lock the door just in case.

Even Mémé, who rarely leaves the house these days, is nowhere in sight. She was having a good morning today. Lucid. She isn't always like that. Sometimes she forgets me, mixes up our names, or calls us something else entirely. Mistakes Clara for her mother, who died in childbirth, or her aunt, taken by the illness that led to the priest's murder. Sometimes the names aren't ones we even know. Ghost names from a past we weren't alive for.

I'm about to suggest going into the village square to find out where everyone is when Clara crosses the room and wraps her arms around me, holding the back of my neck with one hand, the other arm pulling me in tight. It's the kind of hug that needs no words, that presses all its relief and fear and love into me without them. It's a reminder that we are here and alive and in this together.

When she pulls away, she turns back to Charlotte, who is sitting at the hearth, as quiet as a grave. "Charlotte." Clara kneels in front of her and takes her hands. "May I ask you some questions?"

I slide down to kneel beside Clara as Charlotte nods.

"They might be hard questions." Clara's voice is calming, the one she uses when someone comes in with a cracked-open head or cracked-open heart.

Charlotte nods again, bites her lip.

"Your sister—Hélène—is she safe at home?"

My heart and eyebrows jump. Sister? Nom de Dieu. I hadn't even thought about who else might be trapped in that evil man's house, who else might—even now—be cowering away from his rage. I know who Hélène is. She's just a little younger than us, out selling candles on market day, all bouncy blond curls and kind hazel eyes. We're friendly, if not friends. But I didn't realize she was connected to Charlotte and Pascal.

The calm that had started to spread across my skin with Clara's hug evaporates into thin air.

Charlotte's brow furrows, and her face collapses in on itself, grief as deep as the gorges, sharp as a tooth. She shakes her head as silent sobs shudder through her, and Clara rubs comforting circles into her hands. Then Clara moves to sit beside Charlotte on the hearth, pulling the smaller girl to her side and running a hand through her hair as she weeps into Clara's shoulder.

Clara's eyes find mine, and I can read her intention as clearly as I know my own.

She can't save one girl and leave another behind.

She must have known right away, as soon as she saw Charlotte. Clara never forgets a name, a face, a family tie. She must have known there was more than one girl trapped in that house.

My mind is racing all over again, my body cold with uncertainty. What are we going to do? I've taken us off the cliff with no

40

plan. And now it isn't one girl who needs us, but *two*. We can't possibly rescue Hélène, too, can we? If hiding Charlotte is half-impossible, what does it mean if there are two of them?

I open my mouth to ask those questions, but Clara shakes her head ever so slightly. And she's right. Charlotte doesn't need to hear me say that this is impossible, that we're trapped, that I don't know what to do next.

So I wait as Charlotte cries herself out on Clara's shoulder. Cries herself to sleep. Clara holds her, breathing deep, until I lift the smaller girl and take her to the bed, laying her gently on the blankets, her brown hair spreading around her like a nest of pine needles.

Then Clara and I retreat to the opposite corner of the room, heads bent together. I rub circles into her hands with my thumbs, a gesture she once told me comforts her. It's a comfort that grounds me, too.

"What are we going to do?" My whisper is pinched.

"I don't know."

"Someone will find her here."

"I know." Clara pauses, then pulls back and puts her hands on my shoulders. "I think you already know what I'm thinking."

"My house." I say it, and I hate it.

She nods.

"It's falling apart. What is she—seven? She can't be out there on her own."

Clara shakes her head. "She's eight. You and I were already taking the sheep out by ourselves by seven."

"But not living in a house by ourselves."

"We could go with her."

"Oh yeah, because that's not suspicious at all. It won't draw any attention to us—moving into the village's cursed house when I have been avoiding it for so many years."

"All right, Joséphine, give me a better choice. We can't send her home. We can't leave her sister there. You're right that they'll find her here. What can we do?"

I close my mouth tight, hating all the possibilities. Hating that all it took was a couple hours to transform my life from hard but nice to utterly impossible.

"I think we need more information," I say finally. "Everyone's gone. I think they're in the village square. I think they know about Pascal being dead, and they're deciding what to do. If we had been home when we heard the news, we'd have gone straight there. We should now."

Clara nods. "I agree, but it's *you,* not we. Someone needs to stay with her." She points her chin toward the exhausted, sleeping pile that is Charlotte and the cheeky lamb who has now done the forbidden thing of climbing onto our mattress to lie beside her.

I nod, move to leave, but Clara's voice catches me at the door, a joke and not a joke. "Try not to do anything reckless. I'm tired of saving people today."

When I reach the square, the priest is preaching. Fire-eyed, passion-flushed, little flecks of spittle flying from his mouth. And if what he's saying is right, all of this is my fault.

"Mark my words." His voice echoes off stone walls as he stands at the top of the cathedral's grand stone steps, waving his arms, expressive. "Parents have been neglecting their children's Christian education! The shameless—*shameless*—immorality of these young girls! The way they run around like God can't see the lust in their hearts!"

Behind him, the cathedral looms, all dark stone, sharp spires, and intimidating detail. The richest thing in the village. A literal reminder—as the highest point in Mende—that God is far above us and so are the men who speak directly with Him. A reminder also—with its intricate whorls and artistic flourishes—that God can afford beauty when the rest of us can barely afford food.

The priest is looking straight at me as he spits the word *lust* into the morning. Bastard. Straight at me *and Mémé,* who I've sidled up beside—strong, no-nonsense Mémé. As if she is part of the problem. Rage flashes through me, hot, and if he keeps it up, I am going to march up there and punch him in the jaw. *Hard.* Like that-time-Jean-tried-to-kiss-me-without-permission hard. Fighting-with-the-boys-when-they-tried-to-steal-our-grain hard. The goal: two eyes the color of forest shadows, blue black.

"That's what's brought the wrath of God down on Gévaudan—unfaithful parents, unfaithful girls! The beast—the beast!—is the anger *you* provoked." He stabs the air with a finger, and the crowd flinches back.

The beast has been killing girls, mostly. So the priest's indictment inspires a lot of bobbing heads and masculine murmurs of agreement in the crowd: if the creature is God's punishment for our sins, it only makes sense that the people it's killing are the sinners. The boys and men it has taken along the way just casualties of women uncontrolled.

"You are culpable, parents. You are guilty, girls. Repent! Repent! *Repent!* The beast will not retreat into the forest. . . . It will not leave us to our lives . . . until all of Gévaudan is cleansed! Until children *obey* their parents. Until women *submit* to their husbands. Your rebellion is killing your children."

The large cobblestone square with its cold, stone buildings is silent as a held breath, people white-knuckled in fear, clutching skirts or children's hands. They're soaking it in, drinking him up. Believing that God would send a wild animal to eat us all up because of lust inside a heart. Never mind the other sins. The ones that punch and bite and stab and break the people all around us. The one that actually killed Pascal, maimed him. Never mind those. They're masculine. Forgivable. Soft curves—they are the problem; they are the thing that makes God rage.

Just like any other man.

I reach for Mémé's hand, and she squeezes mine, her eyes still trained on the man raving before us all. From this angle, it's so easy to tell that she and Clara are related. Same heart-shaped face. Same golden-brown eyes and deep-brown skin. Same halo of hair peeking out from beneath their caps, only Mémé's is stark white now. She's an older, sharper, flintier version of my softhearted best friend.

"Something's happened," she whispers to me now. "He's just taking his sweet time getting to the point. Man loves a show."

The right corner of my mouth twitches upward, and I squeeze her hand back.

"I've just received word that the beast has taken another victim," the priest continues, his voice dropping to a lower register.

A series of gasps ripples through the crowd before everyone falls silent again, rapt.

"Young Pascal. His promising future gone. Oh, alas! Imagine how you've broken God's heart for Him to take a boy in the prime of his life. Imagine how you've broken all our hearts!" He points again into the crowd, sweeping his finger across us all and pausing, pointedly, on me. His eyes narrow, finger like a gun taking aim. His hate finding its target once again.

If you didn't know better, you'd think his ire was simply because I am a girl, the very creature he believes responsible for the danger. All lustful heart and foolish whims. But the truth is that our enmity goes deeper than that. He knows I don't like him—and he cannot stand it. Cannot stand not to be worshipped. Cannot stand that when he put his hands on my derrière last year, I whipped around and bit him. Hard. There's still a scar on his hand where he put it up to defend himself from me and instead found my teeth wrapped around it.

I find that scar deeply satisfying—the only satisfying thing about him. "Why?" he screamed then, as he pulled his knuckles from my jaws. And I answered him plainly, his blood on my teeth, "All's fair in love and forcing men to keep their hands off me." I didn't say more, but he understood the rest, the unsaid things behind the bite. I am not your friend, your toy, your pet. I am not a quiet thing for your taking. I am a feral thing, a bitey, clawing, screaming thing. And the more people know it, the better.

Ultimately, perhaps, his hate for me is really hate for himself, for the way he cannot hide himself from me. I am the evidence of the lust in *his* heart. And he knows that I know that he isn't any different from the rest of them.

"The beast—" He starts back in on his tirade, but this time he's interrupted by the only other people in the village who don't seem to take him seriously: a group of boys somewhere between boyhood and manhood that Clara and I call the pranksters. Boys it's never safe to listen to, because they think the height of humor is sending you on a wild-goose chase, handing you salt in place of sugar, claiming something is wine until you take a swig and realize it's vinegar. If what you want is on the right, they will tell you it is on the left. If you need to look up, they will tell you to look down. The humor is a delight when your enemy is on the receiving end and endlessly irritating when you are.

"What happened to the two old ladies out in the field?" Louis is the interrupter. A cheeky seventeen-year-old with gold-brown skin and bright green eyes. The most beautiful person in the village, outshined only by Clara. Which is part of why he gets away with all he does. That and simply being a boy.

The priest presses his lips together and narrows his eyes, unamused by the question. But my heart stutters, skittish and dread-soaked. Were there more casualties today? I sweep my eyes across the square. Which old ladies are missing? Who isn't accounted for?

My answer comes swiftly, from another prankster. "A man met them in the field and dropped his trousers!"

Ah, a joke. I should have known.

A chorus of gasps, sighs, disapproval, and inappropriate laughter moves through the crowd.

"And what did those little old ladies do?" one prankster yells, all mock horror.

"The first lady had a stroke!" another returns.

"But what about the second?" Louis feigns shock.

"Alas, but she couldn't reach!" The skinniest, youngest boy calls out the punchline and drops into a bow.

They roar, then, with laughter, not minding if they are the only people amused by the joke.

"You should be ashamed of yourselves, jesting when a boy lies dead!" The priest's face has gone even redder, if that's possible. I don't believe he cares about Pascal. He's angry that the crowd's attention isn't focused entirely on him.

Louis drops his head a fraction then, seemingly shamed. But another of the boys speaks up, throwing a fist into the air. "It's what Pascal would have wanted!"

The others hurrah. "For Pascal!"

"For Pascal!"

It's this shout that shakes loose more of my own knowledge of Pascal, the vague familiarity of his face finally sliding into place. I've seen him come to Clara—for medicine or advice— yes, but this is the other way I know him. Not as a prankster himself, really, but somewhat adjacent to them. Newly in their orbit. Very occasionally taking part in their antics.

These are his friends.

This is—however strange and inappropriate—their tribute.

The priest opens his mouth, no doubt to scold them further,

but a wail sings through the courtyard and swallows his words. Another interruption, but this one reminding us not of jokes and living boys and antics the rest of us roll our eyes at—but smacking those things down. Reminding us that death has come to the doorstep today. And perhaps it isn't done taking its due.

We all turn toward the sound like a field of tall reeds changing their leaning as the wind shifts. There's a girl stumbling between the houses and into the square, her face tear-swollen, puffy, and red. Her hair is honey blond, her nose tipped up at the end. I've never seen her so miserable, and it takes me a moment to realize who she is.

Charlotte and Pascal's sister. Fourteen-year-old Hélène.

Another sob shudders through her as we all watch, her shoulders heaving and a second wail escaping like a wild thing unchained. A wind. A storm. An act of nature that cannot be held back.

In her hand, held up to us, stretched out: an uneven, shredded piece of fabric so drenched in mud and blood that its original color has been lost.

It is the same strip of fabric I cut off Charlotte's skirt not two hours ago, and my heart goes cold with it, the memory of the anger and terror and now a new feeling: guilt. Because I have saved Charlotte, but I have also done *this* to her sister. I have pulled this terrible noise from her heart. I have made her believe that Charlotte is dead.

There are different types of love in this world, suitable for different purposes. Clara's love is a bandage, a salve. It heals and soothes. Mémé's is a practical thing with no space for nonsense.

It feeds and clothes. And mine is this: sharp-edged, explosive, impulsive. A thing that saves and destroys all at once.

I'm sorry, Hélène. I'm so sorry.

The crowd is frozen, staring, plunged into a quiet so deep we might as well be underwater.

"My sister," Hélène gasps into the air, holding the flimsy cloth out toward us all. "It wasn't just Pascal the beast killed. Charlotte is gone, too. All that's left is blood."

Guilt and relief weave together in a complicated knot. Because I have hurt her, but the cloth in her hands, the words on her lips, can mean only one thing: they've found our staged attack scene—and believe our brutal lie.

Charlotte is safe.

For now.

6

HÉLÈNE FALLS TO HER KNEES, AND IT'S LIKE THE ACTION RE-
leases us all from a spell. Mémé is the first to rush forward, take
Hélène in her arms, and lift her to her feet.

"Now, ma chérie, come with me. You don't need to be crying here in a dirty square. We'll get you some tea." Mémé steers
Hélène's tiny frame away from the gaping villagers and toward
the path home.

*Oh là là là là là, Mémé, just this once be less of a good per-
son!* We can't bring Hélène to the house where her supposedly
dead little sister is hiding.

Of course, Mémé has no way to know about any of that. Like
always, she sees a hurting girl, and she takes action. Tea and
broth and warm fires, healing what she can and holding grace
for every hurt that's left. The woman is sixty-two years old and
still managed to chop wood this past winter when both Clara
and I went down with a hellish flu.

As I turn to follow Mémé, the crowd's murmurs grow louder, their shock turning to a new flurry of emotions. Feminine voices call out "poor child" and "her poor father." Masculine voices start to roil with anger. They growl about the ineptitude of the towns before us whose men weren't man enough to stop the beast before it made it here. One man calls out blame for the monarchy, which has never protected us a day in our lives. Others cheer their agreement.

The priest hushes them, then starts back in on his tirade, a few last words chasing us on our way out of the square. *Repent, sinners, repent.*

And oh, if only it were that easy. If only I could bare my soul to God in exchange for an answer. "How do we save Charlotte?" I'd ask Him. Or smaller, more urgent: "How can I keep Hélène from coming to the house, discovering her sister before we've found a way to keep her safe, get her away?" Or bigger, bolder: "How can we save Hélène, too?"

For a moment, I consider letting Hélène find Charlotte, putting her out of her misery. Taking her with us right now. But there are too many gaps in that plan, too many chances for this whole fragile enterprise to fall apart. What if she screams and brings everyone running? What if she insists Charlotte go home with her? We don't know enough yet to bring her in on the secret. And there's no way we could save her today, too. Two deaths have been staged in Mende in one morning; getting away with staging a third only hours later . . . it's simply not possible. Even the world's most robust carnivore would be sated by now. We'd need a whole pack of beasts to explain away the death and disappearance of three children in one day.

No, I have to keep Charlotte hidden, even from her sister. Until we know more.

Hélène has stopped crying and now moves alongside Mémé like a ghost as I continue to scour my mind for a way to stop their slow progress toward the house. Perhaps I could say Clara is ill. But then if Hélène tells anyone and Clara is seen traipsing around the village, we look suspicious. Perhaps a sheep is ill? But then Mémé might ask our neighbor Amani to come over, with her near-magical ability to know exactly what is wrong with a sheep and how to soothe it. Hiding Charlotte from Amani would be just as hard—if not harder—than hiding her from her shock-blanched sister. Mon Dieu, why is this so difficult? Sometimes I think God's in league with the pranksters, laughing at the impossible situations He's orchestrated for us.

My other option is to leave Mémé, somehow get home before them, and take Charlotte away. But if they found the bloody cloth, they'll be out looking for her, without a doubt. Everyone on high alert. Taking Charlotte out of the house means trying to avoid dozens of people instead of just one.

I press my nails into my palms in frustration. My stomach is all knots. It's been less than half a day, and we're already going to be caught. Charlotte, I'm sorry you found yourself such an incompetent savior.

Hélène stops then, so suddenly I almost run into her. She breathes out long and loud, presses a hand to her chest, and leans forward, racked again with sobs. Mémé stops alongside her, rubbing circles into her back.

Well, I suppose this is my chance. Perhaps a two-minute head start.

I whisper to Mémé, "I'll go start the fire, get the kettle on."

She squints at me—suspicious or surprised—because I'm normally not the one to think of something like that. But she's too caught up in caring for poor Hélène to ask me why I've suddenly developed a Clara-like helpfulness.

I wait until I round the corner of a row of homes before I break into a run.

Charlotte is still asleep—pink-cheeked, mouth wide, the cheeky lamb tucked in the crook of her arm—when I spill chaotically into the room. "They're coming. We have to hide her."

"What? Who?" Clara is up like a shot, and Charlotte startles, opens her eyes.

"Charlotte—" I shake my head at Clara and reach for Charlotte, casting my eyes wildly around the room. Sheep in the kitchen. Mattress on the floor. Wooden chairs. Handwoven rugs. Nothing substantial enough to provide real cover.

I turn to Clara, the lump in my throat growing larger by the moment. "Where do we put her?"

"Up." Clara points to the rafters above our heads.

They're thick, sure, but not so thick that she'll be perfectly hidden from every angle. It's risky as all hell. But it's also a better option than any I can see.

"Don't you remember? I used to climb up there and hide from you when we were playing as children."

I bark an involuntary laugh. "You never told me where you were those times I couldn't find you."

She shrugs. "Had to keep some of my secrets."

"Charlotte." Clara turns toward the girl, now awake and staring wide-eyed and frightened again. Clara kneels, eye to eye with her. "You need to go up on the rafter and lie down flat, as flat as you can make yourself. Pretend you are the rafter. You're part of the house. Don't move. And don't come down until we say so—no matter what. All right?"

There's no time to waste, so Clara and I reach for Charlotte then, hoisting her toward the rafters. Charlotte grabs hold and scrambles up, surprisingly agile.

"Good. Now lie down, mon amie. Stay as quiet as you can," Clara coos into the ceiling.

Charlotte does as she's told, pressing herself to the rafter, and it's a better hiding place than I expected. I can see her, but only because I'm looking. If you *weren't* looking for her, the little fingers, the tuft of hair . . . it might be subtle enough not to see. And Hélène won't be looking, not if she's in the shape I left her in.

It might work.

I shake myself out of my thoughts and rush to the hearth. A fire. I told Mémé I would start the fire, start a kettle. I busy myself doing just that.

Clara moves beside me. "Who exactly is coming to our house?"

"Mémé," I say, striking the flint into familiar spark. "And—"

Before I can finish the sentence, the door opens, admitting Mémé and a tear-soaked, defeated-looking Hélène.

Clara's mouth drops open, and she looks wildly between us. I can imagine her thoughts tracing the same patterns as my own. First, perhaps: Why are we hiding Charlotte? Isn't Hélène safe? Then, a pause: Is Hélène a danger to us? Should we tell her? Clara must come to the same conclusions I have—or at least choose to wait out the questions—because she says nothing, just rushes to the door to help Mémé with Hélène.

Clara takes her by the hand and leads her to one of the chairs at our little table, angling it away from the beam. Clever. Relief loosens the anxious flutter in my chest as I place the kettle over the now-respectable fire.

"Now," Mémé says, settling into the chair opposite Hélène and taking her hands. "You've had a shock."

"Both of them are gone." Hélène's voice is weak, cracked around the edges. "They're looking for Charlotte's body now. There was nothing but blood and cloth left. But it was her dress. I know. I sewed it for her."

As Hélène speaks, I can see Charlotte's fingers tighten on the beam, and my heart spikes. *No, no, no, Charlotte. Stay hidden. Mon Dieu, stay hidden.*

A fat tear rolls down Hélène's right cheek. "They won't find her, will they? If it's the beast . . . she's too little, so easy for it to carry away. We won't even be able to bury her body."

"Child, there's no use thinking about that kind of thing. Nothing you can do to change it." Mémé takes the bowl of tea from Clara's outstretched hand and presses it into Hélène's.

"I think Pascal tried to save her. He must have. He *would* have. He loved her so much. He was that kind of brother."

Above us on the rafter, Charlotte's face comes slowly into

view, and I can tell from the way her jaw is starting to set that this whole thing is about to be over. This is a girl who wants to be held by her sister, to comfort her. A girl about to show herself. I try to catch her eye, shake my head just enough to bring her back to her senses, but she only has eyes for her sister.

"I think it's my fault." Hélène's voice is unbearably small. "Pascal had a dream last week—a nightmare—about darkness dropping over us all like a curtain. All the light in the world went out. I didn't know what it meant, but I knew it was something . . . ominous. I should have kept Charlotte in the house. I should have locked them both in."

"Child, there is no sense in blaming yourself." Mémé takes Hélène's hand and pats it firmly.

Above us, Charlotte opens her mouth as if to speak, but Mémé beats her to it, leaning toward Hélène. "Your poor father. The man must be devastated. Two children taken at once. He lost your mother, too, just a few years past, didn't he? It's a lot for a person to bear." She's speaking from experience, having outlived her own children, her husband.

Above me, Charlotte pauses at the mention of her father. *Yes*, I think. *Yes, Mémé, keep talking about the man she's hiding from. Remind her why she's up there.*

I tear my eyes from Charlotte and address Hélène, desperate. "Yes, tell us about your father."

I can tell it's a stilted way to enter the conversation by the way Clara cringes, and Mémé makes a face at me as if to say *Child, which wild mushroom did you eat this morning?* But it's the only thing I can think to do that might stop Charlotte from revealing herself. Give her more reminders of the man she's hiding from.

Hélène doesn't notice everyone else's awkwardness. She only pauses, stares into her tea, and mumbles, "Yeah, poor Papa. He's a good man. Doesn't deserve this."

Charlotte's eyes widen above me, and she stops her slow movement toward her sister, blinks fast, then disappears back onto the beam, only slightly visible again.

I let out a shaky breath. Mon Dieu, that was close. And . . . *a good man*? She called him a good man. I was right to be cautious. If Hélène truly believes in her father's goodness, she'd take Charlotte back to him, wouldn't she? She'd raise the alarm if we let her. We are right to keep Charlotte hidden—at least until we can find out more.

Hélène stays a little longer, collecting herself. And then she hands Mémé the empty bowl, thanks us for our hospitality, and says she wants to join the search for Charlotte. Clara tries to talk her out of it, tells her she's in no shape to be out there, that it's too risky, but Hélène only shakes her head and pulls our front door open.

"Merci again." Her voice is quiet as she pulls the door closed behind her.

"That poor, poor child," Mémé clucks, standing and pressing her hands to her diaphragm.

Clara throws me a significant look as she reaches for her grandmother's shoulder. "Mémé, we have to tell you something. You should sit back down."

But before she can, there's a shifting noise above us, and we all look up as Charlotte—having apparently decided that Mémé is safe—sits bolt upright on the beam.

Mémé goes bug-eyed, her jaw dropping comically as her gaze darts between the three of us.

"What in the earth and heavens above did you two do?"

7

WHEN WE EXPLAIN THE SITUATION TO MÉMÉ, HER EYES GO flinty.

"Wretched man," she says first. Then, "Monster." Then, "I'm proud of you, girls. You did the right thing."

She doesn't say anything else, just goes to work coaxing tea down Charlotte's throat and starting soup on the hearth. She forces Charlotte to eat the last of our bread because "growing girls need real sustenance, especially after a shock."

By now, the sheep are bleating a protest. They didn't get enough grazing time today, and they are never shy about letting us know when that happens.

"You girls go. I'll stay with Charlotte." Mémé waves us toward the sheep, who yell another protest in response. Then, tipping Charlotte's chin up with a finger, she smiles kindly. "You are safe with me, ma chérie. Don't fret."

Clara and I gather the sheep again and step into the day, which is bright, sunny, and bird-chirp-soaked because nature doesn't know any better. Or doesn't care that this little village is having a terrible day.

We nudge the sheep away from our usual routes—all of them too close to the scene of this morning's crimes—and to the riverbank, where clovers and grasses have grown a bit wild. The sheep *blea* their approval. My fool lamb startles at nothing and jumps into the river, and I jump in behind him, calf-deep, to fish him out.

"Can you go one hour without trying to kill yourself and me in the bargain, please?" I tut.

"BLEAAAA."

Eugénie, a girl just a little older than us, grazes her own sheep on the opposite bank. She waves, her body language somewhere between friendly and sad. She's another of the priest's usual targets, probably because she's so curvy and has been since long before any of the rest of us. She's also a girl who speaks her mind, which likely makes her number two on his hate list. Only usurped by me because I bit the man.

Both Clara and I wave back, but she's already busying herself with an older ewe who has managed to get a foot stuck in between the roots of a small tree that hangs over the water.

Clara occupies herself foraging alongside the sheep for edible plants to take home, as we always do, and I fall into step beside her. We keep our voices low so that they don't carry to Eugénie or anyone else who might be about.

"We need a plan," I say.

"How are you feeling?" Clara says at the same time.

We both laugh. How perfectly typical this is. How exactly *us*. Clara checking on the state of that little battered thing I call a heart. Me diving straight into the action.

She raises her eyebrows as if to say, *You first.*

Reluctantly, I let go of the urgent need to make a plan, to fix things, to have it all figured out, and I let her question in. How *am* I feeling?

Tired. My skin is stretched out with it, my head heavy. I could close my eyes and sleep for a year.

Angry. My jaw is tight with that, just waiting for another target to sink my teeth into. This village—this goddamn village— full of gossip and yet never telling the right secrets, the ones that could save us. I'm angry at all of us. The man who did this, of course, but every man who hurts anyone in any way, too. The man who hurt Charlotte. The men who killed the old priest. The new priest, who put his hands on me. And I'm angry at the rest of us for letting it happen. Not knowing or not caring enough to save the Charlottes and the Hélènes.

I reach deeper and find—

A stomach still in knots. A shiver stuck under my skin.

"Scared," I admit.

"Of what?" she whispers, as we both spot some edible mushrooms growing at the base of a tree and stoop to pluck them.

The obvious answers are there on the tip of my tongue. The murderer who's leading searches for his missing daughter. The unknown, wild thing that's killing shepherdesses. But those aren't really the fear that's rooting down inside me now. Clara knows it, which is why she asked instead of assuming. She always seems to know.

"I'm afraid we won't be able to save her." Tears spring to my eyes with the admission. "I'm afraid—" I take a deep breath. "I'm afraid that I'll fail her like my father failed me."

The other fear, the ever-present one, doesn't cross my lips. I'm afraid I'll fail Charlotte, yes. But there's another anxiety tied up with the first: of failing Clara, too. Of her realizing—like my father must have realized—that I am not worth staying for.

Clara leans across the space between us and kisses my cheek, calming the thoughts without even knowing them. "If we do fail, at least we tried. That's more than he did. You already did more than he did."

"I love you, Clara." The words sing through all the other feelings, the truest truth at the bottom of my heart.

"And I you. Forever."

"And ever," I complete our refrain.

"Amen." Clara glances to the sky.

"BLEAAA," the fool lamb agrees.

I scowl at him, then return Clara's cheek kiss. "And you? What are you feeling?"

"I feel like I'm a thousand years old."

I press the last of the mushrooms into the burlap bag over my shoulder and lace my fingers through hers, waiting for her to go on.

She closes her eyes slowly, opens them again just as slow. "I've been taking care of everyone since I was so little. I always had to. And I still do. I can't let Charlotte or Hélène suffer. But

I'm so tired. I just wish—" She laughs at herself. "I just wish I could live the way other people seem to, worrying only about themselves. And at the same time I *don't* wish that, because I wouldn't be me if I didn't care. So I guess I just wish I was less tired. Or people needed me less."

"If people needed you less, what would you do with your time?" I tease.

Despite my teasing tone, Clara looks thoughtful. "Garden. Learn to weave as deftly as the neighbors. Fall asleep in your arms early every night." She smiles. "And as long as we're dreaming about impossible things, I'd wish for our bellies to always be full and the weather always warm."

I unlace our fingers and draw her into a hug, where we stay until the three youngest lambs—my fool baby and two lambs Clara bottle-fed when their mother rejected them who now believe that Clara is their mother—wander over and start bumping gently into our legs. A reminder of exactly what Clara is tired of: how much every creature in this damn village needs her attention.

I realize, with a small twist in my gut, that I'm part of the problem here. Not only relying so much on her, perhaps, but my impulsiveness is what got us into this situation with Charlotte and Hélène. It's not just myself I'm burdening when I jump off a cliff on impulse. It's always Clara, too. It's always her pulling me up a cliff with a branch, hiding little girls on rafters, digging me out of the sinkhole I jumped into.

I kiss her cheek again because I can't think of how else to say *thank you* and *I'm sorry*; then I pull away and scowl down at the pushy lambs. "All right, you. Can't handle yourselves for more than ten minutes, eh?"

Clara laughs, stooping down to pet them. "Don't listen to her. She loves it when you bump around her ankles with your fuzzy little baby heads."

As we start to move the sheep along the riverbank, edging away from the village, I return to the practicalities of the situation I've put us in. "We need a plan—soon."

"I know. And I think you know, after what happened today, that I was right before. We can't keep her at the house. We have to take her to yours."

The muscles in my back and neck tense without my permission. "I know." Even as I agree with her, every part of me rings a warning.

"We have to take her as soon as possible. Tomorrow, early, unless there are still search parties out."

I nod my assent, and she grabs my hand, holds my gaze as she says, "It'll be all right. I know how you feel about that place. But you'll be all right. I promise."

I nod again, though my jaw is tight, then tease out the thread of our other problem. "Charlotte's young to be on her own, but if we can get Hélène out, too, she can care for her. Do you think she meant what she said about their papa being a good man?"

Clara's mouth arcs wryly upward. "It's amazing the delusion people are capable of. I've had people tell me in one breath that their sweetheart is the one who pulled an arm out of socket and in the next breath that they want to marry him."

We both stop to watch the sheep, silent for a long moment.

"So we figure out if Hélène is in danger and if it's safe to take her out of that house. And then . . ." I trail off, because there's a big blank space after that. None of this was a plan.

"Then we figure out how to keep them fed," Clara says.

She's right. It's hard enough to keep ourselves fed. Coming to the end of summer doesn't leave us much time to store up enough food to get them through winter.

She goes on, as if she read my mind, "I think we have to get them out of the village before winter."

My eyebrows arc in surprise, and the familiar fear flutters in my stomach like so many wings. *Out* is always a dangerous conversation. *Out* is leaving. *Out* is abandonment. "Get them out where?" I try to keep my voice steady.

"South, I think. You remember Belle used to tell you all about the coast. It's warm there."

I snort. "Yeah, if you trust Belle. Which I don't know why anyone would."

My former foster sister is something of a sore topic for me ever since her father dragged me off to live with them for a few months, calling it "Christian charity" and "saving an orphan" and ripping me away from the only people I cared about. I needed Belle to be on my side then, but she only ever tattled to her papa that I was ungrateful.

"You couldn't trust her with your secrets, sure, but you don't think she lied about the places she'd been, do you?" Clara cocks her head.

"No," I begrudgingly agree. "I think she was telling the truth, maybe embellished a little, but the truth."

"So that's our answer, then. The sunny south. We have to find a way to get them south."

The enormity of it crashes into me. Clara's right that we can't hide them here forever. The only logical conclusion is that we have to get them *away*. But Gévaudan is my whole world, and there's something dizzying and impossible about even trying to contemplate what a journey like that looks like. And still that little flutter of fear that I both know is irrational and also somehow believe: that Clara might also choose to go south, slip through my fingers like Papa did.

Still I try to help with her plan. "I suppose we find a way to send them on with a merchant next time one passes through the village?"

Clara nods. "Or a theatrical troupe."

I smile at that, the memory of the wonder of a live performance calming some of the jittery feelings in my chest. "That troupe only came here once."

"Yeah, well, maybe I would like to see them again, and if I say it out loud, they'll show up and solve our problem. The girls can sign on to clean up horse poop or something." Clara winks.

I laugh. Something about her saying "the girls" makes it clear to me that the thought of leaving hasn't crossed her mind. Just my mind playing tricks on me again. Just the deep scar of my father's departure ever convincing me that anyone else I love will eventually walk away, too.

The worst of my tension recedes. "Perfect plan. No critiques from me."

We loop the sheep back toward home, and Clara grows a little somber again. "Joséphine?"

"Yeah?"

"Whatever happens, just know I love you, all right?"

I stop walking and give her my full attention, lean in to press our foreheads together. "I love you, too, Clara. More than anything."

"Forever."

"And ever."

"Amen."

8

THE SCREAM IS A GUTTURAL, HEART-DEEP SOUND. IT IS TER-
ror and despair and a ripping, shredding loss distilled into sound
and wrenched from the deepest part of a person.

It wrests me from sleep, punches through dreams into my
gut and lungs.

I'm back in the cabin, watching my brother's last breath take
shape and rise into the eaves. I'm back at the window, watching
Papa disappear into the snow like a ghost. I'm back in the snowdrift, crawling inch by inch toward Clara's house. I'm back in
every nightmare I've had since. My body feels them all, weighing
me down. Dizzying.

And then I realize that *I'm not back there.* I'm here on the
straw mattress between Clara and Charlotte. The screams don't
belong to me. They're not coming from my pain.

Charlotte.

She's sweating, trembling, pulling herself up beside me, knees to her chest, arms tight around them, her face pressed into her kneecaps as she breathes unsteadily.

A nightmare. No surprise after what she's been through. But—the realization tears through me even as my breath starts to find its normal pace—*we cannot have her screaming here.* It's everything I was afraid of. We're too close to the other houses. All it would take is one neighbor knowing that the scream wasn't mine or Clara's or Mémé's. One neighbor lucid enough in the night to understand that someone else is in this tiny cottage. Someone who shouldn't be here. Or even one neighbor who thought it *was* us and that it was more than a nightmare. A Good Samaritan busting through the door and in on our secret.

I eye the door, sick to my stomach.

Clara's awake now, already wrapping her arms around Charlotte, promising her it was a dream, that she is safe. I should have done that. But instead I am frozen here, trying to separate myself from the past and my future fears enough to act in the now. Finally, I unfreeze enough to thread my fingers through Charlotte's as Clara rocks her gently back into sleep and then lays her beside Mémé, who has somehow slept through the whole thing.

When Charlotte's breathing has evened, Clara and I lie back down facing each other.

"One more hour of sleep, and then we'll take her before the sun comes up," Clara whispers, reaching out to brush a rogue hair off my face and tuck it behind my ear.

I nod. There is no other option.

She pauses. "Joséphine."

"Yeah?"

"I'm scared."

I lean my forehead in to touch hers. "Me too."

9

AFTER EVERYTHING, WE OVERSLEEP. NORMALLY WE TAKE the sheep out before the sun is even up, but now it's peeking over the horizon, turning the world orange. Even the fool lamb taking up residence next to my head sometime after the scream didn't wake me.

I curse under my breath as I slip from the warmth of the blanket to the chill morning air of late summer, press my feet to cool stone.

Save for the cheeky little bugger, the rest of the sheep are exactly where they should be: clustered in the stone kitchen like a couple dozen piles of fluff. Mémé is up and busying herself with the fire, Charlotte still curled in the blankets like a cat.

Mémé watches as I ease myself from the mattress and start to dress.

"Be a bit quieter, dear," she says, motioning to Charlotte. "Joséphine is still sleeping."

I stop, my heart sinking. The confusion is back, just like that. After such a lucid few days.

"Mémé, *I'm* Joséphine."

Mémé waves a dismissive hand at me. "I really don't understand your generation's jests, Celine."

I bite my lip. Celine is a name she calls me often during these episodes. We've never successfully gotten her to explain who that is.

Clara rises from the bed, easing the cheeky lamb off with her, and crosses to kiss Mémé gently on the forehead.

"Love you, Mémé," she whispers.

"I love you, too, Simone."

Clara's face is pained at the mention of her mother, but she doesn't say anything. When Mémé is like this, the only thing you can do is wait for it to pass.

Clara crosses to where I'm pulling on boots. "I think," she whispers, "that we need to check that there aren't a bunch of search parties about before we go marching out with her."

"I think you're right."

"If there are too many people out, we can take her tonight, when the sun goes down."

"I agree, but with Mémé like this, do you think we can leave Charlotte with her? What if she brings a neighbor over or tries to take Charlotte somewhere?"

Clara bites her lip, then turns to her grandmother and crosses the few steps between them. "Mémé, Joséphine isn't feeling well. Can you make sure she stays in bed and gets her rest? I think it's contagious, so nobody else should come by."

Mémé looks sharply at the bed. "Dear me, I didn't know. Why didn't you say something sooner? I'll start the tea."

Clara reaches out to squeeze her arm. "Merci, Mémé."

"I think that'll work," she says to me. "But just in case, let's go quickly."

We slip out the door and into gently warming sun, our footsteps finding familiar rhythm and our hands slipping effortlessly into each other's as we weave along the edge of the village. We pass the occasional artisan working in their yard or with their door open to coax in some sunshine, one of the neighbors getting a late start with her sheep. But no search parties. No unruly groups of men with pikes and flint-eyed stares.

Just as we are about to turn back for the cottage, a voice rings out.

Louis. Prankster. Would-be charmer. "Mes amours, haven't you heard? It's not safe for such tender, feminine things to be out of the house alone these days."

He slips around the corner of a nearby house and into step beside us, and I roll my eyes, but Clara smiles. It's a familiar smile, the kind Clara readily bestows on people. The one that cracks their secrets open, endears them to her instantly. But there is something else there, too, I realize with a small jolt. A familiarity I didn't realize they had. A special tenderness toward this boy.

Why?

I haven't seen him stopping by the house for remedies or chats. I don't think he's been spilling his personal secrets or bringing her an ailing relative to comfort.

Could it be that Clara has *feelings* for this boy? My heart skips a beat, and my palms go instantly sweaty. The rest of the village seems to have a crush on him. But merde, Clara should have more sense than that. The idea of falling in love with anyone in this village makes me queasy . . . and a prankster? The worst of a lot of bad options.

"Not safe for tender masculine things around here, either," I answer, thinking of Pascal.

Pain flashes across his face, and I remember—with a little regret at how casually I just mentioned the boy's fate—that Louis and Pascal were friends.

"Louis, how are you?" Clara's voice matches her smile, all softness and welcome as she reaches her free hand out to squeeze his shoulder.

Oh là là là là. No, Clara, *no.*

He cocks his head at her, not giving in to the seriousness of the question. "Well, I'm fine—and you're *fine.* But we're all about to be less fine." He wiggles his eyebrows.

I take the bait, partly because I want to know what "less fine" means to him and partly because I want him and Clara to stop locking eyes. "What's that supposed to mean?"

He grins. "Just that Lafont is on his way and a contingent of soldiers not a day's march behind him. They say the beast can kill a man with its breath alone, but I've heard the same for soldiers, and our village is about to play host to a whole company of them." He waves a hand dramatically in front of his nose.

I'm not sure which piece of information I hate more. Lafont—our regional government official, my former foster father—rarely comes here, which is how I like it. I haven't seen him in years, and still my stomach clenches with the probably unreasonable thought that he might try to take me away again. And soldiers coming . . . that can't be good, either. Not for hiding Charlotte, not for saving Hélène if we find that she wants to be saved. I suppose there's hope in it—the soldiers decidedly more likely than the village's men to catch the beast and put an end to so many casually brutal deaths. But something about the idea of so many armed men here in Mende makes my skin crawl. Couldn't they hunt the beast from Saint-Alban or Marvejols? Or Saugues, where there have been so many more attacks than here?

"Why are they coming *here*?" I snap.

Maybe it's a foolish question. Obviously, we have a beast problem. The exact kind of problem men like to solve, the kind that requires their violence. But nobody ever cared about us before . . . why now?

Louis wiggles his eyebrows again, clearly enjoying having so much gossip to share. "The papers picked up the story of our beast. We're famous now. Denisot says it's the first time a story from France has made it all the way to Germany."

My eyebrows arc skyward. The papers never pick up rural stories. It's the cities they spend their time on—and the cares of people in them. I know because when I lived with Lafont, reading those stories was part of my requisite daily lessons. Never mind that the tales of those cities felt completely alien to my own life. I never saw a single story that felt like it *mattered*. The illustrations were of menageries, shows—tigers and monkeys, tightrope walkers and contortionists. Never a long night of lambing or the sharp angles of a gorge or the concentrating face of a candle maker hard at work. Never the darkness we live with daily here, the ever-present possibility that our last breath is one wolf attack, ice storm, or fistfight away.

"Louis!" Another prankster pokes his head around the corner of a house. "Thought that was your voice. Did you hear that *Duhamel* is coming with the soldiers?" There's more than the usual amount of awe in the boy's voice.

"No way!" Louis throws up a triumphant fist.

"Who's Duhamel?" I ask.

Both boys gawk at me.

"Only the most decorated knight in France, best hunter in the kingdom," the second boy answers.

I nod, though that doesn't answer much. Anyone these boys hero-worship could easily be a rogue or pretender.

"Nah, come off it, Denisot," Louis disagrees loudly. "The *d'Ennevals* are the best hunters. Duhamel is a hero, no doubt, but *best* is a title reserved for the men who took down the largest wolf France has ever seen."

Denisot makes a dismissive noise. "Duhamel is a real hunter. The d'Ennevals took that wolf with bloodhounds and tricks."

"Since when do you look down on tricks?" I raise an eyebrow at the pranksters.

Grins spread across both faces, eyes sparking.

"Good point, this one." Louis points a thumb at me and looks at Denisot.

"Speaking of hunters . . ." Clara, ever more focused than me, moves the conversation seamlessly to the information we need. "Are people out hunting for it now? Still searching for the little girl?"

For the briefest moment, the grin slips from Louis's face, replaced by something raw. But then the mirth flickers back into place, and I wonder if I imagined it.

"No," Louis says after a beat.

"That little girl is long gone," his friend adds. "No point in keeping on looking."

Anger flashes in Louis's eyes then. "Zut. Don't be a prick, Denisot. She's not a missing house cat. She's a little girl—and your friend's little sister."

Denisot shrinks back from his friend, hands up. "All right, all right."

Clara and I exchange a glance. I don't know whether to be angry that the village has stopped looking so quickly, given up on Charlotte so easily, or relieved because no search parties means a clear path through the forest to my house, where Charlotte will be so much more well hidden. I'm also curious about Louis's anger. This boy, who is so rarely serious about anything from what I've seen, seems serious about this. I wonder if he has a little sister. Perhaps Charlotte reminds him of that, of the danger someone he loves might be in, too.

Before Clara and I start walking again, she reaches out to squeeze Louis's shoulder. "We need to take the sheep out. Take care of yourself, all right?"

He nods, then moves toward Denisot, the two disappearing around a corner, off—no doubt—to some mischief.

"Poor boy," Clara says softly as we point our faces and feet toward home.

I press my lips together, something strange and defensive rising in my chest. "You're too nice, Clara. There are other people doing worse here than Louis."

She only smiles sadly and takes my hand.

Back home, Clara ushers the sheep toward the door where I wait, holding it open—both of us quiet so as not to wake Mémé, who sometimes sleeps long and hard or at random times these days. Especially on the bad days, when she's confused.

Clara's sheep file out first, braver or more trusting than mine. Mine use them as cover, like the imps they are. I imagine they're thinking: *If there's a wolf out there, better them than me.*

I raise a disapproving eyebrow at them, but I don't speak. Mémé deserves her rest. I won't be the one to deny her another hour of sleep.

After I triple-check that the coast is clear, Charlotte follows my sheep out and I close the door behind us. We walk as quickly as we can up the hill behind the cottage and into the trees, where a game trail carves through thick brush out of sight of the houses.

Out of sight of the houses means safety from Charlotte's papa and *less* safety from the creature we've blamed for her disappearance. I become acutely aware of it the moment the village disappears behind us. Thorns snag at my ankles, and dread snags at my heart. My mind can't help but flash me pictures of what would be a deeply ironic end to this whole thing. Killed by the very creature we've been using as cover. Our necks in the vise of a powerful jaw. Our chests pressed to the earth by paws the size of a head. Our end bloody and bleak.

I shake the images away, nudging the straggler sheep at the end of the line, and we march, each of us silent and separated by clusters of sheep, who make mildly irritated noises. They're used to our shorter routes to the tastiest grasses, not used to the snagging thorns and the way the scree on this trail shifts under their feet. Only the oldest among them have ever gone this way. That's how long I've been avoiding it myself. While our herd is generally amicable, my sheep in particular hate change. They know better than to run off, but their huffing is meant to let me know they do not approve.

Well, I don't, either, sheep, but we're all just going to have to cope.

"Joséphine." Charlotte whispers my name, speaking for the first time all morning.

I stop and face her, stooping so that we're eye to eye. "Yes, mon amie?"

"What if he hurts Hélène?" Charlotte's knuckles tighten on Clara's hand.

Clara squeezes that hand reassuringly. "We'll get her away, too. Don't worry, little love."

"But I should have come out at the house. I shouldn't have hidden from her."

Clara and I exchange a look, still uncertain.

"We asked you to hide. You did such a good job," I answer, reaching my hand forward to take Charlotte's free one and squeeze my own reassurances into it. "First, we need to get you to the cottage where you'll be safe. Then we will figure out how to bring Hélène."

"You promise?"

I hold her gaze. "I promise."

I squeeze her hand one more time and then rise to my feet and lead us onward. My boots tapping lightly on packed red dirt, sheep still huffing their impatience at me as we go.

The closer we get to my house, the fewer signs of humanity we see. The more the hair rises across my arms, the back of my neck. *Danger,* my heart whispers. *Danger.*

There's a reason I nearly died up here. The same reason my father loved it. It's isolated, surrounded on all sides by trees. An old cart path is overgrown completely now, young trees and thick brush taking up residence. Ferns obscuring knife-sharp stones that would stab through the soles of the boots of anyone who took that way. The second path, the one we're following, is a thin, trampled, weaving thing—red as a wound—that emerges behind our old barn.

It's warm outside, but my skin is clammy as we grow close. My breath ragged. Through the trees, I see the dark wood of the barn, its broad side weather-worn and the slope of the roof thickly overgrown with vines and ferns. My stomach clenches involuntarily.

We're here. And I'm not sure what I'm afraid will happen, but *I am afraid.* Of the place itself, I guess. Of what happened here.

Of what my father did, leaving me behind, and maybe of

what it means about me. That I'm not just discarded but *discardable*. The kind of girl who couldn't even inspire enough love for my own blood to save me. Is that fear or sadness raking its claws along the other side of my heart's door?

As we spill from the forest into the clearing around the barn and house, half mud and half weeds, my stomach tightens, my muscles clenched and ready to flee. There is no danger here. No beast standing in the clearing, teeth bared. But my body clings to the *memory* of danger, and all I want is to turn and run. The worst of those memories flash before my eyes—and I feel every one of them lodge deep inside me. I feel ice like needles under desperate fingernails, see my brother's chest go still, smell Papa's sweat as he leaned down to kiss me goodbye, forever. Dread and grief sink like twin boulders in my gut, impossibly heavy.

I try to ignore the feelings, focus on what's here and now. Beside the barn, weather-worn fence posts are draped in lacy fungus, an eerie gray-green color. Above them, pine boughs shiver in a light wind. Below, a bed of shed pine needles is the rust-red color of drying blood.

This is the place he disappeared, my dread-soaked heart reminds me. Now, rust-red and viper-green. Then, covered in snow so high that it nearly swallowed the fence posts. The world beyond it stark white and fading gray shadow. My breath is coming too fast, and I'm dizzy. I close my eyes to block out the place, but I can still see it clearly. This time with Papa silhouetted against the white. He morphs into Clara in my mind, the person I'd be most devastated to see walk into the forest without me. It's like I'm in one of the worst of my nightmares, only I'm awake.

This is why I didn't want to come here. This is why I *couldn't* come here.

I lean forward, hands on knees, trying to make the feeling stop, trying not to cry.

Clara's hand comes down soft on my shoulder, and instead of stopping the tears, it looses them. I sink to the dark-red-and-black dirt, breathing long and deep through my nose. I can feel myself shaking, but I can't stop it. Can't stop the burn in my throat, the tightening behind one eye.

Clara sinks down with me, and then—as if she's the one saving me and not the other way around—Charlotte joins us, wrapping skinny arms around my waist and pressing her face into my right shoulder.

I push my fingernails sharp into my palms. *The clearing is only a clearing,* I remind myself. *The house only a house. The barn only a barn.* My father is gone. This place cannot take him again.

But what if it takes Clara? I know the thought is nonsensical, but I can't keep it from flipping my stomach again.

"I love you," Clara whispers, as if she can read my mind.

"And I you." I return the sentiment between long, ragged breaths as my heart starts a slow descent toward its normal pattern.

"Forever." She kisses the place where the tears have traced their way down my left cheek.

"And ever."

"Amen."

I open my eyes and try to see the place as Clara does. Not

tainted, not cursed. Not a nest of memories like so many spiders. It isn't falling apart nearly as much as I imagined. It's sturdy, if filthy. Through the open door of the cottage, I can see nests in corners, cobwebs stretched from beam to beam, ceiling to floor. But these are fixable things. Clara is right; Charlotte will be safe here for now.

Charlotte will be safe. I cling to that thought, use it as a weapon against the others.

When my breathing is normal again and the darkness has released my vision, I let Clara help me to my feet, and the three of us approach the cottage. My fool lamb and two other youngsters follow us through the door of the house and take a path through the room perfectly calculated to cover them in as many cobwebs as possible. The normalcy of it is grounding, if further proof that that there's no thought in any of their little fluffy heads.

The little fool trots up to me and baas loudly.

"Look, you did that to yourself. I'm not sticking my hands in there and getting a spider bite," I answer.

"BLAAAA," he returns, louder.

"You should have thought of that before you decided to open up your own personal Spider Inn."

Behind me, Charlotte giggles. The lamb looks as disgruntled as a lamb can look and takes another lap around the room, followed by his fellows.

Clara draws close again and touches my elbow. "You going to be all right?"

I press conviction I don't feel into my nod. Because more

than one thing can be true at once, and my two truths are these: I am not all right, *and* Charlotte will be safe here.

She squeezes my elbow. "I'm proud of you."

I only laugh. Proud of what? This barely-held-together mess of a person who feels danger when there is none?

For the next few hours, we work, trading off between indoor and outdoor duties. I still jump at strange noises, feel waves of nausea at certain views, but they don't incapacitate me, and I pull my weight. Clara watches the sheep as they graze around the house and barn while I clean the chimney flue—the inside of the dirty chimney strangely comforting since it holds no memories for me. I watch the sheep as Clara chops wood for the hearth. Charlotte stays inside on our stern orders and scrubs the stone floor, sweeps away whatever spiderwebs the lambs haven't already mopped up with their bodies. She brings up her sister twice more, her voice always strained, and it's clear that's what's on her mind. My anger flares for the man who made this eight-year-old child feel that she is responsible for her sister's safety. Flares again because he's the reason I have to be here, facing this place that makes me want to tear off my own skin.

When we're done with our scrubbing and chopping and furniture rearranging and the lambs have dusted the whole room with their damn empty heads, it almost looks like a home again—just barer. Less full of people and trinkets. Only a few possessions left behind—a small table, two chairs, a moth-ravaged blanket, an old kettle that needs a serious scrub.

Luckily, we brought a few things with us. Blankets, a flint, bowls, some food. Charlotte will be all right here, at least while we figure out what to do.

After a few more instructions for Charlotte—stay quiet, stay inside as much as you can, only light a fire in the hearth if there's a storm or the temperature drops dangerously low—and a promise to come back each day, we leave.

Clara and I pull the door closed behind us and sigh in unison. I think both sighs mean the same thing: *it's going to be all right.* For the first time since we found Pascal's body, my own body relaxes into that belief, the feeling that the immediate danger has passed. Charlotte is safe now. She's here, far from prying eyes. The house is secure enough to keep her both hidden and protected. She knows how to make a fire, how to brew tea, how to forage for edible plants—we made her demonstrate each skill. And while it still feels unfair to leave her alone with her nightmares—no Mémé to spoon her in the night, no Clara to reassure her with whispers, not even a fool lamb to try to comfort her by stepping on her face—she's safer here than she'd be with us. And perhaps, if all goes according to plan, Hélène will be here with her soon. Big sister. Big spoon.

I hold out a hand for Clara and whistle loudly at my sheep. "Time to go home, ladies."

A quick head count tells me the only one missing from my flock is the cheeky lamb. Because of course he is.

After an unbothered few seconds of searching, I find him with his head stuck in the barn door and scowl, scolding, "You'd be dead if it weren't for me; I hope you know that."

"BLEEAAAAA."

"Glad you agree."

I lean down to see how he even managed this newest feat of idiocy, and it looks like he had to turn his head completely sideways to get it in between the beams, like a goddamn contortionist.

"Clara, can you come help me . . . ," I start to ask but trail off at the end.

Once again, something is wrong. Something my heart picks up on before my mind. Like the butterflies dipped in blood. Everything looks correct until you peer a bit closer.

I place a hand on the lamb's back to calm him as I stare at the side of the barn, letting my mind catch up with my animal instinct. The thing now screaming at me to run.

It feels different than the terror of my arrival. That was the terror of memory, the unspecified dread of the place. This is an urgent, instinctual, present fear. Like I'm a deer who heard the crack of a branch under predator feet.

It isn't until Clara gasps behind me that my understanding of why slips into place.

On the side of the barn, alongside the scars of wood worn down by time, neglected and abandoned, are other scars. Deep and dangerous.

The scars of claws pressed into and raked down the wood.

An animal stretching, sharpening its weapons.

This stretch, this kind of clawing, is a thing that wolves never do. A reason that the small portion of the village that believes this beast is merely a wolf pack grown bold is dead wrong. Emphasis on dead.

I press a hand to the deeply scarred wall, feel those scars in my own soul.

Until now, the beast could have been anywhere. The deaths

attributed to him here were not orchestrated by him. The rest of the village doesn't know that, but we do. He might have taken up residence in Paris for all Clara and I knew.

But now.

Now.

We know.

The beast is here.

10

THE DAY LAFONT ARRIVES IS THE DAY THE BEAST STRIKES
again. This time, I believe, for real.

We know because a scream like a knife's edge slices through
the village and into each of us. It is long and high and desperate,
like no other scream I've ever heard. Not a moment of terror,
but a stretched-out series of moments. Death coming but not
coming quickly enough.

A young man—twenty years old, candle maker, new father—
has been separated from his head. The rest of him a shredded
mess. The head nowhere to be found. Carried off by the time
the first person who'd heard the cry had rushed to its source.
It's unusual, the beast taking a man—and a grown one at that—
and I wonder if the creature has grown bolder, going after larger
prey now.

Clara and I are on our way to check on Charlotte—who is

still hiding in my cottage because there's nowhere else to put her, despite the signs that the beast was there—when we see people rushing toward the square and we follow.

Around us, speculation flies. "It's a serial killer dressed in wolfskin!" one man yells in the square. "A demon summoned from hell because we lost the war," another whispers. "A witch," some hiss, triggering an instant knot in my stomach. "A witch just like the old priest. A friend of his hell-bent on revenge."

They would keep their girls indoors if they could, I know. If we didn't have to graze the sheep or risk starving this winter. These families would lock their children up inside and board up the windows against that stalking evil.

Since they can't afford to do so, the past few days have been full of compromises. Children sent out in groups instead of solo. Shepherdesses grazing their sheep on the nearest land instead of the farther, nicer fields. That won't last long before the land is overgrazed but it's a temporary talisman against some of the village's fears.

"It's worse than the fever," a woman rushing ahead of me says in pained wonder. "I didn't think any curse would be worse than the fever."

"I'd take a fever any day over what that poor man just suffered," her companion answers as we all turn a corner and spread out into the square.

When we reach the church steps, I pull up short.

Étienne Lafont in his shockingly clean new clothes, polished boots, and politician's smile stands on the church steps next to our beady-eyed priest. Though the pranksters said he was on his way, something about seeing him here is still startling. We so rarely host him here in Mende. We have little to offer a man so well positioned. He spends his time at his grand house in Le Puy and sometimes travels even as far as Lyon or Paris or the sea.

To everyone here, this man means money and power. A visit from him means something has gone terribly wrong. But to me, he means something else, too. Obligation and something akin to powerlessness. The year my family died was a terrible one here. They weren't the only casualties. And so Étienne came—to survey the scene of our collective devastation. That was when his sense of Christian duty tore me away from the family I'd made.

"God tells us to help widows and orphans," he announced when he showed up on Mémé's doorstep and dragged me, sobbing and screaming, to a carriage so fancy it might as well have been solid gold. I hated every swirl of paint, every perfect stitch on the cushions, every glamorous inch of that carriage. Still hate it with a hate that's bigger than my own body. It spills over when I see those touches of glamour.

I lived with him and his daughter, Belle, for two excruciating months. They made it their mission to make me better—*normal,* they said. And I could feel the full weight of their disapproval at every nightmare, every tear, every time I thought about my house, my brother, my mother, and got so dizzy that I needed to sit down on the floor then and there. All I wanted every minute of every day was to go *home.*

Not to my house, but to Clara's. To Mémé, who listened to what I said. To Clara, who made me laugh and dance with her. To the aunties who lived in the houses around us, scolding good-naturedly when our antics left us dust-drenched or battle-scarred.

I ran away from Lafont five times. I didn't even know how to get back to Mende, but I tried. Nobody can ever accuse me of not trying. I can feel the blisters on my feet just as vividly as I feel the ice under my fingernails. Both escapes were essential to my survival.

Eventually, I won the battle. Finally, Étienne threw his hands up and said, "God can't save those beyond saving."

And so being beyond God's saving grace was what saved me in the end.

Now Lafont speaks to the crowd, and I listen, hating that he's here but knowing his presence also means information. "I know that there have been many losses lately in our great region. Three in Mende here, so many more in our neighboring villages. And as we pray for their souls and for an end to this scourge on our homes"—he motions to the priest, standing at the other side of the church staircase and nodding along—"God has also called upon us to act and act decisively. The king has heard our despair, and he is sending his best hunters, his soldiers, to end this so-called beast and bring its corpse back to Paris."

A ripple of approval moves through the crowd, growing in volume. I glance around me, nodding at the aunties, the village butcher, the women who weave our wool. Eugénie is there, looking on with interest. She has a split lip and a fresh bruise on her neck, but she doesn't look pained. I wonder, fleetingly, what happened. To my surprise, I also see Belle in the crowd. Her father doesn't usually bring her on short trips, so that doesn't bode well. She's wearing a spotlessly clean dress and shined leather shoes and—a new and strange addition—a bright red bird sitting on her right shoulder.

Lafont goes on, tugging my attention back in his direction. "The soldiers will be here shortly, and I expect everyone to pay them their due respect. Each of you will take a soldier into your home. Feed them. Shelter them. They are our salvation." He pauses on the last sentence and lifts his hands for emphasis.

A murmur passes through the crowd, and I turn to Clara, wide-eyed. Did he just say that we'd be *housing soldiers*? And *feeding* them? What delusion is this man living in?

A gruff older man echoes my own thoughts, holding up a disbelieving hand in Lafont's direction. "Soldiers in our homes, you say? We barely have room for ourselves!"

A chorus of agreement rises.

Lafont lifts a hand, "Now, now, is that any way to—"

"Feed them? We almost starved last winter. I don't have the stores to feed another mouth end of summer like this." A female voice this time, one of the weavers.

"The king is the richest man in France. He can't send his men with their own stores?"

"Yeah!"

"True!"

"Now, listen—" Lafont tries to regain control of the crowd.

"Lafont, this feels a lot like the time you tried to tell us to put together a permanent beast patrol at night and we told you to fuck off." This time it's a prankster piping in, laughter at the edges of his tone.

Snickers of amused agreement ripple through the crowd. As usual, when the pranksters have their sights set on someone else, we all love them. Speaking our mind for us. We're afraid of the beast, but not more afraid of it than starvation.

"What's to keep us from telling you to fuck right off now?" the boy asks, emboldened by the crowd's reaction.

Lafont flushes pink. "I should think the edict of the king is quite enough for all of us. But—" He raises a hand again and shouts over the growing burble of voices, the insults starting to flow ever faster. "BUT—if that isn't enough for you, there's this."

Lafont looks imperious now. "The king is offering a reward of *four thousand livres.*"

At that, the whole crowd goes silent. So silent and so sudden that it feels like being struck temporarily deaf. And maybe I *have* been struck deaf. It would make more sense than what just actually happened.

Four thousand livres. It's more money than any of us here have seen in our lives. The kind of riches that could get a person out of here. No more living on the edge of starvation, the edge of freezing.

Lafont looks satisfied to have all our attention back. "Yes, four thousand livres to the man who kills the beast. Treat your soldiers well, and they may share their bounty. Kill the beast yourself and it's yours."

Irritation bunches through me. So it isn't four thousand livres for us for housing soldiers, as he first implied. It's for whichever man does the violence the king needs. And we're all just supposed to *hope* whatever man does it also takes pity on the people whose cellar he's been plundering? I must be the only one thinking this way, since no one else challenges him.

"The soldiers will be here soon. I suggest you prepare a place for them." Lafont waves a hand as if he's dismissing us all.

As the crowd starts to thin, everyone returning to their shepherding and weaving and caretaking tasks, I find my attention back on Belle. The one still person in a sea of retreating backs. Her bird preens itself as she watches her father speaking to the priest.

"Speak like a lady," the creature suddenly screeches in perfect French, and I feel my mouth drop open.

"Did that bird . . . just talk?" Clara is beside me, looking as bewildered as I feel.

"It definitely did."

"How?"

I shake my head.

Clara is apparently dead set on finding out. She starts purposefully toward Belle. And while I don't particularly want to talk to Belle—now or ever—after a beat, I follow.

Belle's eyebrows flash upward in surprise when she sees us coming. "Well, well, well, here come the last people I'd expect a bonjour from." She skips the usual cheek kisses, and Clara doesn't object. Unusual for her, but Belle is the only person Clara seems to hate. Well, her and her father. No real surprise since Clara is the one who had to put me back together when they finally gave up on keeping me. I was a mess when I came to Clara through the ice tunnel and a mess all over again when Lafont finally returned me to Mémé's door. Despite all their talk of Christian charity, the

Lafonts didn't even leave us with some grain or money or one of the fancy cakes they'd trot out at their parties to impress the guests.

I wouldn't have expected them to give us a cake, but two months in that house had taught me just how much they had. How much they could have afforded to share if they'd wanted to.

Now, it seems, they've moved up in the world even further. The strawberry-red bird with a near-human voice must be some kind of luxury item.

"What is it?" Clara says after an awkward moment, reaching a hand tentatively toward the bird. "Did it just talk?"

Belle grins. "He does talk, in fact. His name is Jean, and he is a macaw. It's a type of parrot." She turns her head slightly toward the bird. "Jean, say something for the girls."

We wait, but Jean only cocks his head slightly, staring at us with one beady black eye.

"Jean, I said the ladies want to hear from you." An irritated edge creeps in over Belle's pride, and while I do very much want to hear the bird say something again, that desire battles hard with my glee at Belle's annoyance over being ignored.

Jean ignores her once again, reaching his charcoal beak into the bright feathers to groom himself.

Clara looks how I feel: both disappointed and smirky. And that pushes me over the edge into full enjoyment of the situation. Because I love Clara's pettiness, and I love it especially when it's directed at Belle. There's something gorgeous about seeing her smirk at the other girl's expense.

"Well, he must not like you very much." Belle tries to recover her bruised pride.

"Or maybe he's an animal, not a toy." Clara bats her eyes as she says it.

Belle fake-smiles back.

"Where'd you get him from?" I ask after a few seconds, curiosity overpowering my enjoyment of the tense silence.

"He's from a menagerie. Papa convinced them to part with him after we saw him perform."

"What's a menagerie?" Clara asks.

Belle laughs as if not knowing is the most ridiculous thing in the world. And for her, I suppose it is. She doesn't know how small the world can be in a village like ours. A theater company set up camp here once, but menageries are far beyond the reach of Mende. The only reason I know about them is because of the papers and advertisements she and her father forced on me during my lessons.

I break in before Belle can give an unbearably smug answer. "Menageries are a bit like the theater, but all animals—no human performers. Birds like hers. Tigers and lions. Monkeys. They ship them across whole oceans to perform."

Belle looks triumphant, staring at Clara and expecting something. Awe, I suppose.

Instead, Clara looks pained. "That's . . . awful."

Belle jerks her head slightly back as if Clara slapped her. "What do you mean? It's amazing! We can see the animals of the world. Not be small-minded like people in these tiny villages."

Jean chooses that moment to chime in. "Speak like a lady."

I exhale a small laugh, but Clara isn't deterred by the interruption. "And what if the 'animals of the world' wanted to stay home? You people, I swear. You never think that anything—anyone—other than yourself has their own life."

"Rich coming from a shepherdess. How are your sheep different than my parrot?"

Clara huffs in disbelief. "At least shepherdesses understand animals. I know not to take a sheep and make it try to live in the water or in a cellar or on the roof of my house. Because it's an animal with needs, and it needs a certain way of living. You don't know what this animal needs." She motions toward Jean, and he flaps his wings.

"Mon Dieu," screams the bird.

Mon Dieu, indeed, sir.

Belle rolls her eyes. "Understanding sheep doesn't make you an expert on anything else. Perhaps leave that to the people who have actually seen these animals before. Everyone who's anyone has an exotic pet. I think important people like the king know more about it than a few shepherdesses."

"Why are you even here, Belle?" I ask, taking Clara's hand because I know sometimes Belle's jabs about being a shepherdess get to her. Even though they shouldn't.

"Papa said he's here until they catch the oversize wolf that's been running around out here. He didn't want me home alone with the tutors that long. So I'm here for the duration." She flits her gaze between our faces. "Unfortunately."

Wolf. It's interesting that she still thinks that's what it could be. Even with so many eyewitnesses saying it is something else. Even with it stalking people and never sheep. I could tell her it's not. Could tell her we saw the claw marks. But Belle only believes what Belle wants to believe, and with Charlotte hiding out, the less we say about anything, the less attention we draw to ourselves, the better.

"Well, nice seeing you, Belle," I say, starting to pull Clara—who looks like she might try to rescue Belle's bird from her at any moment—back toward the house.

"Wish I could say the same, *sister.*" Belle says *sister* like she actually means *spider.* "Try not to get yourselves in trouble and embarrass Papa while we're here."

I stop, tighten my grip on Clara, and, just like that, our roles reverse, Clara gently tugging me away while my anger sparks brighter against the flint that is my former foster sister.

Belle loves that anger. She thrives on it. Seeing it rise now brings a smile to her smug face. "What? I needed to say something. Can't have you rushing off into the forest with your little pike trying to take down the wolf yourself."

"Mon Dieu!" screams the bird.

"And what if I did?" I retort, fully turned back toward her now.

"Then I imagine you'd die a bloody death. Leave it to the men. We're just girls. There's nothing we can do here. That's why there are soldiers coming."

My anger has gone from spark to flame. Perhaps *she* can't do anything, this rich girl who has been protected her whole life. Never made her own meals, followed a lamb off a cliff, held back a wolf at the end of a pike, stared it down.

But I have.

I wasn't planning on going after the beast, but this disdain for the idea that a girl *could* be the one to take it down is misplaced as hell. I'm not the only girl in Gévaudan who has seen the cold eyes of death and won the staring match. Clara has pressed her hands to bleeding men's wounds and saved their lives. She's stitched a sheep's claw-sliced flesh back together with a sewing needle. Mémé killed a viper with her bare hands. She's conjured meals from almost nothing, kept us alive on little more than air. Not to mention that the only two known instances of successfully fighting off the beast were by a band of children and a young woman: Marie-Jeanne Valet. I can picture it even though I wasn't there those few months ago: Marie-Jeanne coming to her sister's defense with only a pike. Soaked to the bone from battling the beast at the edge of the river, falling in, flying out with a battle cry. Bloody and wet and furious and screaming. Her bayonet striking at the center of the thing's wide chest. It ran away bleeding, too battle-weary to take her on. Her little sister, safe. Her self, *safe.*

The story of the boys was similar. A rowdy little band of too-skinny children face to face with the beast, attacking it with stones and pikes and even fists when it tried to take first one then another of them. They tired it out, cut it enough times, and it retreated.

The triumphant were not men, not even teenage boys. *Ten-year-old children and women not past twenty.* That's who has foiled the beast. Not all the men who've claimed they shot it and then it got right back up and kept on killing.

"Don't be a fool." My voice is sharp as I contradict Belle. "Marie-Jeanne Valet was a girl, too. She fought the beast off with her bayonet, saved her sister's life."

She tosses up a casual hand, and her bird flaps wildly,

disturbed by the gesture. "And that's why they call her the Maid of Gévaudan. She's Jeanne d'Arc, Joséphine. A legend. Not just a girl."

"My point exactly. Any of us can be a legend. You don't know until you're faced with the evil thing you have to destroy."

"Mon Dieu, mon Dieu, mon Dieu!" shrieks the bird.

"Mon Dieu," I agree.

Then I give in to the pressure Clara's putting on my arm, and I follow her through what's left of the crowd.

As soon as we're out of the village, my anger fizzles, replaced by a soft, sick dread deep in my belly. We step into the cool canopy of the forest, our feet pressing indents into soft mud coaxed into existence by a light rain the night before, and I whisper the concern that's building in me. "You don't think soldiers will try to take over my house, do you? Is Charlotte still safe there?"

Clara bites her lip. "I think they would try if they knew about it. But I don't think anyone is going to tell them. And if they're all assigned to our houses, nobody will be looking for another place to stay, right? I think . . . I hope that's not something we need to worry about."

I laugh, a strange, ironic sound. "I mean, thank God, since we have enough things to worry about."

11

IT'S BEEN TWO DAYS SINCE LAFONT ARRIVED AND, IF RUMOR can be trusted, today is the day that the delayed soldiers will join him. I'm still worried about us housing them, feeding them. I'm still on edge about what it might mean to have them scouring the forests for the beast when we're hiding a vulnerable little girl. But part of me is relieved, too. Because perhaps they can lift the heavy fog of fear that's settled on the village.

There are so many fewer open doorways with songs floating from them. Children are hushed when they scream-laugh, kept indoors to play at the hearth instead of the yard. More than one mother comes to the square vacant-eyed, haunted by the reality that her children—the ones in the fields with the sheep, the ones she can't afford to lock away at home, lest they all starve this winter—could be next.

Clara and I pick our way through the too-quiet streets, our

steps echoing off cobbles as we move toward the square to trade some chard for carrots.

It's unsettling, the silence. But even more unsettling is the state of the square as we turn the corner and come into view of the cathedral. A ghost town with a population of one. A single figure—slight, pale—hands clasped around the candles she must be out to deliver.

It's Hélène. If possible, she looks even smaller than the last time we saw her, like the days between have stolen little pieces of her soul, left her little more than a hungry ghost. She sees us watching her and raises a hand in greeting, and without consulting, we both move toward her. We've tried to find her more than a few times, but the stars were never aligned in our favor. She was always out delivering candles or at the house with her father. Never alone, never within reach.

The center of Mende isn't normally the best place for a private conversation, but today our bad fortune is also our good fortune. Fear has given us the space to talk.

"Hélène." Clara leans in and kisses both cheeks, leaving a comforting hand on the younger girl's shoulder. "How are you feeling?"

Hélène laughs, the sound bitter and hollow. "So sad that it shreds me into pieces. Then so numb that I wonder if I will ever feel again. Then so guilty that I'm not honoring their memories because I'm not sad enough. Then so angry that I could kill the beast myself, with my bare hands."

The honesty is unexpected and shocking, like a cold plunge into the river. It slices through me, leaves me speechless in its wake.

Clara doesn't have the same problem. "It's not on you."

"It *is* on me." Hélène makes a fist and presses it to her lips as if she can keep the words from spilling out. "I couldn't keep them safe."

Clara and I share a significant look. Does she mean safe from the beast—or from their father?

In my peripheral vision, I see some of the usual morning crowd filtering quietly into the square. Women meeting to trade what they have for what they need. Others here for news, for rumors, for a scrap of knowledge that might make a difference.

"You couldn't have known what would happen." Clara's voice is soft, keeping our conversation private even as the square slowly starts to hum.

"I could. I *did*. I . . . I think maybe Papa—"

Bang! A shot silences Hélène and sends a flinch shuddering through us all. Several people shout in alarm. And I whip around to look as a broad-shouldered man in his thirties rides into the square, his horse snorting and musket pointed skyward. His skin is tawny, his eyes blue, his hair a slightly lighter shade of red than my own. But the most noticeable thing about him is the way his shoulders pull back, chest and chin jutting forward. This is a man who believes wholeheartedly in the next words he says.

"Good people of Gévaudan, your salvation has arrived!"

Behind him, soldiers file into the square, some on horseback, others on foot. They're younger than I expected, some probably our age, very few anywhere close to as old as their leader. They're rowdy and bright-eyed, shoving each other good-naturedly, swinging their muskets with an alarmingly casual air, and speaking fast and strange.

It takes me a moment to realize they're not speaking French. And then to realize that I don't think they're even all speaking one language. There's one group speaking something that is thick and deep and guttural. Another light and musical and I can catch a word here or there, though pronounced so strangely that I'm not sure if I'm understanding right.

I glance at Hélène and Clara, both gaping at the display as the square starts to fill not only with soldiers but with the curious faces of our neighbors, drawn in by the ruckus. I wish I could ask Hélène what she was about to say, but our barely private conversation has now become not-at-all private. *I think maybe Papa . . .* How were you going to finish that sentence, Hélène? You think he hurt them? Is that what you were about to say? Or something less close to the truth? You think he misses them? You think he loved them?

The frustration of the interruption tightens across my skin, and then another interruption dashes any hope I have of restarting the conversation even at a whisper. Eugénie sidles up to us, still sporting a slightly bruised lip, still—as always—walking with purpose, confidence.

"I wish I could be one of them," she says, using her chin to point at the soldiers. Then, to the sky, she calls, "Saint Joseph, do you hear me?"

I draw my eyebrows together. "What?"

"The soldiers." She waves a hand at the unruly bunch. "They left home, traveled. Someone else feeds them and houses them. Takes them places. Soldiers don't starve to death. Nobody bothers them."

Clara frowns. "I think the English 'bothered them' quite a bit. They say we lost thousands of soldiers in the war."

"But we lost them fighting, at least. They're not . . ." Eugénie searches for the word. "Just waiting around for something to happen to them."

"You'd rather face down British guns than stay here?" I ask, that tight feeling returning to my gut, whispering, *Danger, danger, don't give Clara any ideas.*

Eugénie is apparently clear on her answer. She reaches up to touch her swollen lip, looks me straight in the eyes. "Anything would be better than living here."

We all fall silent, watching her. Is Eugénie suggesting what I think she is? That the swollen lip, the bruised neck, are the result of living here. That someone here is hurting her. Like someone here hurt Pascal and Charlotte and Hélène?

"Some say the beast is actually a man." She turns her eyes away from us and watches the soldiers. Then, more quietly, "I believe it."

When her eyes meet mine again, they're troubled. She's probably deciding she's said too much. Been too bold.

I turn and glance at Hélène, who looks like she's seen a ghost, and Clara, watching with her usual compassion, as Eugénie sidles away as fast as she came.

It all happened so fast, it's only now that the truth smashes headlong into me, the anger flashing hot at its heels. *Someone is most definitely hurting Eugénie.* Oh la vache—is every man in this village hurting every girl? Have we all been keeping the exact same secrets? The busted lips from a spooked sheep, the burns from candle wax, the tears from "being emotional creatures." Are they all cover for the same evil?

Clara opens her mouth to say something to Hélène, but again we're interrupted, this time by the sharp shout of a man's voice ringing through the noisy square. "Hélène, get over here!"

Hélène jolts like she's been hit, opens her mouth, closes it, and rushes away from us across the cobblestones. Her papa waits, stone-faced, and reaches for her shoulder as she approaches, but she shies away, follows him out of the square and toward her house.

Clara leans over and slides her arm around my rib cage, pulling me tight to her side and whispering into my neck. "She's terrified."

I nod.

"We need to get her out of there."

I nod again.

"Soon."

I nod a third time, squeeze her hand. "Clara?"

"Yeah?"

"I don't think we can stop with just Charlotte and Hélène." I aim my gaze pointedly at Eugénie, standing across the square, her lips quirked in an impish smile at a young, bewildered-looking soldier.

I say it before even thinking it through. Which I suppose is normal for me now. Off the cliff, through the ice, hands in the dirt and blood shredding a skirt to pieces. I am all impulse.

Clara leans over to kiss my cheek. "You know I agree. But, Joséphine, I don't know how. It's going to be hard enough to feed

Charlotte and Hélène and keep them hidden. Hard enough to find a way to get them away somewhere."

"I know. But anything else feels like I'm feeding Eugénie straight to the wolves. You saw her lip, heard what she just implied."

Clara presses her forehead to my neck. "You know, everyone in the village thinks you're so tough. But you're just an old softy in there."

I snort. "Tell that to the teeth marks on our priest."

She laughs back. "True. Really, you're like a predator. A wolf or a barn cat. Soft when you want to be, fatal when you don't."

She's not wrong. But even as she calls me soft for wanting to help them, I know the truth: it's the *fatal* part of me that wants it, not the soft part. I want to leave my teeth marks on the souls of each of those men, make them scared to put their hands on another girl.

As we stand there, her head tucked neatly into my neck, several candle makers sidle up to us.

"Did you hear?" The first leans in, conspiratorial.

"Hear what?" Clara pulls away to face the woman.

"They saw it—the beast. Jeanne and Jean, while they were doing their washing and hanging it out in the garden."

My chest tightens. This is the first indicator of the beast since that man died a few days ago. A reminder that the creature is still with us. I spend so much time worried about the men here that I almost forget sometimes. The danger is in the village, but it's in the woods, too. The beast isn't just cover for men's misdeeds or our rescues. It's a living, breathing, killing creature watching from the shadows. Biding its time.

Clara is the first to speak in the heavy silence after the woman's words. "What did they say about it?"

There's both darkness and delight in her tone when she answers. Dread in the words, pleasure in being the first to tell us. "They said the head is big enough to crack a skull like a walnut."

The other woman chimes in. "It's bigger than anyone else told us. Jeanne said the size of three or four grown men. A giant."

Clara bites her lip, and I reach for her hand, fear stretching tight across my midsection. Have we made a terrible mistake, using this creature as our scapegoat? An even more terrible mistake leaving Charlotte in a remote cottage? A creature that size could easily break down a door, couldn't it? Snap her head like a walnut. A worse fate, perhaps, than the one we're trying to save her from.

My fear is cold and tight, like that seizing feeling in your lungs when you jump into a lake on a crisp fall day. The water so frigid that it steals your breath, makes your lungs forget how to take in more.

"You girls be careful out there," the first woman says, her eyes hooded with worry. "We're talking to all the young shepherdesses. We think you all should try to graze near the soldiers now that they're here. Or at least near the village."

Unthinkingly, I shake my head. "If they saw it while they were hanging things in their own garden, staying close to the village won't save any of us."

Both women looked pained. Clara gives me a look that asks,

Really? Because she'd choose the comfort of silence or thanking them for their idea over my blunt dismissal of it.

"Just . . . be careful." The second woman reaches out to pat both Clara and me on the arms. "It's still here. And it's even worse than we thought."

12

DUHAMEL—PRANKSTER HERO, RENOWNED HUNTER, KNIGHT, the most respected man who has ever left footprints in the dirt of Mende—is an absolute *asshole.*

I hated him when he rode into the village on a strong, blond horse and announced that our salvation had arrived. And I hate him again now, a short time later, when the rest of the village has filled the square. The two women who came to issue us warning have faded into the crowd to warn other girls. The priest and Lafont stand on the church steps beside Duhamel, both quiet in deference. And the crowd hushes as the most respected hunter in France makes another proclamation.

"Tomorrow we feast! A celebration of our arrival and the impending doom of this beast that has been plaguing France. The king will not stand for it! I will not stand for it! Prepare the sheep!"

A warm, hopeful sound travels through the gathering crowd.

Around us, people speak at varying volumes, saying "Finally!" and "He's the best hunter in France," and "Here to save the children."

Beside me, the butcher looks particularly delighted by the proclamation of a feast. "Has the king already purchased the sheep or . . ." He glances around the square.

Duhamel twists his face in a way that is probably meant to look indulgent but just comes off patronizing. "My dear man, we're here to save you. Is the village so ungrateful that you can't feed the men—the patriots—who keep you safe?"

The crowd ripples with a dozen sounds. A few shouts of approval, yes. The lingering hope and relief of hearing that they're here to save us. But as his words sink in, there's also a hum of worry. A reflection of my own fear of empty winter bellies, weak muscles, that gnawing feeling you get when you know your body is eating itself because there is nothing else for it to consume. So it draws energy from fat and muscle, and you shrink and shrink until you are a ghoul. Skin and bones and hollow eyes.

Beside me, Clara looks as upset as I feel. If these men plan to save us by starving us, they're off to a good start.

Neither of us says a word, but one of our neighbors does. An old white woman with milky eyes and knobby knuckles that remind me of tree roots. She's a particularly good gardener, and we all trade for her vegetables. In fact, it was her we were looking for this morning for our own trade. She drives a hard bargain, so perhaps it's no surprise that she's the one to speak first.

"Young man, stop with this foolishness and pay people for their sheep. I'm sure the king is paying you for your"—she waves a hand dismissively at the soldiers—"talents." The way she says the last word leaves no mystery as to how she feels about their so-called talents. *Foolish waste of time* would have been an equally apt description in her mind.

"Show some respect, Madeline," a man near her growls.

"Yeah," another chimes in. "If you're going to ask a question, at least ask it in a respectful way."

The woman—Madeline—motions to the men who've spoken. "Monsieur Duhamel, these fools might not know what's good for them, but I do. It's not them who'll starve this winter. It's their little girls. We appreciate what you are here to do." She sounds like she doesn't mean the last part nearly as much as the first. "But coin is called for here. If you can pay for those fancy little hats, you can pay for a sheep."

Duhamel's smile is a terrifying thing. There's no mirth, no crinkling at the edges of his eyes. Only bared teeth, a predator's sign of strength.

He doesn't answer her, merely steps slowly, purposefully down the church stairs and across the cobbles, the crowd parting to give him a clear path to Madeline. Even the men who defended him before fall silent.

When he reaches her, it's the rest of us he addresses. "The king will not stand for disrespect." He says the words with little malice, but he draws his sword as he does, and that's enough malice for anyone.

The sound of four-dozen soldiers drawing their own swords around the square sings through the air.

Most of the village—me and Clara included—stands frozen

112

in the wake of it, gaping, shocked at how quickly this escalated. I can almost hear their thoughts: He's only waving it around for effect, right? He wouldn't actually hurt an old woman for taking the wrong tone with him, would he? A few voices at the edge of the crowd must believe that he would. They gasp out "No" and "What are you doing?" just before the sword comes down, whistling through the air.

She starts to turn, but she's too slow. The flat of the blade strikes her on the back so hard that the metal breaks, the tip spinning off and cutting three bystanders on its way to the ground. Madeline falls to her hands and knees with a crack and a shocked exhale.

In the wake of it, we all stare in disbelief.

"I'm here to save you, you ignorant fools," Duhamel berates us over the woman's pained moaning as her family rushes forward to pull her away—the only people brave enough to do so.

The people closest to him scramble back, pushing the whole crowd farther from Duhamel as the family gently guides Madeline toward the edge of the square. Clara squeezes my hand and then releases it, moving toward them. In seconds, she'll be all whispered assurances as she guides them toward the house, where she can assess the damage, try to heal what can be healed.

But what can be healed now? Now that we know exactly who Duhamel actually is. The greatest hunter in France—a veteran, a knight—who broke his sword over the back of an old peasant woman who couldn't have harmed him if she tried.

This is the man sent to save us all?

Lafont is the one to break the silence, his tone nervous and conciliatory. "Now, now, Duhamel, I'm sure this is all a misunderstanding. The village would be happy to host your feast, and we are so grateful that you are here. Isn't that right?"

Lafont is looking at us all expectantly, and however we all feel at this moment, a murmur of agreement rises weakly through the square. A few voices ring out louder than others, men who seem to still hero-worship the knight before us, even with what he just did.

Duhamel retrieves the second piece of his sword and returns to the church steps. Back to his rightful place, above us, looking down.

The soldiers sheathe their weapons.

I can tell Lafont will be charged with choosing who loses a sheep today. I think—bitterly—that it's unlikely to be the men who spoke up on Duhamel's behalf. More likely to be Madeline, maybe those of us who helped her, too. Which means Clara. The thought makes me sick.

Lafont, Duhamel, and the priest are speaking now, heads down and together. The rest of the square slowly shifts, as if we have all been in a trance. To my left, I watch several concerned-looking neighbors veer toward our house, leading two of the people who were cut by the rogue tip on its way to the earth. To my right, a cluster of soldiers have turned their attention to Eugénie, who has her hip thrust out and her lip pouted. As I watch, the boys all lean forward to hear something she says.

My stomach turns at the sight. These boys just helped a man hurt an old lady, and Eugénie is still bright-eyed and flirtatious. How can she act like they aren't the enemy? How can anyone?

It's clear that not everyone feels the same. Many of the men in the square have started up conversations with the soldiers. Some laugh. Others listen politely. Those who are hurt or afraid or angry simply leave, and far too many people stay.

From behind me, so close it makes me jump, Belle's bird chimes in over the growing murmur of voices. "Speak like a lady!"

I turn and find Belle sitting on a wooden cart, the bird bouncing side to side on her shoulder as if he can hear music we can't. She looks—unsettled. Twisting her hands together, uncharacteristically quiet. She's even forgotten to sit straight, the greatest sin in her household.

"Mon Dieu!" Jean greets me as I approach.

"Mon Dieu to you as well."

"How do you take your tea?" he caws.

"With sugar if you have some," I return.

He bobs a little dance.

Belle makes a face at me. "He just says random things. He doesn't understand you."

I shrug. "Not any different than talking to most people, then."

She worries at the edge of her sleeve. "What do you want, Joséphine?"

"To check on you." I'm a little startled to realize that is why I came over here. Because I may not like Belle, but she's not all right. I don't know if it's because she watched what the rest of us watched just now or if it's something else. But here I am.

She eyes me with suspicion. "Check on me how?"

"You seem . . . worried. Upset."

"Mon Dieu!" Jean lifts a single leg into the air.

Belle stops fiddling with her sleeve, sits up straighter. "I'm

115

fine. I just—I—I think it's probably like Papa says. Girls shouldn't have to see certain things."

I squint a little at her. "Like men hitting little old ladies hard enough to break metal?"

She swallows. "I mean, he had his reasons. It's not our place to question them. But yes, if you must know, I don't think *I* needed to see it."

"And what about the little old lady in question? Is it inappropriate for *her* to see the violence? Can it be inappropriate for ladies to see violence and yet somehow appropriate for them to be the target of it?"

"I don't want to talk about this anymore."

"Mon Dieu!" Jean whistles.

Part of me wants to keep pushing, but part of me is tired. I should go be with Clara. Belle clearly doesn't want my help or my perspective.

I start to turn away.

"We're famous now. Gévaudan, I mean," Belle says before I can leave, her voice a little desperate. Like she doesn't want to talk about what just happened, but she also doesn't want me to leave her alone. "Even the *Courrier d'Avignon* is publishing stories about the beast. Papa said it's the first time Gévaudan has ever made the papers."

She says it like she expects me to think this is interesting news—even exciting—but what could be less exciting than being the center of everyone else's morbid fascination? My stomach turns.

What must it be like to be Belle? To be at the center of everything but know it cannot touch you? To feel the discomfort of watching a little old lady hit but never think that *you* might be next. To be less than a mile from where a man's body was found without a head and know that the creature that hunted him can never hunt you. Because you're never alone. Your life doesn't depend on taking out sheep, facing the wild. The danger cannot touch you.

Her safety is a shield for her, but also a weapon. A way for her to dismiss our fear, our gut-deep knowledge that the rest of us could be next. To her, a newspaper story means she's ever so slightly more important. To me, it means the death toll here has reached a fever pitch.

Belle doesn't notice the disgust wrinkled into my nose. Or if she does, she doesn't let it deter her. She's standing up now, straight-backed, her voice regaining its confident edge. As if she's shoved the memory of Madeline as far from her mind as possible. "I do wish we didn't have to come this far down. But I suppose it'll be history-making to be here when they haul in the wolf. I wonder if someone from the paper will want to interview us."

"Said like a true rich girl." I huff an exhausted laugh. "You do realize this thing is *killing people,* right?"

"Rich?" She scoffs, completely herself again as she motions to the bright bird ever on her shoulder. "I'm not rich. All the noble girls have monkeys or servals. Parrots are for poor girls."

I can't help but laugh. Out loud, in her face. It bubbles out of me—rage and disbelief in a sound like mirth. "You've got to be kidding. Girls here are *starving to death.* And you think you aren't rich because your papa didn't get you a monkey."

Belle opens her mouth to retort, but Lafont clears his throat behind me. Apparently I was too distracted to notice him cross-ing the square. "Ah, Joséphine. Good to see you." His tone is formal. "I hope all is well."

A bizarre thing to say to someone whose village has lost three people in the past week, but all right, Lafont.

"How do you take your tea?" Jean squawks.

It would be funny if I weren't standing in front of the man who tried to kidnap me in the name of Christian charity. My body is too tight to smile or even respond. Even looking at him this close makes me feel like running. Every muscle tensed for the possibility. I turn my eyes to his nicely polished boots in-stead.

"Mon Dieu! Speak like a lady!" Jean screams.

Don't tell me what to do, bird.

When I don't say anything, Lafont goes on. "I'd like to intro-duce you to Walter—the soldier you'll be hosting."

My eyes drift up to the boy's face. He's probably a little older than me, seventeen or eighteen, with bushy brown eyebrows and flat, unwashed brown hair, skin shiny and red with sunburn from the long march to Mende. His expression is . . . nothing. A purposeful blankness as he stands at attention like Lafont is a commanding officer of some sort instead of a politician.

Belle doesn't seem to mind. She smiles sweetly and flutters her eyelashes at him.

Bird, this would be the moment for the *mon Dieu!* You're sleeping on the job, sir.

"Walter, Joséphine will introduce you to your hosts. And for now, I leave you." Lafont starts to turn away, but then thinks bet-ter of it and turns back. "Ah, and Joséphine, Belle here is going to need a lady's maid. Hers fell ill this morning, and of course I don't want to subject her to contagion. If you know any available girls with appropriate manners in the village, please send them to me."

I fight a desire to tell him that no one in Mende will meet their exacting standards. But I'm sure that they pay well enough, and someone will be smart enough to fake those manners. Eugénie, perhaps, if she wasn't so busy flirting with the soldiers in our peripheral vision, her head tossed back in laughter as they all stare wonderingly at her delicate throat.

After a long pause, I realize he isn't going to leave until I respond. "I'll let you know if I think of anyone." My voice is tight, but it does the trick. Lafont turns on his heel and marches away, beckoning Belle to follow, which she reluctantly does, smiling sweetly at Walter as she goes.

"Mon Dieu!" Jean screams, late to his cue.

"Come on, then." I sigh the words and motion for Walter to follow me. I'm not sure if they'll want us at the house yet. Would it traumatize poor Madeline more to have a soldier march in while she's being treated? I decide to take this boy the long way and veer us both down an alley toward the river.

"Have you seen the beast?" His French is deeply accented.

"No," I say. But is that really true? I have seen the beast that killed Pascal, who might have killed Charlotte if we hadn't hidden her away. For that matter, I've seen Duhamel break his sword across a woman's back. Seen a priest stand by and watch. Seen Eugénie's split lip, heard the word *man* drip with disdain. So yes, I've seen so many beasts in the past week alone.

"They say at least a dozen men have shot it already, and still it stands and flees. They say perhaps it's bulletproof. Or invincible."

"Or maybe those men were just bad shots. Or braggarts." I turn us along the riverbank, kicking at some pebbles.

He looks disgruntled. "Perhaps I don't understand your words. Are you as arrogant as that woman in the square? Are the girls here not taught to hold their tongues? If so, I see why they think a witch might be hiding out in this town."

The words have their intended effect, and I go silent, heart beating sickly as my thoughts snag on the brutal death of our last "witch." It was foolish of me to assume I could talk to this boy like I talk to the other boys around here. This boy who carries a musket on his shoulder, who used it to guard a man as he hit an old lady. Merde, I really need to think before I speak. Not for my sake. If he wants to hit me with the musket or his fists, I'll fight back and damn the consequences. But it's not just me who can get into trouble here. It's also Clara and Mémé—and Charlotte if they look closely enough.

"I'm sorry," I say. "I shouldn't have disrespected those men." The words are flat and there's no truth in them, and I wish I were a better actress, but the boy doesn't seem to need honesty. Just compliance with his wishes.

He nods, smiles. "Very good."

We pick our way across boulders, rocks, and stones in a variety of sizes along the river's edge, each worn smooth by a thousand years of rushing water, a thousand footfalls across their faces—of men and wolves and deer and mice. Anything that needs a drink or wants to eat a drinker. The ones closest to the water are slick with lacy green algae, the ones higher up on the bank bleached white and gray like old bones.

Walter is clumsy, knocking the stones out of place, generating the kind of racket that makes me deeply question what his qualifications are for stalking an animal like the beast. I'm about to open my mouth and tell him to at least *try* to walk quieter when I hear it. Amid the sound of rocks knocking against each other like a clapping crowd, something else bangs against the stone.

Something hollow, different. A wrong note in the middle of a familiar song.

I turn toward the noise and watch something white clatter down boulders toward the water. I move toward it before I even realize what it is. This stone that is not a stone.

I reach down and hook my fingers around the thin edge.

It's a human skull. Clean, white, emptied. Cracked in a way that sends me visions of sharp teeth and crushing jaws. Beasts large enough to crack a head like a walnut.

Just two days ago, they found a man without a head. Now I have a head without a man. It doesn't take book learning to know what this foolish, clumsy soldier has accidentally unearthed.

I hold it up to him, speechless.

His face blanches to match the bone.

13

IF THE SKULL COULD SPEAK, WHAT WOULD IT TELL US? Would it describe the beast the way that the soldiers do? A thing that takes a shot and stands right back up. A thing that can leap whole gorges—which no wolf can do. Would it call the creature the wrath of God or the wrath of nature or something else altogether?

"It walks on its hind legs," Walter tells us in the flickering light of the fire, his French strange but understandable. "It can snap apart a human skull in a single bite."

Clara and I exchange a look as the boy finishes the last of the lentils that were supposed to last us two days. He takes that look as fear of the beast and goes on. "Talons on its paws, they say. A tail like a snake! And it's bulletproof."

"Sounds formidable, young man." Mémé nibbles slowly on her own lentils, making them last.

From the kitchen, the sheep bleat out their own inscrutable conversations, which usually have to do with which ewe's baby is where in the cluster. I glance over to see my motherless fool bleating right along with them, even though there's no one he needs to report his whereabouts to.

"Whoever kills it will be rich. Famous, too. Like Duhamel. Imagine having the king's ear." He has a faraway look on his face.

Clara hands me the lentil bowl we're sharing now that we have the soldier in the house. She tried to leave me more than half, but I pass it straight back. "Not hungry."

She gives me a look but knows she won't win the fight and won't waste the lentils, so she continues eating.

"The reward is four thousand livres. Can you imagine?" The boy thrusts his empty bowl toward me. "Any more?"

I press my lips together to keep from screaming.

"Désolé. That's all we have, I'm afraid," Clara answers, reaching across me to take the bowl.

Finding the skull, taking it to Duhamel, and being praised for his great find (never mind that it was mine) has put the boy in a good mood all afternoon and now into evening. Madeline and her family were gone when we arrived, and Clara and I managed to slip away to graze the sheep and visit Charlotte with some stores for a couple hours, but every moment before and after has been full of his chatter.

He's still talking, even now, this time reciting some great feat or another of Duhamel's, when he's interrupted by a pounding at the door. "Open up, king's men."

Like it could be anyone else. None of our neighbors would

hit the door half as hard, half as self-importantly. Even the pranksters knock like normal humans.

Clara opens the door, and I stand just over her shoulder.

The two young men invite themselves in, pushing past us without even asking, tracking dirt onto a floor that Mémé swept while we were out this afternoon. Clara's face flashes annoyance, and I'm sure my expression mirrors hers.

"Your home has been selected for the honor of giving a sheep to our brave men."

Of course it has. Just as I predicted. But I suppose Clara didn't predict it, because her face falls from irritation to dismay. And I know why. She *loves* these sheep. Sure, sometimes we have to sell one to the butcher. But mostly our sheep are here for wool, milk, cheese. We spend so much of every day with them. We reach our hands inside them to guide breech babies out. Stretch our pikes out in front of them to protect from wolves. We dislodge stone from hooves, trim rogue nails, pet their small, friendly heads. Some of them we raised, too. When their mothers died or rejected them. It happens. And there's a special bond there, when you've woken every two hours all night to make sure they are warm and feed them from a makeshift linen nipple.

They stare at us—the soldiers and the sheep—waiting. And I don't know which option is worse: making us choose who goes or doing it themselves. I suppose we have to choose. If they do, they could end up leaving one of the babies motherless.

Mémé sets her bowl down then. "I don't suppose we can talk you fellows out of this?"

They look confused. "Madame, we have our orders. Can't

disobey orders. And you should be honored. Lafont chose you personally."

"Did he now." It's a question with no question mark. Mémé unimpressed.

"Yes, madame." The boy doesn't read the sarcasm.

Mémé stares at him hard for a moment, then moves to the kitchen, touching the heads of each sheep as if blessing them one by one.

"Take one of mine," I tell her. "Not Clara's."

Clara doesn't object, only reaches for my hand.

Mémé clicks her tongue and drops a rope around the neck of an ewe that we suspect has become sterile. It's a practical choice, but the thing about being a shepherdess is that even practical choices can hurt your heart. I can see it on Mémé's and Clara's faces even as I feel it in my own body. A tight spot in my throat. A sourness in my belly. Ironically, I suppose it's good I haven't eaten. Nothing in there to churn.

I press my own hand to the ewe's head as Mémé leads her to us. The other sheep, confused, mill about. Two try to follow their friend and have to be nudged back by Mémé.

Goodbye, you were a good sheep.

The boys nod and take the rope. "Walter, meet us at dawn at the square. Don't be late. We're riding out to find the beast first thing."

Walter nods and the boys march away, Clara and I standing in the crack of the door, pressed together, watching the ewe as she follows, stops, looks back, and is pulled forward. It feels different than other times we've had to butcher a sheep. Those times were about survival. But this—this feels wasteful. Especially after I've seen how these boys eat, how easy it is for them to take for granted that the lentils were for a single meal instead of three days and three people.

In the morning, Walter leaves as early as we do. He points his feet toward the village square, and we point ourselves into the forest, to Charlotte. She needs to know that there's no foraging today. It won't be safe with the soldiers scouring the trees. She'll have to stay hidden.

Our bags are bulging with supplies, things we don't want the soldiers to take. Food not just for Charlotte but for us. Keeping something there will keep it safe from the soldiers, buy us some small amount of time if they keep eating their way through our stores. My stomach growls just thinking about the food since I didn't eat supper.

We walk in silence longer than we need to, but once the village is well and fully behind us, Clara lets out a long, slow breath.

"I don't know where to start," she says as we walk.

I make a hum noise meant to urge her on.

"We need to talk to Hélène, for real and today. If they catch the beast, our window is gone. And without Hélène, I don't think we will get Charlotte safely out. An eight-year-old handed over to a merchant to deliver down south by herself? There are too many bad outcomes there. I can't do it."

"But with Hélène she'll be safer," I agree.

"We have another problem, though." She nudges the sheep on.

"Only one?"

"Food."

"Oh, that one." I try for humor, but it comes out flat.

"Even if Hélène and Charlotte can forage . . . which will depend on how long these soldiers are here . . . it's not going to be enough."

I nod, then offer up a suggestion I hate almost as much as I hated putting Charlotte in my house. "Lafont is looking for a lady's maid for Belle. If you took the job, we'd have a little more money for food."

Clara stops walking and raises her eyebrows at me. "Me? You know they won't take me."

I grit my teeth. Lafont is the worst. Clara's right. It was clear when he took me under the guise of Christian charity that part of his motive was to make himself look good and part was because he didn't like seeing a little white girl raised in a brown home. We haven't seen the Lafonts in years, but there's nothing in their recent behavior that makes me think either of them has changed. Belle still oblivious and embarrassingly bold about her ignorance. Her father definitely still not man enough to stop a knight from harming an old lady on his watch and almost certainly also still "concerned" about "all the foreigners" in Mende. Never mind that most of them were born here.

"I hate them," I mutter as we continue walking.

"Me too. But I think you're right that we need them. Or their money, really. Which means *you* need to be the one to go work for Belle."

I make a face. God, it just gets worse and worse. Not only is there a ravenous animal scouring the countryside for shepherdess-shaped snacks, but we've got a little girl to keep alive, another to rescue. And did I say the other day that I thought we should try to help Eugénie, too? Ha! My delusion knows no bounds.

"How am I going to keep the sheep, save Hélène, feed her and Charlotte, and work for Belle?"

Clara emerges into the clearing ahead of me, starts nudging the sheep around the barn. "I'll have to manage the sheep on my own. You'll work for Belle. And we'll both do what we need to do for the girls. Together we can do it."

"And what if we can't?" I bump the fool lamb gently with my calf to keep him from wandering away from the group as I emerge from the woods.

"There is no *can't* anymore." Clara pauses. "We have to."

14

"PASCAL WAS A VEGETARIAN." CHARLOTTE SITS CROSS-legged in front of the hearth and speaks without preamble. It's the first time she's talked about him since everything. Really the first time she's started a conversation instead of just answering our questions or asking when Hélène is coming.

Clara drops to the same position across from her as I stand in the doorway, half listening, half watching the sheep graze the edges of the overgrown clearing around the house. My eyes on them, then on the tree line beyond, the shifting shadows that could be a hidden carnivore. The recent sighting has sobered me, and I still can't shake the vigilance that spikes whenever I'm at the cottage. Even now that I'm here almost every day. The combination leaves me stretched as thin as worn-out thread, a breath away from snapping.

Clara, as always, is holding it together much better than I

am. Her voice floats out the door, so soothing. It makes perfect sense that the entire town trusts her with their secrets. "Do you want to tell us more about him?"

"They sent him away last year to train as a soldier. But they sent him back because he wouldn't shoot a gun. He said he wanted to come back anyway. Even though they have more food in the army. But he met a man from far away and the man ate only vegetables. So Pascal did, too, ever since that. Because he didn't want to hurt anything in this world." In my periphery, Charlotte blinks fast. "He gave me his portion when we did have meat at the table. Said growing girls need more food than grown boys."

It hurts me to hear it, and I wonder how much more it must hurt Charlotte to say it. Or maybe it hurts less to say it than to keep it in. I never can tell which is more unbearable: saying the thing that makes you sad or trying to pretend you aren't sad.

My own brother wasn't like Pascal. He wasn't a soft heart. More like the kind of brother who'd put out his foot to trip you and laugh when you fell. But also the kind of brother who'd kick somebody else if they did the same thing. Like he could pick on me, but nobody else could. I wish I remembered more about him. It's been so long that most of my memories are hazy, except the day he died. What a horrible way to remember someone. Not as a person, but as a ghost rising into the eaves.

I wish he were here now—a feeling that lodges in my throat like the stale bread we try to coax into edible form by dipping it into soup. He'd be a prankster, no doubt. But a fiercely protective one. I bet he'd kick anyone who wanted to hurt Clara or Charlotte, too.

Charlotte's voice rises again, the words tattered, broken things whose echoes slice through my own heart. "I couldn't save him."

Oh, Charlotte. Neither could I.

Clara reaches across the space to hold Charlotte's smaller hands in hers. "It wasn't your job to."

"I hate being so small." Charlotte pulls her hands back, presses them into her stomach. "I hate that I couldn't stop him. I couldn't *ever* stop him."

Her words slice into me again. She's talking about her father, but she might as well be talking about mine. I couldn't stop him, either. Couldn't make him stay. Couldn't make him save me. Love me. Are those the unspoken truths in between her words, too? She couldn't stop him from hurting Pascal. But she also couldn't make him love her. I know the shape of that wound.

"Pascal would want me to be brave," she goes on. "He wouldn't like that Hélène was there alone. He would want me to go get her." Charlotte breathes fast now, uneven. She's terrified of the idea, it's clear. Terrified but also feeling the heaviness of *should.* At such a horribly young age, she is trying to take it on herself. I know the shape of that feeling, too.

I turn to face her, my voice resolute. "Charlotte, we'll get Hélène. Soon, I promise. We're just trying to find the right moment when she's alone."

"It's taking so long." She presses her hands to her face, breathes hard and loud. "What if he kills her, too?"

God, there's the anger again, rising out to push out even the fear. I want to rip that man limb from limb.

Clara takes the smaller girl in her arms and whispers

131

something comforting I can't quite make out, and I move out the door, scanning the trees, doing my regular sheep head count. One, two, three, the fool lamb, five, six . . .

BANG. A shot rings through the crisp afternoon air, flinging birds from trees in a panic. The sheep scream and run frantically toward me. Clara's face appears at the door.

"Stay inside," I say, moving aside and ushering the sheep into the shelter of the house. No more shots ring out as I count each precious sheep, feeling wrong when I end the tally on twenty-four since they took number twenty-five yesterday. I close the door behind them, keep them in. Keep them safe. From a rogue bullet launched from an overeager soldier's gun or the beast itself if that's what they're shooting at.

Somewhere in my gut, I know I should stay with Clara and Charlotte and the sheep. But I need to know what the danger is, what's happening. So instead, I run toward the sound.

No other shots ring through the air. Birds settle back into trees. But I still follow the murmur of men's voices, growing louder and more urgent.

"Goddamn it, goddamn it, we must have just missed him. Clever devil!" It's Duhamel speaking as I make it to the empty field where his fifty dragoons range around him.

As I emerge from the trees, someone shouts and muskets swing in my direction. My breath catches in my throat and—

BANG.

It's loud, and my heart slams into my chest, but nothing else happens. I look down at my body, press my hands to hot skin, coarse cloth. No blood. No wound. If this is how good of a shot they all are, no wonder the beast keeps walking away after being supposedly gunned down.

They lower their muskets, and Walter starts toward me, looking angry. The rest return their gaze to Duhamel and something else. Another wrong thing in the landscape that takes me a moment to take in. The thing that has stopped them here, I imagine. Perhaps the same thing that inexplicably called to me to run toward the shot. The knowledge that I'd find *something terrible*—something that is only less terrible because I know what it is instead of letting my imagination run wild—at the end of the run.

It's another body. A girl only a little younger than I am, her eyes like glass, skin the gray of a thin sheen of dust. Her center has been destroyed, but her head is here, staring serenely at a dozen dandelion clouds. I don't know her, have never seen her in my life. Which I'm pretty sure means she isn't from our village. She's a neighboring village girl wandered too far.

Around her, sheep have stampeded, released their bladders and bowels in fear, retreated to the far side of the field, where some graze now and others still scream their dismay. I wonder if they tried and failed to defend her. Sheep do that sometimes. If the shepherdess is in danger, they gather up their courage. We protect them from wolves, yes, but they protect us, too. I've always thought my sheep think that I'm one of them, and now I think it again, watching these sheep mourn their girl. They believe they've lost one of their own, I can feel it in my soul. Is this what my fool lamb would do if it were me lying glassy-eyed staring at the sky?

It *could have* been me. Not just in her place, killed by the beast, but also killed by a bullet. These soldiers are jumpy. And running toward them was a foolhardy choice. I suppose the lamb comes by his foolishness honestly since they say animals reflect their keepers.

And what does the beast reflect, I wonder?

Walter reaches me and grabs me roughly by the shoulder. "What are you doing here? This is not a place for little girls!"

Little girls? I'm what—a year younger than him? I'm so tired of boys like this. Normally, my indignation would burn hot and fast, and I'd probably hit him. But I can still see the girl behind him, staring at the sky, and I feel simply . . . exhausted. Probably for the best. If I talk back to him, will we lose another sheep? I wonder what will become of *her* sheep. Will the soldiers return them to her family or steal them for the feast?

I don't ask, though. I don't talk back. I don't even answer.

Instead, I shake his hand off, turn, and retreat the way I came.

15

CLARA IS ANGRY.

If you didn't know her, you wouldn't see it. Because Clara doesn't scream her rage into the sky, confront you with it, bite your knuckles, kick your shins. She sits with her anger, stares it in the face, and lets it build.

I can see the early spark of that anger in the high set of her shoulders, the thin slant of her lips. She's angry that another girl is gone and there is a whole field of soldiers just staring at her corpse. She's angry that one of those fools almost shot me. She's angry on behalf of Charlotte and Hélène and Eugénie and probably some dozen other village girls she's keeping secrets for. And now she's angry most of all at me. Because I ran toward the shot instead of away, and because she couldn't follow. I left her with the sheep and the child, and she couldn't leave either behind.

She's painfully polite to me on our way back from Charlotte, even when I try to explain myself, and I wish she'd just say how utterly furious she is. *Let it out, Clara! Scream if you need to.* I know that's not how she works, but I want it to be.

On our way home, we pass Hélène's house for the millionth time and find no one there. Just empty windows covered in heavy leather flaps staring us down like eye sockets, stone façade bleached like bone. The sheep bleat their irritation at us for the detour, but we have one more to make. It's market morning, and we'll stop by the square. To trade for things we need and to trade for information. Because market morning brings people from all the surrounding villages, sometimes even merchants from farther afield. It's a place for news as much as a place for handmade soap and jarred sweet peaches.

As we approach the square, a familiar silhouette waves to us from the edge of the bustling crowd. Amani—our neighbor, the sheep-healing magician, and one of Mémé's closest friends— raises a friendly hand as she guides Mémé toward us by the elbow. Their laughter spills across the cobbles like a single sunbeam on a dark day. I watch it unknot something in Clara, her shoulders dropping an inch, then two, as we aim for the two older women.

Amani tuts as we usher the sheep into one of the temporary pens they put up at the edges of the square during market day. Most grunt unhappily at being in close proximity to another pen full of someone else's sheep, but the little fool lamb is a decided fan of strangers and shoves his head forcefully between the wooden slats to scream a hello at the other sheep, who sidle away from him.

"You girls look exhausted." Amani drops Mémé's elbow and kisses each of us on the cheeks.

Mémé chuckles. "Who isn't?"

"You're not wrong. But these girls are sixteen." Amani pats Mémé's elbow, which is still crooked in front of her. "They should be full of energy! Don't you remember sixteen?"

Mémé laughs. "You know I don't, Madeline."

My heart drops. Mémé seems so lucid right now, and yet she's mixing up names again.

Amani doesn't miss a beat or show any distress, though. "It's Amani, my love. Don't you go trying to prove your old age by getting my name wrong, now. I know you're as spry as they come. You aren't fooling a soul in this circle."

Mémé furrows her brow but chooses to glance over her shoulder at the square instead of answering.

"Now, you two about ready for the feast?" Amani asks. "They said it's at sundown. Don't be late, or those boys will eat everything they stole. If they're going to take our stores, we might as well get a mouthful out of it."

We nod in unison, and my stomach growls as if to agree with her.

"Madeline—" Mémé starts again with the wrong name.

Before she can finish her thought, there's a loud slam from the square and a ripple of noise in response. People gasping, dropping things, ending their conversations, and whipping their heads toward the sound.

We do the same, craning our necks to see what's happened. And the only reason we get our answer is because it's playing out on the upraised steps of the church. It was the heavy oak church door that slammed open and into the stone façade. In the doorway now, a man—the priest—wrestles with a smaller figure.

It's Hélène, her golden curls locked in his fist as he drags her out of the building, her cap askew. My heart stops.

"Oh la vache," Mémé says behind me. "This must be about the little girl staying with us. They have the same sad eyes."

Clara and I whip our heads around to stare at Mémé. I know she's having a confusing day, but how can she not realize what's just said?

Amani only pats her hand. "My love, don't go getting senile on us right now. Jo's the girl who stays with you. You raised her. That girl on the steps, her sister was taken by the beast. Poor dear. And now—what is that horrible man doing?"

I don't know what to say or where to look, but at least Amani doesn't seem to have thought anything of Mémé's proclamation. I return my attention to the church, crane to see as the priest releases Hélène's hair and throws her down on the steps, her knees connecting to the stone with an echoing, horrible crack.

I don't think anymore, just rush forward, start pushing into the edges of the too-thick crowd as she hits the stone steps with her knees and cries out in fear and pain.

Someone calls my name behind me, but I keep pushing my way through the throng. My throat nearly closes, and I feel dizzy, my mind flashing pictures of my own encounter with that evil, evil man. His hands on me, my teeth on him. The fear, the rage.

"Demon!" the priest screams, his voice as painful as the scrape of metal on metal. "Ungrateful!"

The murmuring crowd falls silent. A man shoves me when I try to pass him, and I stumble into the corner of a market stall, the pain sharp against my hip.

"The devil is the father of lies!" The priest is addressing the crowd now as Hélène curls in on herself on the steps, clutching at her knees. "And THIS is his daughter! Daughter of lies!"

I'm trying to find a path through the crowd when I feel a hand strong and hard on my shoulder. I turn to push it off, to push forward, but it's Clara.

"Stop," she whispers fiercely. "You can't involve yourself in front of everyone."

Tears of rage burn behind my eyes, but her words make it through the fury. She's asking me, without saying her name, to think of Charlotte. To not draw attention to us. I fist my hands and try not to scream.

"This girl came to me to defame a good man. But I do not deal in lies. Lucifer, I will not hear it!" The priest rages into the sky.

At the front of the crowd, I see him then. Charlotte and Hélène's papa, his face red as a beet, his eyes trained on his daughter's tiny form. My stomach turns.

Clara slips her hand into mine, pries my fingers apart, and interlaces them with hers—tight.

"Has the Lord's word not told you to obey your parents? To honor your father? And here you are spreading lies about the man who brought you into this world, who keeps you safe!"

Safe? I want to scream. That man is the danger, not the protector. I squeeze Clara's hand and blink tears from my eyes. I want to feel the priest's blood between my teeth again. I want to hear him scream. Why is no one else doing anything? I can't because of Charlotte, but there are a hundred people here and not a single one has moved to help her, to stop him, to ask what he means when he says she's lied.

It stabs into me, the realization that was always there and is now laid so bare in front of us: *the village will not protect us.* We knew it. We must have known it. Because it never occurred to Clara or me to take Charlotte's safety into anyone's hands but our own. But the silence across this square, the nods of approval from so many of the adults, the way not a single person moves forward, it turns the quiet certainty to a screaming reality.

No matter what happens, we are on our own. Saving Charlotte and Hélène will be our task and our task alone. No one here can be trusted.

"Go!" The priest waves at Hélène, now scrambling to her feet. "Go and repent, child! Perhaps God will see fit to save your soul. He is more merciful than I would be!"

I start forward again without thinking, but Clara holds my hand tight, pulls me back.

Hélène's father marches up the steps and grabs her roughly by the arm, yanking hard and forcing her to trip down the stairs.

I turn to Clara, so many words I want to say stopping before they reach my mouth. Because what is safe to say here and now? I settle on a single word, knowing she will feel my full meaning. "Tonight."

Tonight we take her. Tonight we stage Hélène's death. Tonight we put an end to one more girl's suffering and reunite sisters that we should have reunited days ago.

God, please let her survive 'til then.

At twilight, the soldiers stand in rowdy, ragged groups in the field across the bridge from the village, roasting our sheep on slow-moving spits over rage-roaring fires. Above them, stars wink into sight in a growing inky blackness. Beyond them, the creeping dark glares out from the forest. The beast is too smart to emerge in front of a crowd, but I wonder if it crouches somewhere just beyond the firelight, eyes shining, biding its time.

Clara and I stay just long enough for some of the boys— drunk on local liquor from who even knows what source—to give us chunks of meat and roasted potatoes. The first thing I've eaten all day, and I almost cry at how good it tastes. Clara insisted we eat before going for Hélène, and now I am so grateful I could kiss her. Still, I'm antsy, and we don't linger any longer than we have to.

We eat as we walk, winding away from the ruckus of soldiers and village. Nearly everyone is at the feast. We were hoping that would include Hélène's father, leaving her alone at the house, but we couldn't find his or her face in the crowd, and we must assume the worst: he's at home with her. Which means we'll have to wait until he's asleep to slip her away.

It isn't enough to wait for the right timing anymore. We know she's in danger, and we know she knows what her father did—that she was trying to tell the priest. That's what he meant by "defame a good man." It's the only thing he could have meant. And if something else happens to her because we waited . . . well, that's not something either Clara or I can live with. Maybe especially me. I can't be just like my own father—walking away when I could choose to save someone instead.

The village is dark and quiet, our footsteps echoing softly off the stone around us. My heart beats an uneven rhythm while raindrops fall unevenly to match it. And then, as we reach the opposite side of the village from where we live, another tip-tap joins our feet, the rain, and my heart.

Footsteps.

Small ones.

I know before I see her what has happened. She's gotten scared, impatient. She traced the path through the woods, came here to rescue Hélène because we were taking too long.

"Charlotte, you can't be here," Clara whispers fiercely.

"You need me," Charlotte answers, her face glistening with rain, her voice set. "She won't go with you unless I'm here."

There's no way to know if it's true, but what I do know is that Charlotte being here puts *Charlotte* in danger. And we've done so much to keep her out of it. I'm angry at her, even though it's not her fault we're in this situation. It *is* her fault that she left the house when we told her not to.

"Anyone could have seen you, Charlotte," I say.

"No one did." She shakes her head.

"How can you be sure?"

"Pascal said I'm the best at hiding, and Pascal never lied."

His name stops us all, and for a moment the only sound is the rain growing louder. As I blink drops off my eyelashes, I realize the growing pace of the rain means the feast will be over. They'll all be grabbing the food and rushing back to their homes soon.

Our chances of getting caught are looking better by the moment. And we don't have time to talk Charlotte out of coming. Not to mention that sending her back means sending her through the nighttime forest by herself. Besides, she might be right. Maybe we need her. Maybe Hélène won't come with two girls she barely knows.

"All right, we better move fast." I motion to the storm. "The village will be full of people running home any minute."

Clara and Charlotte both nod, rain-drenched now with water rushing off their chins.

This time when we approach Hélène's house, light flickers inside. A flame in the hearth. We slip around the side of the house farthest from the other entryways, and I motion for Clara and Charlotte to duck alongside the stone as I slowly move to peer inside.

I see him first, and my heart leaps into my throat. Charlotte's father, *murderer*. He's asleep in a chair next to the fire, a bottle of some kind of liquor tucked in between his arm and stomach like he's protecting it even in sleep. His head is tipped back, mouth open.

I let some of the tension release in a slow breath through my nose as I scan the rest of the room and find Hélène's back turned to me as she busies herself with some kind of preserves she's jarring. The supplies spread around her red as blood. Strawberry, I suppose. Or wild berry. Or something of that ilk.

I move from the window and squat beside Charlotte and Clara. "Your father's asleep. Hélène's awake. We have to be very quiet."

Charlotte takes a deep breath. "I'll get her. Let me get her."

I glance at Clara, and she nods in agreement, so I follow her lead, letting Charlotte slip ahead of us around the corner and to the back door. Clara gently holds me back. "Let them see each other for a second first."

I nod again, take a few steps away from the house so that I can see inside without being seen, and watch as Charlotte presses her hands to the door, undoes the latch, and swings it open. The warm light of the fire flickers across her face, sparkles off the rain as it runs rivulets down her cheeks, off her chin, and down each elbow.

"Hélène," Charlotte breathes, and Hélène jolts, pauses, then turns.

When she sees Charlotte, she freezes and the world goes quiet, like everything around us is holding its breath. Even the rain seems to pause in the sky, frozen for a heartbeat as the two sisters lock eyes.

Hélène will come to us now, slip into shoes and coat, out the door and into the night. Charlotte was right, and I was wrong. We needed her all along.

But no.

The held breath of the world cracks and shatters. The rain pounds downward. The night splits in two—*before* and *after*—as Hélène releases a bloodcurdling scream.

16

CHARLOTTE'S PAPA ROARS OUT OF SLEEP, AND WE *RUN*.

Clara leads the way through sharp, dark branches, over snaking roots, and I follow, Charlotte's wrist in my grip. I'm pulling her on, her body slightly resisting, like she's not sure if she should run or go back for her sister.

"Why did she scream?" she whimpers as we go. "Why did she scream?" Then, "We have to go back."

But her father is awake now—and the soldier staying in their house could be back any moment. The whole lot of them could be back, mounting their horses and riding into the forest after us.

There's no other option but to run. From the real beasts this village is hiding. The man who killed his son and went back for his knives. The soldiers under Duhamel's command, capable of breaking a sword over an old woman's back.

I stumble over roots in the dark, scrape against tree bark, bite my cheek and taste blood. The ground grows slicker as the rain falls faster, and more than once we have to slow to keep from falling into the muck. The sticking, sucking mud snatches at our feet as if it wants us to be caught.

When we reach my house, I pull Charlotte inside behind us, close the door, and lean my back against it, my breathing labored. Whole body trembling. Water pools immediately underneath me, running off my clothes like a waterfall. Mud slicks across the previously clean floor. Clara and Charlotte are twin falls of their own, each of us making our own miniature streams that start with us and follow the contours of the wood into the corners of the room.

"We have to get home." Clara is the first to speak as we catch our breath.

My whole body rebels against the idea, tensing, heating. "No. What if they find us wandering the woods so late? They'll know. They'll find us out."

"And if they *don't* find us home in our bed when Walter gets back? What then?" She presses a hand to her heart. "If there's a search party, we can't be missing. They won't look for Charlotte here, but they would look for *you*."

She's right, and I hate it. I want to curl into a corner and cry and sleep, holding Charlotte and Clara tight to me.

But now we have to leave Charlotte—again—and still without her sister. In more danger than ever. But more danger still if I stay.

"Charlotte." I kneel to be eye to eye with the younger girl, her

146

face wet with not just rain but tears, too. "You have to stay. We will get Hélène out, but not tonight. You have to stay now, you understand?"

She cries harder but nods, and before I know it, Clara has pulled me back into the storm, pressed the door closed behind us, and we are running back the way we came, fighting mud and branches, thorns and tangled roots. I wonder if the beast hunts in rainstorms. I wonder if Charlotte's father is hunting us even now.

I wonder if we'll survive the night.

17

NO SEARCH PARTIES SLAM THEIR FISTS INTO OUR DOOR. NO soldiers shout through the night. But neither Clara nor I sleep. Walter gets home a little after we do, all three of us drenched to the bone. He's in a good mood, though, belly full and first day of the hunt complete. They found nothing more than a dead girl, and yet he lauds all their courage, chatters on about thinking they spotted the evil thing and finding it was only a squirrel or rabbit, but how he's confident Duhamel will lead them to victory in the end.

None of us have enough energy to join his one-man conversation. Clara and I too drained and terrified from what just happened, Mémé even more confused than she was earlier today. When he first got back, she called Walter "Pierre" and asked if he'd brought her any sweets. It's anyone's guess who Pierre is, but when Walter called her crazy, I wanted so badly to hit him.

This foolish boy who doesn't know what it feels like to watch a strong, confident woman slip in and out of herself.

I want to ask him what the soldiers know, but that would only give us away. So I listen to his fool stories, waiting, until it's clear to me that he knows nothing about tonight. We won't get any information from him.

Just like his first night in our home, we offer Walter the mattress and he doesn't decline. Mémé curls on her side on some wool blankets in front of the hearth, and Clara and I slip in beside her, just a little farther from the warmth of the fire and with a couple fewer blankets than anyone else.

Walter and Mémé are snoring now, but I know Clara isn't sleeping, because I can feel her twitching, wakeful, at my side. I imagine her mind looks much like my own—a storm of terrible possibilities. Did Hélène see us, or did she only see her sister? If she did see us, did she recognize us? Is her father on his way here even as I wonder about it?

My gut twists with the knowledge that I started all of this. I dragged Clara into it. If Charlotte's father is on his way to our house with a bag full of knives, it's my fault.

Then my mind wanders to Charlotte. How is she feeling, out there alone? Will she keep her promise—stay in the house this time? Or will she run off and reveal herself to her sister again? There's a helpless sort of fear in the question. I can't stop her if she does, can't know what she is doing. Please, God, don't let all of this be for nothing. Please, Charlotte, stay.

149

Along our normal route the next morning, two soldiers halt us in our tracks, and my heart flies into my throat.

They know something. They must know something. Is this the end, then? We decided to go out as normal, pretend everything was business as usual. But I knew in my gut it wouldn't work. And now: soldiers twice our size holding up their hands in a confident gesture that means *stop.*

Clara's voice is steadier than my own would be. "Gentlemen, what's the problem?"

"Mademoiselle, we cannot allow you to pass. The field ahead is where we've set our trap for the creature. Too much ruckus might scare it off."

It takes a moment for my mind to catch up with his meaning; this isn't about Charlotte, and it isn't about last night.

"What kind of trap?" Clara's thoughts are several steps ahead of mine.

The boys share a look, seem to decide it's all right to give us more detail. The first answers, "They say the beast returns to its kills. We've poisoned the girl's body, and we're standing guard to keep people away. If the creature comes for her, it will surely die."

The second looks smug. "Duhamel is truly a genius."

There's a swooping sensation in my belly as though I've missed a step. Did he just say they are *using the girl's body as bait?* Tainting it with poison? He said it without a hint of remorse or empathy. Said it like she's just a thing to be used. And it's moments like these that I wonder if there will ever be a time when I don't want to cry and scream and hit something all at once.

I may not know the girl's name, but I know there is something callous in how they are treating her death. She was a person, and they only seem to care that she might make a way forward toward their goals. Her death is a means to an end for them.

Clara nudges the sheep around, hers filing after her in an orderly way, mine turning less uniformly, and I follow her. Neither of us responds to the soldiers or says a word as we weave away from our preferred route and toward the riverbank.

As we round the bridge and veer toward the water, I notice a silhouette at the river's edge, seated on a boulder, knees drawn up to its face. It's Louis, I realize as we draw closer, and his body shakes with quiet sobs.

I raise my eyebrows sky-high and stare at Clara. Louis, king jokester, is openly *weeping*?

She doesn't look as surprised as I am, and I remember the familiarity she had with him a few days ago. It pinches at me. Has Clara been keeping a secret from me? I mean, I know she keeps secrets for people who come to her for advice. We all trust her to keep those. But this feels like something else. An intimacy that makes me want to grab her by the elbow and pull her away.

When we step up beside him, Clara reaches out to touch his shoulder, and he jumps from the boulder and stands, blinking at us. He'd been so wrapped up in whatever he was feeling, he hadn't even heard the decidedly-not-quiet approach of the chittery lambs.

He wipes his eyes and slides into a grin, though it looks wrong on his face now.

"Are you all right?" Clara asks.

"Of course!" His voice is unconvincing.

"Did something else happen?" I break in, drawing their attention.

He looks like he's searching for an answer and finally settles on: "They're using that poor girl's body as bait."

It doesn't feel like the real reason this normally happy-go-lucky, laugh-at-the-world boy has curled in on himself like a question mark, alone when I never see him alone. But Clara nods. "It's awful."

"They don't even know her name. Lafont said her family's been found and notified, but even he couldn't remember her name." Louis looks angry instead of hurt now, and I wonder if I misjudged. Maybe this girl's fate has moved him to tears before rage.

"Do they know any of our names?" Clara's answer is cheeky, and, come to think of it, I've never heard Walter call us anything other than "girls."

"Don't get me wrong," Louis says. "I want them to kill it." He's as earnest as I've ever heard him. "I want them to kill it more than anything. To avenge . . . us all. But I don't want them to kill *all of us* in the process. Or turn us into nameless corpses."

"It's wrong," Clara agrees.

"It's evil," I add.

"They've only been here a few days, and already we're low on winter stores at my house. They took one of our sheep for the feast. Lucky us, what an honor." Louis is still bitter and serious, but the sarcasm feels more like the Louis I know. "You'd think I wouldn't care. I already lost everything," he adds, cryptically.

"What do you mean?" I tilt my head.

He waves a hand, an attempt at casual that falls completely flat as he changes the subject at a dizzying pace. "On top of everything else, apparently we've got ghosts in the village now."

Clara blinks fast, trying to catch up. "What?"

Louis makes a sound somewhere between laugh and snort. "Oui, during the storm last night, Hélène saw her dead little sister calling her into the downpour." He waves his fingers in a suggestion of spookiness.

Clara and I exchange a wide-eyed look, and he must take it as interest or fear because he goes on. "Her father says she's just lying again, but I saw her face when she told me about it. She thinks it was real. She thinks her sister is back to haunt them. Maybe haunt us all."

A ghost. *That's* why she screamed. She believes so completely that Charlotte is dead that it never crossed her mind that the little girl crying and calling to her in the night was her real, *living,* flesh-and-blood sister.

"Where is Hélène now?" Clara asks.

Louis shrugs. "Out with the sheep, I assume. That's how I saw her this morning, taking them out. Pascal used to do it, but it's been on her since . . . well, you know. I'm surprised you haven't seen her yourselves. She was going toward that gorge area where you usually are."

I narrow my eyes. "How do you know where we usually are?"

He shrugs again, winks at Clara. "I keep track of all the pretty girls in the village."

I clench a fist.

"Anyway—" His smile still doesn't quite reach his eyes as he takes Clara's hand and kisses the back of it. "If you mademoiselles will excuse me, I have some soldiers I hate and some havoc I'd love to get back to."

And with that, he's gone.

Only minutes after we return the sheep home, Amani pounds on the door and shouts through the wood. "Village square, ladies! We've all been summoned."

Clara goes to help Mémé from where she's settled in the bed, but she waves her away. "More nonsense, no doubt. You girls go. I've had enough nonsense in my life, but not enough naps."

Clara leans over and kisses Mémé's forehead, then follows me out the door, through the maze of alleys, and into the square. The place that so much of our lives have revolved around lately. It's always the place for news, for gathering. But since the beast sidled up to Mende's doorstep, we've been here so much more often than usual.

I'm starting to hate it, these worn-smooth cobblestones, the stone façades stark and bleached in the midday light. The dark-wood doors with their simply carved crosses, tributes to a God who hasn't yet saved us. A God who might even be punishing us, if the priest is to be believed. Even the chimneys stretching into the blue sky, the plant boxes hung from unshuttered windows, herbs and flowers peeking over their sides—the things I normally like about the square—feel cruel. Reminders of a time when we had one fewer probable way to die.

When we arrive, much of the village is already there. Belle stands off to the side of the church steps, Jean on her shoulder whistling a tune and occasionally murmuring something unintelligible. Clara pulls me toward her.

"Belle." Clara nods.

"Clara?" Belle tilts her head curiously.

"Joséphine said your father wants to hire a lady's maid for you, yes?"

Belle's eyes flash surprise. "Yes."

"I think you should hire Joséphine. You already know her. She can read. And I can take her sheep for the time being."

I sigh. I know we talked about this, and I know we need me to do it, but merde, I do not want to. All I want is for the Lafonts to forget I exist, not to see me every day and maybe get attached enough to try and kidnap me again. Though I suppose that's within my control. They won't get attached if I am not a nice person to be around. Which shouldn't be hard, since nothing about Belle ever makes me want to be nice.

Belle looks suspicious. "*You* want to come work for me?"

"Don't get too excited. I could use the money." I probably shouldn't be rude, because I really do need the money, but part of me hopes that she'll say no and force us to figure out another way.

"Speak like a lady." Jean decides to join the conversation.

Belle grins, reaches up to scratch gently at the feathers on his neck. "You always did tell it like it was, Jean. All right, I'll tell Papa. Lord knows my things need washing. You can start this afternoon."

"Can't wait."

Clara nudges me hard in the side, but Belle just smiles at my sarcasm.

Around us, the square has filled with not just our neighbors, but also Duhamel's fifty dragoons, Lafont's attendants, and even some strangers I don't recognize. Perhaps merchants who lingered after the market because Mende's now the "exciting" place to be; perhaps a journalist since the papers now know who we are. Near the back, Eugénie holds court with a circle of soldiers, all of them leaning in, eating up whatever she's saying. Just behind Clara and me, Louis and the other pranksters lean with studied casualness against a stone wall turned gold by the angle of the sun. They're the only villagers who look casual. A quick glance around the square reveals set jaws and deep worry lines. Women clutch at small children. The men have a look that hits me like a fist. The look they had in the days before they went after the priest, demanding he lift the curse he couldn't lift. Calling him witch. Then calling him corpse.

The town is afraid; the town is dangerous. What will they do with their fear this time?

As usual, Duhamel and the priest stand above us on the raised platform before the church. The priest wears his customary look of superiority, but Duhamel looks strangely disgruntled.

It unsettles me even more. What has upset this dangerous man?

Lafont clears his throat, and everyone turns toward him, even the rowdiest soldiers falling silent. "The illustrious Duhamel and his brave dragoons would like you to know that they've heard your complaints and will no longer be using poisoned corpses to lure the evil thing out."

"Yeah, sure, that's about our complaining, not the fact that it didn't work," Louis murmurs behind me.

Denisot chortles. "And not the fact that he's embarrassed at being exposed as a fool."

"I thought you loved him, thought he could do no wrong," I say softly over my shoulder.

Louis grunts. "Never meet your heroes."

"The king has also issued a new decree that I am to pass along to you all." Lafont clears his throat again. "Firearms have been temporarily legalized in Gévaudan. Any man who wishes to go after the beast will be welcome to use one."

A few people clap, others making sounds of approval, and the pranksters behind me whoop with anticipation, but my stomach sinks. It's bad enough that these men have fists and knives and pikes at the ready. What happens to a girl like Hélène when her father's temper reaches a fever pitch and there's a musket in the house? What happens to the next person they turn on, the next priest?

God, we need to get Hélène out of there. I scan the crowd for her but can't catch sight of her golden curls. She's short and so am I, so perhaps she's here and just hidden by so many men head and shoulders above her.

Lafont holds up his hands to calm the crowd, and it works. They're attentive again. "There's more good news. I'm very proud to say that the king has sent us even more hunters. He's serious about taking this creature down and saving the lives of our girls."

Ah yes, the king, great protector of girls. So safe for women that his own wife hasn't shared his bed for several decades.

Based on the priest's sour expression, I imagine he would prefer if all us girls were eaten. And maybe Duhamel agrees because his scowl deepens.

"With that in mind, may I present to you Jean Charles Marc Antoine Vaumesle d'Enneval and his son Jean-François. We now have the king's *three* best hunters in our midst. Please make them welcome." Lafont flourishes a hand toward the church, and two men emerge. The first—with the ridiculously long name that lets you know just how rich he is—is old. His face has the look of parched soil, cracked and grayed by the sun. His neck is reminiscent of a rooster's, extra skin flapping. His son appears to be Duhamel's age, and by the way they're staring daggers at each other, I presume they know each other. With their wealth and connections, maybe they even attended the same university.

"Thank you, good people of Gévaudan." As soon as the younger d'Enneval speaks, it's clear that they're Normans—Frenchmen from Normandy, the descendants of Vikings. His accent is thick, some of his word choices strange to a local ear. "I understand that hunting the beast has not yielded the results one would hope for. But never fear, our methods are not . . . so"—he darts a look at Duhamel, who looks as though he's bitten directly into an unripe olive—"*primitive* as those used thus far. We have the latest science on our side, and we will trick the demon thing into running straight into our traps! It will come to us, I assure you, rather than us chasing it."

Duhamel looks as if he'd like to break another sword. But at least this time it'd be pointed at his actual rival. "We'll see whose methods are best, d'Enneval. You crow about your success before you've found any."

Mon Dieu, what children these men are. It's a game of king of the hill on a large scale and with deadly consequences that won't touch them. There are people *dying* here, and just like this morning with the poisoned corpse, these men treat us like we're tools in their quest for glory. Why would it matter who killed the beast? They can't care about the reward, not if they really are the best in France. Four thousand livres will be so little to them. It's fame they're after. And they cannot imagine sharing it, even if that would be the better way to save us all.

"Mon Dieu," Jean mutters at Belle's neck.

"Mon Dieu," I concur, and Belle shoots me an irritated look.

"Speak like a lady," Jean chides me.

"Take your own advice, bird."

Lafont claps his hands and dismisses us back to our day-to-day, but Clara, Belle, and I still watch the stage as the d'Ennevals and Duhamel continue their standoff, just at a lower volume.

"Duhamel, brother, I didn't want to say this in front of the whole village, but the king has asked us to relieve you of your duty."

Duhamel smiles without mirth. "I'm sure if that were true, he would have sent an actual letter. And probably given me more than two days of hunting."

"Two whole days? We'll have the beast within one. Spare yourself the embarrassment, and leave the village before we succeed," the younger d'Enneval returns.

"Oh, I shall leave the village before you succeed. Because you never will."

The men turn away from each other in unison, almost as if it's been choreographed. A perfectly timed number to end their dick-measuring contest.

Even Belle rolls her eyes.

18

LAFONT OFFERS ME THREE TIMES AS MUCH MONEY AS I'D make for a season's wool yield, and I'm sick and giddy all at once. Sick because it's so little for them. They could change all our lives in a second if they wanted to, but they never do. Giddy because it will be enough to take care of Charlotte and Hélène. I only have to put up with Belle a few hours in the afternoons. Wash her things, brush her hair, make her feel important.

That last one is the hardest task, but it'll mostly just require me to do stupid things she demands, all of which she could do herself. *Organize my dresses, Joséphine. Read aloud to me, Joséphine. Brush my hair, Joséphine.*

She and her father are staying in the most opulent house in the village. In Mende, that's not saying much, but it's still substantially nicer than our little cottage, with four separate bedrooms on a second floor, a hearth etched with whorls in the plaster, floors ever polished.

It's Eugénie's house, where she lives with her older brother and her father. The latter inherited wealth somewhere along the way, but he loves cognac and telling tall tales, so everyone in the village has a different version of how they got their nice house. Whatever the answer about the home's origins, I know they don't have enough money to do much beyond keep up the place. Because Eugénie tends sheep just like the rest of us, shears them, sells the wool. Keeps those men fed and warm.

After ushering me inside, the servant—probably someone the Lafonts brought with them—bustles off toward the kitchen without another word, and I wonder what I'm supposed to do. Wait here? Go find Belle?

I hesitate a few seconds and then decide finding Belle is the best option. She might see it as impertinent that I didn't wait, but irritating Belle is a favorite pastime anyway, so either I find her and get to work and she's glad, or I find her and she wishes I waited and she's irritated—either outcome is fine with me.

I pad up the stairs, a couple steps down the upstairs hall, and into Belle's room—and stop in my tracks.

The priest is here.

In Belle's room.

Warning slithers across my skin, tightens a knot in my center, closes my throat. The instant recognition that something is very, very wrong. No man should be alone in Belle's room with her, the priest least of all.

I take in the scene in the space of a heartbeat. They're standing near the window, the priest's back to me. Belle's body language is tight. Her arms wrapped around herself. The smile on her face nowhere close to reaching her eyes. The priest's body leans slightly forward, too close to her. My mind flashes me an image: an animal backed into a corner. Me, when the priest touched me and my body chose fight over flight.

Belle's body has chosen freeze.

The priest hasn't seen me yet, and he reaches out to touch Belle's arm. Her body is so tense that you wouldn't think she could grow tenser, but she does. She is stone and metal and ice. Her shoulders up toward her ears.

She sees me, and the fake smile slips, a half dozen emotions flashing by in the space of a released breath. Panic. Pleading. *Relief.*

The priest sees her looking and glances over his shoulder, then turns sharply.

"You," he says.

"Me," I agree, something sharp finding its way into my tone. Protective.

Belle finds her voice, and it's a small, trembly thing. "Joséphine, good. My"—she searches for a word—"my hair needs attending." She takes a small step to her right, away from the priest, then a larger, faster one. "Father, you'll have to excuse us."

"Indeed." His voice is flat. "Jacqueline—" He uses the wrong name for me on purpose. A power play of some kind. As if I cared.

As he moves across the room, I step out of the doorframe to make way. He stops beside me, and I hold his gaze. *I will bite you again, old man. Don't test me.* I hope he can feel that truth in his bones. He waves me farther from the doorframe, and I take another step back.

The last thing he says, turning back as he passes into the hall, is laced with irritation. "Always in the way, aren't you?"

I don't think he expects me to answer, but I do. "Oui, yes, I am."

His nostrils flare, but he doesn't answer. He keeps going, disappearing into the hall, his feet tapping on the steps. Belle and I are frozen in silence—her a deer afraid that running will bring back the evil thing, me a predator waiting to pounce if he returns—until the sound of the front door opening and closing echoes up the stairs.

I turn to face her.

"MON DIEU!" Jean screams from a perch in the corner of the room, and Belle jolts at the sound.

"Mon Dieu, indeed," I agree. "Belle, what just happened?"

She tries to laugh, but it comes out shaky. "Nothing, of course. What do you think happened?"

"Belle, it's just us here. Nobody's judging you."

"I don't know at all what you mean." She raises her chin.

"You really aren't going to tell me what happened? You looked terrified."

"Terrified? What a silly thing to say. It's just the priest. He's . . . he's . . . he's concerned with my Christian education. I should be grateful for his attention."

I want to smack her out of whatever delusion she's in, but since that kind of thing doesn't usually work, I try to channel Clara instead. What would Clara say?

"All right. If you change your mind and want to talk about it, I'm here." There, that's what Clara would say. Leave space for the person to decide things slowly.

Because I'm me and not Clara, I add, "But what *I* saw happening in this room was a man who shouldn't have even been here backing you into a corner. And when he did that to me, I bit him. You should feel free to do the same."

Belle blanches but doesn't say anything more—just moves to the vanity and frees her hair from its covering, ready for brushing.

19

IT'S TWILIGHT, AND HÉLÈNE IS HOME ALONE.

Finally. *Finally.* We know where she is, and she is where we need her to be.

There's no telling how long it'll last, how quickly her father or the soldier in their house will return from whatever they're doing. As twilight falls, their return only feels more imminent, our task more urgent.

As Clara approaches the door, I stand watch beside a tree on a soft, uneven patch of ground full of finger-thin pine cones in a hundred shades of brown. Behind me, an owl cries in the night. Branches whip and snap in a growing wind. And hair prickles at the back of my neck. I can only hope that when we retreat into these trees, we aren't just serving ourselves up on a platter to the thing we plan to use yet again as an escape. My mind is fatigued with the constant possibility. Death in front of, death behind. Death in every shadow.

The back door opens, spilling candlelight onto cobblestones and dirt.

"Come quickly," Clara says, a whisper through the night. "I'm here to help you."

Hélène asks questions I can only half hear, but Clara interrupts her. "There's no time. We'll tell you on the way. Do you trust me?"

"We?" Hélène's head emerges from the doorway, scanning.

I wave to catch her attention. I am the we.

"Help me how?" she asks when she sees me, uncertain.

"Get you away from your father," I answer.

"He'll come after me." Her voice is laced with fear, and I feel yet again—deep in my gut—that we have made the right choice.

"We'll make it look like it's the beast striking again." Clara motions for Hélène to step outside and—after a brief hesitation—she does, watching as Clara steps forcefully into the house and grabs a bowl and kettle off the table. She returns to us in the doorway, holds eye contact with Hélène for a long moment . . . and then smashes the bowl and kettle as hard as she can on the cobblestones. Both shatter, tea leaking in every direction, shards forming a mosaic on the dark, dampening stone. "There, it's like you opened the door with these in your hands and were attacked."

"Where are we going? Should I bring something?" Hope has crept around the edges of Hélène's voice.

"No." Clara's voice is nervous, urgent, the rattle of dry leaves in a harsh wind. "The longer we stay, the more chance of getting caught. Just come. Just bring yourself." She glances around her, but nothing has moved in the alleys around us, the forest behind me, or the windows of the houses next door. One has candles lit, leather curtain pushed aside, someone probably at home, but no shadow or silhouette has passed across the flickering light.

Hélène pauses for an interminably long moment, then reaches to close the door.

"No," Clara says, breathless. "It has to look like you opened the door for something and were attacked. The glass broken, *the door open.*"

Hélène's eyes dart to the forest as if to ask what's keeping the staged beast attack from becoming a real one. I don't have answers for that question, and after a few heavy moments, she must decide not to ask it. Decide to take her chances with this beast and not the one in her father's heart. She takes Clara's hand and lets us lead her into the trees.

Before we go too far, I turn. "Now, Hélène, I'm going to need you to scream. As loud as you can. And then we run. Any neighbors that hear it will believe the beast got you."

Clara and I both lift our hands to cover our ears as Hélène takes a deep breath, wipes at the single tear that's escaping down her cheek, and shrieks into the night. The scream is everything we wanted. An echo of how she sounded when she saw Charlotte. But instead of despair, it's packed full of fear and fury and *force.* It's so haunting. So believable. I feel her horror in my bones—Pascal's death, her sister's disappearance, her father's fists, perhaps even the loss of her mother years ago. She must have been holding so much inside.

As the scream echoes into the night, Clara reaches her hand out once again, and we run. I lead the way around blue-black trunks in the darkening night, over mud puddles speckled with the reflection of stars.

Hélène is silent, face pale in slivers of moonlight, and I can't help but think the fear across my skin is wrapping itself around hers as well. There is a beast on the loose, and we are in the woods, in the deepening dark. They say it doesn't attack in the woods, a fact I was so certain of in the daylight that first day when Clara warned me away from the edge of the trees. But in the dark as we weave deeper, farther from the village, circling around it, my certainty is gone, replaced by a dull ache in my belly.

It was too easy. How Hélène was finally alone and came with us. It was so easy that it feels like a trick.

When we're far enough away from the village, I finally speak, turning to face Hélène in a small glen with moonlight washing down over us. There's no time to sugarcoat anything. I just need to prepare her enough so that she doesn't scream or run or give us away when we get to Charlotte.

"You were right," I begin. "About your father. He killed Pascal."

Her already-white face goes whiter. "How do you know?"

"Because Charlotte saw him do it," Clara whispers, putting an arm around Hélène's shoulders.

Hélène's brow draws in. "How would you know that?"

"She told us," I say. "She's alive, Hélène."

Hélène's breathing grows fast and loud. So very loud against the familiar night noises of crickets and owls. Her face collapses in on itself, chin trembling, tears building.

"She's alive." She breathes the words. Then again, "She's alive."

"We thought your father might hurt her, too, so we hid her. Like we're going to hide you."

She presses her hands to her mouth, looks away from me and into the forest.

"Breathe," Clara soothes. "Breathe."

"I thought she was dead. I thought it was my fault."

I look at Clara, then back at Hélène. "We can't stay here. It's not safe. Can you walk? We can tell you anything else you want to know—but for now let's go."

Hélène nods through her tears and manages to keep silent as we continue through the dark. We skirt the village by a large margin, and it takes more than an hour to pick our way gingerly around trees and over boulders and across fallen trunks over streams.

And then, finally, we're there. We emerge on the opposite side of where we normally would, facing the front of the house instead of the back of the barn. The clearing is quiet, cold. No flicker of fire from inside the house. No motion or noise.

The feral thing inside me raises its attention. Something not quite right here—something more than my usual unease about the place. Has Charlotte fallen asleep already, smothered the cooking fire because someone happened by? Or perhaps because she heard us coming and didn't know it was us?

Clara leads the way across the clearing and pushes the door open. "Charlotte?"

Behind her, my breath catches in my chest.

The house is empty. And beside the door, near where Clara's hand rests on the doorframe, another—newer—set of claw marks slashes ruggedly down the wood.

Charlotte isn't here, but the beast was.

20

WE CLOSE THE DOOR BEHIND US, SHUTTING OUT THE NIGHT.
There's no blood on the ground, no sign of a struggle. Please,
dear God, let that mean Charlotte is all right. Perhaps the thing
came and she had to climb a tree or hide herself in the barn.
That's the first place I'll check as soon as I catch my breath. Because that must be it: she must be in the barn.

A darkly familiar thought slithers through me. *Unless this
place is cursed.* Unless by bringing her here, I've doomed her.
My mind flashes me the possibilities: Charlotte, like my brother,
releasing her soul into the sky. Charlotte torn apart like the girl
in the field. Charlotte's skull clattering down boulders, carelessly
kicked by a soldier who will never learn her name.

My stomach is as tight as a fist.

"Where is she?" Hélène's voice is an octave higher than normal. "I thought you said she'd be here?"

She should. I shake my head. "I'm going to check the barn. She might have closed herself in there if she heard something."

Hélène presses worried hands together, wide-eyed, as Clara guides her into an ancient chair by the hearth, and I open the door again, staring out into the quiet darkness. I press my fingers to the scarred wood as I close the door behind me, scanning the trees for the glint of an eye, a movement in the night.

Nothing.

Only the distant hoot of an owl, the normal slight stuttering shifts of pine needles on the breeze.

I force myself away from the door. The barn is only steps away, but it feels like a mile. Yet again, I'm pulled back to the day in the ice. Every step a journey, every minute a thousand years. Time was a fluid thing then, and it's the same now.

I step, then pause, listen. Step, pause, listen. When I reach the door, it opens easily, not latched. The interior is inky dark, and I hadn't thought to light a candle before coming out here. My body freezes, unsure what's scarier—leaving the door open to whatever lurks in the night or the possibility of closing the lurking thing in with me.

"Charlotte?" I whisper into the dark with no response. No movement, no sound.

She's not here or she'd answer me. Unless she's here and *can't* answer me.

God. I'm going to have to go inside. My mind flickers into its favorite activity yet again, flashing me the worst-case scenarios. Charlotte lifeless in a corner, found out by her father while we were rescuing her sister. Our efforts having meant nothing in

172

the end. Perhaps worse, Charlotte's body in pieces, found by the other evil thing.

My stomach clenches, and I step deeper into the barn, leaving the door cracked. A foolish choice, perhaps, but the only hint of light in this place. I feel along the edges of the empty room with my feet and arms. I kick nothing but dust and the edge of the wall, feel nothing but rough wood under my hands.

It takes forever to circle the whole place. But there's nothing here. No one here.

I'm relieved—and somehow not. Because is it a good thing that she isn't here, or does it just confirm that something sinister has happened? Another curse. Another person I love disappeared into the night.

I slip out the door and this time move faster across the space between the two buildings, barely glancing at the dark trunks of trees standing watch—

Until a branch cracks behind me, loud as a gunshot in the quiet night. It's like my soul leaves my body, leaping through layers of skin to launch itself above me and watch the scene unfold. I think of my brother again. Was this what it felt like for spirit to jolt from skin and rise into the sky? To know with perfect clarity that this is the moment you die.

Then I turn, my vision returning to myself, and watch as a familiar figure emerges from the trees. Not monster. Not wolf. Not demon. Not man.

A little girl in a tattered dress.

"Charlotte." I cry the name as I bend in half, hands on knees, my body too weak to hold itself up. "Where the hell have you been?"

*

"I couldn't save Pascal." Charlotte's voice is haunted as she steps toward me, her head down. "So I wanted to save Hélène. But she's not there. She's not at the house. What if Papa—"

"Charlotte." Mon Dieu, she thinks Hélène is hurt. "Charlotte, we told you we'd get her out. She's here. She's fine."

Charlotte blinks through her tears, and the door behind me swings open. Warm orange light from a now-active fire in the hearth spills out around the silhouette of her sister.

"Hélène?"

"Charlotte!"

They both stand frozen for a moment, and then Charlotte runs to her sister and they collapse in the doorway, hugging on their knees, crying desperately as they cling to each other.

I take a shaky breath and gently nudge them inside before closing the door behind me and pressing my back against it because I need reassurance that it's there. That we are inside and we did it and we are safe.

We are safe.

I press my hands to the rough wood behind me and watch the sisters as they sob and laugh and shake. Hélène pulls Charlotte away from her, studies her face, collapses into tears again, and then pulls her close.

"You're alive," she murmurs. "You're really alive."

My heart aches, and not just for them. What would it be like to survive with someone else? What if I could hug my brother like that? My mother. I can't even picture it, because it's been so long and their faces have faded now. Indistinct in my mind, like

174

ghosts. I have only tattered remnants of memory. And my heart stretches longingly toward the two sisters, both survivors, both wildly alive.

"Charlotte, did something happen here?" Clara's voice is soft as she helps the two girls onto the blankets by the now-cozy fire, presses bowls of weak tea into their hands.

"What do you mean?" Charlotte wipes her shiny cheeks.

"The claw marks outside the door," I answer for Clara. "They're new."

Charlotte's eyes widen. "What claw marks?"

I glance at the door. If she hasn't seen them, does that mean they happened while she was trying to get to Hélène again? Does it mean the beast is still nearby? Was my fear in the barn more than a fear of the dark, the unknown . . . could it be some animal instinct, some bone-deep knowledge that I was being hunted?

I shiver and exchange a look with Clara. "If they're fresh claw marks, we should stay."

She licks her lips. "Mémé will worry. She might raise the alarm and send out a search party. And even if she doesn't, Walter will notice that we're gone. We're already out late. I don't think we have much time before our absence is notable."

"Our absence will be more notable if we get eaten." I try for a joke, but it comes out too scary to be funny.

"What do we think it is?" she asks. "The beast."

Despite all the rumors, all the theories, Clara and I have never had this conversation. Because it never mattered. Whatever it was, it was a danger to us, perhaps to the sheep. And choosing a pet theory wouldn't keep us safe. Theories were for people like Belle, who saw the thing as curiosity more than personal danger.

But now—perhaps if we could figure it out, we would be safer. If we knew whether it hunted at night or by day. If we knew whether what they say is true and it was more interested in open spaces than forest—or vice versa.

"Belle thinks it's a wolf," Hélène says, patting her sister's arm like she still can't believe she's real.

I didn't realize Hélène knew Belle. It irritates me that she does, though I'm not sure why. I guess the idea that anyone cares what Belle thinks is irritating.

"Wolves don't sharpen their claws on wooden doorframes and barns and trees," I answer. "And if it's a wolf, it's a really strange one. Nobody's lost a sheep. Why would a wolf go for a person over a sheep? Sheep can't fight back, not really. They're smaller. Easier."

Charlotte's eyes are shiny with fear. "The priest said it's a demon."

I frown at that one. There's no way to prove or disprove a supernatural theory. "Well, if it's that, I don't think there's anything we can do."

"What about a bear?" Clara asks. "I know we don't see them much, but there are some higher up in the hills."

"Bears do sharpen their claws on things," I agree. "But the descriptions don't match at all. People say it's this reddish thing with a mohawk and a long tail. I haven't heard of any bears growing a long tail . . . or a mohawk."

"All right, but people also say it can kill with a single glance and can't be pierced by gunfire. So either it is a demon or some of the parts of the description are wrong," Clara answers.

I let out a long breath, realize that I'm still pressed against the door as if my body is what's keeping whatever is out there at bay. I push away from it, feeling foolish.

"I don't think we're going to figure it out tonight," Clara goes on. "But I do think we have to go, Joséphine. If they send a search party and you are the person being searched for, they'll come here."

"Oui, you're right." I pull my coat tighter around me as Clara comes to join me by the door. My stomach is all knots, but Clara is right. We must risk the beast or risk exposure. And at least if we do the former, the girls stay safe.

"Take care of each other," Clara says to the girls. "Charlotte, you know how to stay hidden. Tomorrow, when it's safe, show your sister how to get onto the eaves in the barn, onto the roof, in case the soldiers come looking."

Charlotte nods, twists her fingers together with Hélène's. I reach for Clara's hand and do the same, and together we open the door and slip into the night, out of one danger and into another.

Clouds move across the moon almost the moment we step onto the sheep trail. There are still stars to see by, but the light is faint and even with the number of times we've walked this same route, we both stumble.

Normally, the tightness in my body eases as we move away from my house. But not tonight. Tonight I am all knots and twitches. Listening for the slightest noise, the barest hint of danger. The only thing that keeps me moving is Clara's warm hand in mine, pulling me onward. We saved Hélène, and we should be celebrating. But tonight the beast feels so much more real than before, so much more present.

As we slip from forest into field, nearing the village, Clara makes a startled, choking noise and I yank hard on her arm, pulling her back from whatever danger has wrestled that sound from her throat. I step in front of her before I even know why she's afraid.

The answer is strange. Ahead and to my right, something massive rises into the sky, tall as the church steeple but thinner than the church. At first, it looks like a tangle of branches, as if trees stood from their places and walked into the field to dance, their limbs tangling together.

"What is it?" Clara whispers just as the answer comes to me.

"It's a cage."

A wooden cage for the world's largest bird. A crude and massive version of the same one in Belle's house.

"How did it get here?" Clara presses warm against my back, her head over my shoulder, breath in my ear.

I shrug, then attempt an answer. "It must be the soldiers. The new hunters. They said they were going to do things differently. They must mean this."

I can't see how it'll help them, having a cage like this. But the realization settles me. This is not something we need to be afraid of. Just another rich man's foolishness.

"We've got to get back." I squeeze Clara's hand and start walking again.

She returns the squeeze and follows.

21

WALTER WASN'T THERE WHEN WE GOT HOME, BUT HE IS here now—as the sun starts to peek above the horizon—helping two other soldiers go through our house like state-sanctioned thieves.

"Does this work?" One rummages through our drawers and holds up a nightgown to Walter.

"I think that's for sleeping," Walter answers.

"If you tell me what you're looking for, maybe I can help," I say, irritation threaded through my voice.

Walter looks at me for the first time since he barged in early this morning. "We need a dress."

Clara looks up and makes a face from where she's been checking one of the ewes, who seemed to be limping this morning.

Across the room, Mémé chimes in. "Child, that's going to need more explanation."

He shrugs. "We were told to bring sheep and dresses, so we're bringing sheep and dresses. Clearly we don't own any, so you'll be donating yours to the cause."

Donating. As if donations were involuntary.

"You're not killing the sheep again, are you?" Clara holds the ewe too tight and gets a BLEA in her face for her trouble.

Walter shrugs again as if it doesn't matter, and the rage curls tight in my chest. We have so little, and he can't even tell us if the "donations" are going to be returned. Are they stuffing our sheep into that cage, hoping to tempt the beast in after them? And what in the world would the army need dresses for?

Walter doesn't deem it necessary to answer her. Instead, his tone goes ominous. "The beast took another girl last night."

My heart speeds up. "Oh?"

"Oh no," Mémé whispers, leaning heavily against the wall as if the news has knocked her over. I feel a pang at the pain we're causing by not being able to tell her the truth. But she's already said things she shouldn't about Charlotte; Clara and I agreed that we can't burden her with any more information.

"Oui, the other sister of that first boy," Walter explains, and I hate him all over again for never learning any of our names.

"Family's cursed." The second soldier's tone is pointed as he rummages foolishly through the chest of blankets as if we keep clothes in there. "That's what they're saying in town."

I open my mouth to ask for more information. How they found out. What precisely people are saying. But before I can, the third soldier makes a triumphant noise, and we all turn toward him.

"Aha!" He raises my cleanest, nicest dress from the bottom drawer of the bureau.

"Well done," Walter cheers, and—without another word or glance for us, and most definitely without a thank-you—we watch as the three boys clomp heavily out of the house with my dress and a deeply irritated ewe who is already screaming her protests as they pull her roughly along on the end of a rope. They leave the door swinging open behind them, and Clara has to jump up and close it because one of the lambs is trying—frantically—to follow its mother.

I only own three dresses, so I guess I'm down to two now. But I hope they bring the ewe back. I want to cry with rage when I think they might not. When I think about how little they value her life and ours. Sometimes I wonder if there was ever a time when I wasn't angry.

"Do you remember our first lambing?" I ask Clara as we lead the sheep through gold-green meadows for their morning graze.

Clara makes an amused noise that tells me she does. "Of course. What made you think of it?"

"I don't know. I guess trying to save the girls is making me think about other times we've had to try to save something. How you're *always* saving someone, something. People who come in and need herbs. Me when I go off cliffs like a fool after my lamb. The girls now. But before all that, the baby."

"I did save her, didn't I?" Clara's voice is soft and proud.

I nod, picturing those tense moments in my mind. When I saw the baby's head out of her mama and nothing else and I made a horrified sound, freezing in my tracks. But Clara—capable even at eight years old—jumped forward and eased the lamb out by the shoulders. Her mama wouldn't clean her, wouldn't warm her, and it was a bitterly cold night. A perfect recipe for a dead lamb, but Clara cleared the baby's airway, unlaced her bodice, and stuffed the lamb against her skin, lending her body heat to the tiny, swollen lamb until the swelling went down and the temperature went up enough for her to feed.

"She was the sweetest baby," Clara reminisces.

I snort. "And the rest of them were devils. After all that, remember the ewes kept trying to steal the baby?"

"Lord." Clara breathes the word like it's the lingering end note of a song. "They're always thieves, but that year was the worst one for it. Remember we had to separate them even in the house?"

"And that one ewe kept biting the real mom to keep her away?"

Clara laughs, and the sound is the best thing I've heard in days. I revel in it, open my mouth to respond when—

"Is that . . ." Clara points across the field, her words trailing off.

We both stop walking and stare.

"Uh, if you are about to ask if that is a sheep wearing my dress, then I think the answer is yes," I answer through an incredulous laugh.

From behind us, a male voice joins the conversation. "Never realized I was attracted to sheep before."

"Joséphine, you've gotten a touch fluffier," another jests. Pranksters.

"Har-har," I fake-laugh.

Louis sidles up to us and throws an arm around Clara's shoulders. Cheeky. "These soldiers, my, my, smartest men in the kingdom. They've decided since they can't catch the beast, they'll trick him. It's a d'Enneval strategy. Genius." He snaps his fingers.

"Is that seriously what they've done? They're dressing up sheep to trick the beast into thinking the sheep are . . . us?" Clara is incredulous.

"Well, at least we know our sheep are coming home tonight, since there's no way this is going to work," I answer.

The pranksters titter with laughter. "Truly, and they keep calling *us* country fools."

"The d'Enneval theory," Louis says, removing his arm from Clara's shoulders and holding up a finger in mock triumph, "is that because the beast's victims have been mostly girls, it's targeting you for a reason. And they can trick it into appearing if they only trick it into thinking there's a live girl for the taking."

I never thought these men were particularly smart, but this is a new level of foolishness. Never mind the part where it ruins our clothes and there's no chance of it working. It's a real marvel how men so well positioned can understand so little about the nature they're up against. They're bragging all over the village about the wolves they've killed, the predators they've faced down. And yet they don't seem to understand the slightest thing about actual animals.

I've faced more than a dozen wolves myself. Watched enough

barn cats, owls, even snakes to know that carnivores take the path of least resistance. Any shepherdess could tell you the same—if a man deigned to listen to us. A sick animal. A pregnant one. An elderly ewe. Or a baby. These are the targets. Not because of their gender or even their age but because they're easier to take down. Slower, smaller, clumsier.

Just like we wouldn't climb all the way down the gorge for dandelions for our salad when they grow right outside the cottage, predators aren't stupid enough to waste their energy on the leanest, fastest, meanest ewe when there is a dopey lamb on the edge of the group paying no attention. It's why every day my own little fool survives is a damn miracle.

"BLEA," he screams as if he can hear my thoughts.

This beast is the same as any other, I'm sure. It isn't taking girls because we're *girls*. It isn't taking girls because the devil told it to. It's like any animal—choosing us because we are smaller and, probably, because it has more access to us. For every man who walks the fields alone in Gévaudan, ten girls do the same. We're the ones alone every day in these lonely spaces.

The sheep across the field reaches the end of its tether and screams its discontent.

"You tell 'em, girl. How dare they make you wear clothes like that." Louis furrows his brow in mock outrage. "Shall I get your dress back?" He looks between Clara and me.

"She'd be happier if you did." I motion to the sheep. "But I imagine you'd be in quite some trouble."

He winks. "I love trouble."

"Clearly."

Louis starts forward, apparently hell-bent on putting himself in the hunters' bad graces, when the sound of horses from our left catches everyone's attention, drawing our gazes away from the sheep and toward those who must be tasked with lying in wait in this foolish trap.

A small group of men, four on foot and two on horseback, stops a few feet from us as our sheep cluster behind Clara and me, unhappy about the unfamiliar men.

"I don't blame you," I murmur softly to them, because my own body prickles with unease at their approach. Though part of me is also glad they're here. Because I need more information than Walter gave us this morning and I'm hoping they'll offer it up. Do they believe the beast took Hélène? Did anyone hear her scream? Has our ruse kept us safe?

I wait for the answers, my stomach a single, pulled-tight knot.

"My lords, the d'Ennevals!" Louis affects an exaggerated bow. "To what do your humble servants owe the pleasure?"

"You're locals?" the younger d'Enneval asks. As if we could be anything else.

My fool lamb decides this question is his cue to scream at the strangers, and Clara—who is closer to him—sweeps him neatly into her arms to calm him while I hold back a smile.

"Oui, monsieur." Denisot ignores the lamb and affects a small bow.

"We need to get to Château de la Baume. Can you point us in the right direction?"

Disappointment overtakes my nerves. These are men on a mission, not men here to tell us more about what's happened, what they believe, whether they've swallowed our lie or choked on it.

Louis and the other boys exchange a look that I know too well. There's a plot behind it. And if these arrogant hunters were paying any real attention, they'd see the danger. Instead, when Louis says, "But of course. We can show you the way!" the d'Ennevals nod in agreement and follow the three boys as they lope off across the field.

"They didn't mention her," Clara whispers, squatting to place a hand on one of her ewes.

"No, they didn't. And I don't want to ask around." I squat to be eye to eye with her.

"Agreed. I don't want to draw attention to all of it . . . but not knowing is making me feel so sick." Clara takes a deep, shaky breath, opens and closes her fists.

I reach over to take her hand, but my fool lamb thinks I'm trying to pet him and wiggles his head into my hand. We both laugh and roll our eyes, releasing just a little of the tension strung tight across our bodies.

"Affection thief," Clara murmurs, pressing her face to his cheeky little head.

"Little bastard," I add.

In the distance, I hear Louis laughing, and Clara and I train our attention back on the retreating men and boys.

"Hmm." Clara squints after them. "Isn't that the way to the bog?"

I raise my eyebrows in response. "Oui. Going to be a fun day for our saviors the d'Ennevals."

22

"MENDE IS OFFICIALLY HAUNTED," EUGÉNIE SAYS AS I CROSS through the door and into her house for another afternoon of making sure Belle never has to do a single thing for herself.

"Oh?" I tilt my head.

This is it. News about Hélène . . .

But no. Belle appears on the stairs and completes Eugénie's thought. "The ghost of the little girl, the first one the beast took here in Mende. They're seeing her everywhere now. Not just at her sister's house."

I'm not sure what bothers me more: the fact that Belle is acting so normal when the last time I saw her she was backed into a corner by the priest, that she doesn't know Charlotte's name, the alarm bells jangling in the back of my mind saying *Charlotte was seen,* or that nobody is giving me information about Hélène.

"Her name was Charlotte." Eugénie is apparently also irritated with Belle.

"How do you take your tea?" Jean chimes in, doing a little jig on Belle's shoulder.

"With roasted bird," Eugénie answers, her eyes a squint.

Belle waves a hand, dismissive. "Well, I heard the ghost of Charlotte has been haunting *several* people. At least three people said they saw it last night in three different places at once."

Well, that's a conveniently impossible scenario. I'm glad Charlotte seems so well relegated to myth, but still—*someone* must have seen her last night if everyone is talking about her like this. And all it would take is for one person to realize it was a real girl and not a ghost . . . and then the attention now trained on the beast could easily be turned toward a new theory: of a live little girl hidden away somewhere. If fifty dragoons were looking for a person instead of an animal, it wouldn't take long to find and check my house. It's only safe because the village doesn't go there, thinking its cursed, and the soldiers have no reason to check it even if they pass by. Because no wolves or bears or demon spawn are taking up residence in tucked-away cottages.

I force a laugh as I follow Belle up the stairs. "You don't really believe in ghosts, do you?"

Belle gives me a sharp look as we reach the top of the staircase and step into the room she's been sharing with Eugénie. "No, but the priest says it could be a demon they saw. Something impersonating the poor girl. Why not? If we already have one potential demon beast running around out here?"

Eugénie snorts. "More than two demons if the soldiers are to be believed. Did you hear what Louis and Denisot did this morning?" She turns to me.

"Well, I did see them offer to show the d'Ennevals the way to the château."

"Mon Dieu!" Jean squawks.

Eugénie snorts again, and there's something very charming about such a pretty girl having such an ugly way of laughing. I find myself grinning despite all the tensions still coiled up under my skin.

"They showed them *something*," she agreed. "Showed them and their horses right into the bog, where they got good and mired. Horses panicked, of course, and threw the d'Ennevals right off into the muck. Then the boys showed them their derrières for good measure."

"Speak like a lady!" Jean twitters.

"Mon Dieu, the things those boys think they can get away with." I shake my head with grudging fondness.

Belle holds out her brush to me and sinks into her vanity seat, a silent command to brush her hair.

"How do you take your tea?" Jean squeaks, reaching out to tap his open beak against the hairbrush as I begin.

"Well," Belle says, ignoring him, "they *didn't* get away with it, did they?"

I look to Eugénie, who shrugs. "They're all crammed up in the jail cell now. If you get a chance to pass by the window, they're rather entertaining. Just giving a recitation of all the wrongs they feel the soldiers have done since coming here. Sheep theft and dress theft and eating the stores and disrespecting the dead. Saint Jerome would be proud."

"Saint Jerome?" I echo. I never did pay enough attention at Mass.

"He's the one who is known for being hot tempered." She salutes.

Belle looks disgruntled. "Ungrateful, that's what those boys are."

"I prefer to think of it as bold." Eugénie leans against the vanity. "If I wasn't hell-bent on getting out of here, I'd probably marry one of those boys. The only men in this village who don't accept the status quo."

Getting out of here. The words leap out at me.

I run the brush through Belle's thick, dark hair but aim my question at Eugénie, not only because I'm curious about her life but also because perhaps she can help me take this vague idea of sending Charlotte and Hélène off with a merchant and turn it into something more concrete. She's not Belle and hasn't seen the world. But she's wealthier than most of us and has family in other places. "Where will you go?"

"Nice." Her eyes sparkle with the answer. "I have an aunt who left for Nice when I was little. She told me when she left that I was always welcome with her. I just need one of those fool soldiers to agree to take me down there."

That explains the flirting. The relentless way I see her surrounded by boys every time she leaves the house, even though I never saw her act like that before they arrived. While we are mapping Charlotte and Hélène's escape, Eugénie is tracing the contours of her own.

But does she really need a soldier? Or does she need *us*? I can picture Eugénie, Hélène, and Charlotte on the back of a wagon heading south. Eugénie providing the destination. Me using the savings I'm collecting here to pay off the merchant.

If that's going to be even a remote possibility, I need to know that people believe Hélène has been taken by the beast. Since no one is offering up the information, I chance the conversation myself.

"The soldiers were at our house this morning," I begin. "They said another girl was taken. Hélène." Saying her name to them makes my heart race, and I hope I haven't made the wrong decision, made myself suspicious somehow by bringing her up.

Based on the way both girls' faces drain of color, they didn't know. Which makes sense. Because why would they be talking about the maybe sightings of a ghost when another girl has disappeared into thin air?

"What happened?" Eugénie speaks first.

I shrug, careful. "The soldiers didn't say much. Just that the beast took her and they think the family is cursed."

"Three people from one family." Eugénie presses a hand to her mouth.

"Maybe that's good news," Belle says.

"What?" Eugénie and I answer in incredulous unison.

Belle turns in her chair to look between us. "Maybe they did something to anger God or the beast itself. And that means the rest of us aren't actually in danger."

I make an involuntary strangled noise. If there is a more privileged, callous perspective on the world than Belle's, I've never encountered it. Hearing about someone else's misfortune and

191

thinking, *Well, at least it wasn't me!* Of course, we all breathe in relief every time it's not us, not someone we love, but there's something different about the way Belle looks at it. Like they've sacrificed themselves for her. Like she deserves that.

She turns back around in her chair and motions for me to keep brushing her hair.

"You know . . ." I start to tell her off as I reach forward to run the brush through her hair again.

"How do you take your tea?" Jean lunges forward and bites my finger.

"Ouch! Mon Dieu!"

Belle turns her head to look. "Guess he doesn't like you."

"Guess that makes two of you."

Belle blinks a few times, opens her mouth like she means to speak, but then glances at Eugénie and closes it again. I wonder what insult was so bad it couldn't be lobbed at me in front of a witness.

As I wander home through gently sloping alleys, the streets are eerily quiet. Even with every danger here, Mende is normally a lively place. Doors thrown open to coax in sun or breeze. Songs floating from windows. Laughing children. The comforting sounds of work getting done. Candles made, cloth woven, hooves cleaned.

But ever since we found Pascal, the quiet has been growing darker, deeper. Another beast in our midst—a nothingness swallowing what was once something. Today, the silence is the thickest I've ever experienced. It scrapes against my nerves, setting my teeth on edge.

I wonder if this is the result of taking Hélène, if we've pushed the village's fear over some invisible edge. No more open doors. No more songs that might draw attention to ourselves. Just tightly shuttered windows, their thick leather curtains secured, and stark, empty stone streets.

My throat is tight, my heart tighter.

And then, the first sign of life I've seen since leaving Belle's house: two women hurrying through the streets, heads bowed, hands clasped. One I recognize as Denisot's mother, the other a weaver who I remember giving out daisy chains in the square when I was too small to do anything other than toddle after my brother.

"Bonjour," I offer as they approach, and both look up with sunken eyes. A sign of little sleep. Too much fear.

"You shouldn't be out here alone," Denisot's mother says, stopping beside me.

"Didn't you hear—another girl was taken?" The other woman's voice is strangled.

"Who?" I ask the question, though I know the answer.

"Poor, dear Hélène." Denisot's mother darts her eyes around the street as if Hélène's name might call the thing that took her. I suppose in a way she's right. I am the thing that took her. I am the beast that planted this fear in these hearts. And I am ravenous to hear her name from their mouths, to know what they think happened.

"It was the beast?" I ask.

"What else?" The other woman looks like she might cry. "They're saying the family must be cursed. Three children from one home . . . that can't be coincidence."

Nerves jitter through me. Rumors of a curse aren't bad for us, but questions about why one family has lost all its children might be. They come too close to truth.

I should end the conversation now, but I feel shaky with the desire for more. To know everything this village is thinking. Every angle from which they might come for us. "Cursed?"

"Some say by God, but . . . the curse could be human, too. Demonic possession or . . . witch."

Denisot's mother reaches for the other woman's elbow. "Come on. We shouldn't talk of such things, not out here on the street. We should get inside. And you too." She motions her chin at me. "Don't be outside more than you have to be."

With that, the women start walking again, passing quickly around a corner and out of sight, leaving me once again with the thick, heavy, choking silence. And words that might keep us safe—or might make us less safe.

Curse. Demonic possession.

Witch.

23

THUNDER ROLLS LIKE A GROWL THROUGH THE DARK THROAT that is our sky, streaked red and gray by twilight. When I got home from Belle's, Mémé was visiting with Amani and Clara was out with the sheep. Later than usual. Too late.

There are so many possible things that could be wrong right now, so I didn't wait for Clara to get home. I pointed myself like a compass toward my house and took off into the growing dark. Around me, now, the wind howls, weaving through tree trunks, smacking leaves into my face as I go. Fat raindrops spill from the sky and then stop again. And my heart beats in time with my footsteps. Fast.

Please, Clara, be at the house with the girls and the sheep. Please simply have lost track of time.

Behind me, a branch cracks, and I whip around, holding out my pike. Something flashes, shiny in the dark. Eyes, I think. But then they're gone. And it's impossible to tell if they belong to owl or squirrel peering out from a hollow in a tree or some-. thing worse. I hold out my pike for another long moment as the raindrops fall faster, drowning out any other night noise. Then I go, following the now-so-familiar trail to the house, and emerge behind the barn.

As usual, the last few steps into the clearing hit me like a gut punch, twist my stomach into knots. But as I slip around the corner of the barn, warm light spills from the windows and a faint bleating rises above the rain, and the tension in my chest and shoulders lightens.

The sheep are here, inside, which means Clara is here, inside. The curse of this place hasn't taken her or Charlotte or Hélène, and every day it doesn't take her, the place feels the barest breath lighter. Safer.

I open the door to three startled but happy faces and a bunch of goofy fluffballs snuggled up near the hearth.

"Mon Dieu, you're soaked." Clara rushes to close the door behind me and pull me farther into the warmth of the room.

"Clara, I thought you would be home before the storm."

She shakes her head. "Sorry. I guess I wasn't paying attention. I couldn't pull myself away."

I turn to see the sisters as I've never seen them before, their faces lit up with mirth, cheeks pink, eyes bright. They're holding hands like they still can't believe, even twenty-four hours later, that they are together and safe.

I can see why Clara didn't want to leave. The joy beaming off them makes me want to cry. And *we did this.* Clara and me. We saved them.

Outside, the rain howls down even harder, thunder smashing through air, wind shaking window covers. But in here it's all lightness and joy. Like a summer day before all of this happened, back when Clara and I could just lean against boulders and trace the shapes of clouds. When I'd ask Clara what she wanted, and she'd say *a whole tub full of lentils* or *a perfumed bath* like I described from Belle's house or *to see the ocean*. And we'd laugh at the beautiful impossibilities. Still watchful over our flock, but not nearly as tense as we've grown this past week.

The memory makes me want to cry.

Is that all it's been—a week? It feels like a year.

I peel off the outer layers of my soaked-through clothes and lower myself onto the wool blankets with the girls. They both reach toward me and squeeze my arm.

"Thank you," Hélène says, holding my gaze. "Thank you so much."

I take the longest, deepest, most grateful breath of my life. It's like that thank-you is a poultice over a long-scarred part of my heart. The part that stopped believing that people could save each other on the day my father walked out of the cabin and left me to die.

We *can* save each other. We are, as Clara likes to say, more powerful than we think.

She sits beside me, her head on my shoulder, and I pull the uneaten lunch from Belle's from my satchel and pass around the bounty. Creamy cheese, fresh-baked bread, ripe berries. Extravagant compared to our normal fare.

For the next hour, everything is perfect. We close our eyes and savor each bite. We stoke the fire to keep out the chill creeping in around the doorframe from the storm raging outside. My clothes and hair dry in the heat, and my heart thaws in the warmth of the conversation.

Hélène tells us about her passion for dream interpretation, how every morning she used to chide Pascal and Charlotte to share whatever they could remember. Charlotte emerges further from her worried shell, no longer the too-grown girl worried about her sister. Her eyes stay locked on Hélène, and I can see the hero worship in them. The desperate, fierce love. The love that drove her out of the safety of this cabin two nights in a row because she couldn't bear to leave Hélène in danger for a single additional day.

Clara and I are mostly quiet, soaking them in. Content to close our eyes and feel the burst of tart, sweet berries on our tongues, to revel in the quiet, warm moment curled up together on a blanket, fingers tangled in fingers, lips kissing foreheads and temples and shoulders because we are just so impossibly grateful to be here, alive, safe, ourselves.

"I love you," I whisper to Clara after Hélène has coaxed one of Clara's dreams out and is crafting an interpretation involving secret wealth.

"Forever," she agrees, her lips brushing my cheek.

"And ever."

"Amen."

As if to punctuate the end of our quiet, happy moment, a new noise breaks through the steady pouring of the rain, the threatening boom of the thunder.

A pounding, shuddering, door-shaking *BANG*.

Then: again.

It takes a moment for fear to rise up and swallow the warmth in my chest. For the smiles to drop from our faces, our attention to turn toward the sound.

A third joy-smashing, doom-bringing *BANG* rings through the space, and I stand before I even know I am moving, placing myself between Clara and the noise.

Because someone—or something—has slammed into the front door.

Three times.

And now it opens.

24

WOULD IT BE BETTER TO FACE MAN OR BEAST? WHICH ONE do I hope is now crashing into the cottage, roaring with fury?

It doesn't matter, because we have no choice. Standing in the doorway, rain blowing in around his silhouette, is a man.

Charlotte screams. Hélène thrusts her sister behind her on instinct.

Their father's face is thunderous rage, his eyes wild.

"You bitch." He takes two steps in and reaches for Clara, who has stepped up beside me and is now closest to him, but I cannot allow it. I, too, am made of rage, made *for* rage.

I scream as I launch myself into him, knocking his arm away from Clara and pushing him two unsteady steps backward.

"Everyone, let's just calm down. Calm down." Clara puts up her hands, positioning herself between this furious man and the two girls we thought we'd saved from him.

Ha. As if life could ever let us save them. It spits in the face of the girl I was just an hour ago, happy, thinking she'd done a good thing. Now I stand frozen in front of a monster as he glares across the room at the three girls behind me. The sheep scream and stamp in distress from the corner.

"You thought you could run away, is that it?" His voice booms above the downpour that's streaming in through the open doorway, the door swaying with the wind and water. I have the bizarre impulse to close it. Close out the beast somewhere outside. But then I'd be closing in another. My stomach churns with the impossible choice.

Clara tries to reason with him. "Sir, you are clearly very upset, and I think we should all sit and calmly discuss this."

"Sit? Sit with the bitches who stole my children?"

"No one stole us!" Charlotte screams from behind me. "You killed Pascal. I saw you!"

His face twitches, his knuckles gone pale. My eyes follow each movement, my body tensing like a cat's.

"You always were a liar," he snarls at Charlotte. "And you"— his eyes move to Hélène—"a whore just like your mother. No one will believe either of you."

"Fine, all right. Then you can just go and leave them here, and no one will believe them. They won't tell anyone." Clara's voice trembles behind me.

He turns as if to go but only laughs, facing the door and closing it with a finality that tells me all I need to know about what is going to come next. "Damn right none of you will tell anyone a damn thing."

When he swings that first punch, I duck and dive straight into him, ramming my shoulder as hard as I can into his stomach and up into his diaphragm. Same as I did to Denisot when we were kids and he kissed me without permission.

Then, it knocked Denisot onto the floor and stopped him entirely. Now, it seems to make this much larger man even angrier. I feel his hand in my hair, wrenching me up and away and then smashing my head into the wall. Splinters scream into my skin, and I stumble onto my knees as he releases me.

Clara's on him now, pulling him away from me, and Hélène is hovering nearby, as if she wants to help but is too scared to do more than flail her hands at him and jump back when he stumbles toward her. Charlotte is frozen.

But the sheep—my sheep—are not. They scream, shrill and urgent, and charge.

People who don't spend time around sheep think they're foolish creatures, quiet, tame. But a few villages away, one girl's sheep saved her from the beast. We go to war for them and they for us.

Now about half of our sheep charge forward, screaming their intent, heads lowered. They slam into his shins and knees, knocking the man off balance, and I jump back into the fray, pushing him hard to finish the job. He flies sideways into a wall and then to the floor.

The fall only seems to make him angrier. He lifts himself to his knees, then feet, and grabs me by the neck this time, slamming me into the rough wood of the wall and pressing, his hand harsh and strong against my throat as my heart beats in my ears. Pressure builds in my face, disorienting.

I can see Clara trying to pull him off, the sheep still screaming at his feet, the fool lamb smashing his tiny head into the
man's shin, still trying to help as I claw at his hands, trying to
remove them from my throat. Trying to breathe.

Spots dance in my vision, and I try to think. My instinct is
wrong here. I won't get his hands off. I need to do something
else. I need a weapon. I need to hit him. I need to—

I curl my fingers and lash out, driving two fingers into each
of his eyes.

He screams and releases my throat, and I choke in a fiery
breath.

If I didn't know it before, I know it now: this man is going
to kill us. Or we'll have to kill him. There are no other options.
There is no driving him back. His rage is too big, a thing un-
caged, unreasonable. We have made him feel a fool, and we
will pay.

I lunge across the agitated sea of sheep to the blanket where
what's left of the tea has spilled from knocked-over bowls, what's
left of the bread has been trampled under hooves.

Behind me, I feel hands claw at my back. My progress stops
abruptly when he grabs hold of my skirt and pulls me backward.

But I have what I was lunging for.

I have my weapon.

I whirl to face him and aim. This man tried to crush the
breath from my throat, and so that is where I strike: his throat.
The cheese knife is tiny, but a throat is fragile. I rip into his once,
twice, a third time. His hands, like mine, go to his neck by instinct. As if he can stop what's happening.

He cannot.

Everyone in the room freezes except the sheep as he grasps ineffectively at the blood now streaming down his chest, soaking his shirt. Clara steps back, then back again. Away. I grip the knife in my fist, breathing hard and raggedly and painfully. His blood is hot on my face, my hands, my body. Hot and slick and thick and smelling nauseatingly metallic.

When he falls, he falls hard, breaking a chair on his way down, sending the sheep scurrying. The noise—the choking, gasping, gurgling final breath—is the worst part. That and the blood snaking across the floor.

He stops twitching, and I finally let myself step backward, once, twice, three times. I drop the knife onto a windowsill and press a shaking hand to my chest.

I know without a doubt before we've even checked him:

I've just killed a man.

25

"WHAT DO WE DO?" HÉLÈNE IS THE ONE TO WHISPER IT, THE first one to find her voice in the blood-soaked, rain-drenched room.

I can feel my heartbeat in my ravaged throat, feel the blood sticky on my hand and arm. I stare at her a moment, blinking, trying to swallow. I lean over, retching, but nothing comes up. And when I straighten again and speak, my voice is hoarse and strange in my throat. "We do exactly what he did to Pascal. We move the body. We blame the beast."

Something featherlight touches the back of my arm, and I jolt away. But when I turn it's only Charlotte, reaching out a hand to touch my arm.

Charlotte. Hélène. I just killed their father in front of them.

I want to come out of my skin, rip away from this world, follow my brother's soul into the sky, a vapor.

I killed a man. I killed *their father*. I'm not a savior; I'm a murderer. I wanted to help, and now I'm covered in blood. My hands, my arm, my very soul.

Charlotte reaches across the space between us again, touches my arm lightly. Her eyes are haunted, her small chest rising and falling so fast, like a bird's. "I'm sorry."

It takes me a moment to realize what she's said. "What?"

"I'm so sorry. He hurt you because of me. And I couldn't save you. Just like I couldn't save Pascal."

Hélène kneels and takes her sister's hand. I kneel, too, slowly, painfully, the initial rush of the fight fading into pain in a thousand places. The splinters in my face, the tenderness at my throat, a throbbing in my hip and another at my back where I must have hit when he threw me against the wall.

"It's not your fault," I rasp, reaching for Charlotte's other hand.

Instead, I find her in my arms, pressing her face into my shoulder, her arms around my torso. Hélène joins her, her touch softer, more aware of how hurt I must be. And then I feel Clara behind me, sliding to her knees and kissing the back of my head.

We sit there, a tangled ball of shocked and wounded feelings and limbs, blood and bruises and splinters. Safe again, for now. Soaking up strength from each other's embraces.

Something breaks inside me then, and I cry.

For the girl I was just an hour ago, who hadn't yet had to plunge a knife into a man's neck. For the girls we all could have been if life were a different thing. If we weren't born in Gévaudan. If we didn't have fathers who left us or blamed us, harmed us, attacked us.

I feel Clara guide me off my knees and to the hearth, and I realize I'm shivering. I am starting to fall to pieces—and I *can't*. Not yet.

Not when there's still a body growing cold in the corner, blood still seeping slowly across the floorboards. I take a deep breath and let it out shakily. "We have to get his body away from here."

"We can wait out the storm," Clara assures me.

I shake my head. "No, we need to use the storm as cover."

As if in agreement, thunder crashes above.

"Help me get him outside." My voice scrapes roughly from my throat.

Clara takes her own deep breath and pushes it loudly out, steeling herself. To my surprise, Hélène and Charlotte step forward, too.

"You don't have to help," Clara tells them. "He's you father. We understand if you can't help."

Hélène sets her jaw. "He was a monster, not a father."

Charlotte makes an animal noise of rage and kicks the corpse's leg. "He killed Pascal."

So it's decided, then. Clara doesn't try to wave them off again. Instead, she simply reopens the door to the wild wind and pelting rain, and the four of us lift and drag the body into the clearing.

Once we're all through the door, Clara closes it behind us, shutting the sheep—and the light—in. It's dark as an ink stain except when lightning flashes through the sky. We won't make it far, I realize. In my haste to remove him from the house, I hadn't really thought about what it meant to drag a corpse through the woods, about how far we'd need to take him in order to keep searchers away from the girls. Not to mention how the smell of blood might call to a predator—if not the beast, then the wolves, a bear. Yes, I was right that we need the storm as cover. But Clara was also right that we need to wait it out.

We make it to the edge of the clearing, and I yell through the downpour. "Drop him here. We can't take him farther tonight."

Legs, arms, head thunk heavy against the mud-slick ground. I wipe my hands on my soaked-through underthings, use the edges of them to try and scrub blood from where it sits sticky on my skin.

Another flash of lightning reveals the forest in front of me. Tall, dark trunks reach into the sky. Pine needles shudder violently against the wind. And—

Is that a person?

Someone stumbling along the game trail, hand thrown up against the whipping branches.

Clara sees it, too. I know because of the way she sucks in a breath and turns to face me, her eyes wide as another flash of lightning slashes through the night.

She asks the question we should have asked when Charlotte and Hélène's father barreled into the cottage.

"Joséphine . . . how did he know where to find us?"

26

I SHOULDN'T HAVE LEFT THE KNIFE INSIDE. SHOULDN'T HAVE let Hélène and Charlotte come out with us. Maybe shouldn't have come outside at all. Though being inside wouldn't save us from the shadow of a man growing ever closer through the night.

I can hear the sheep screaming inside the house, feel Clara's hand reaching for mine.

"Go," I whisper, turning to the girls. Because whoever this is coming toward us, they don't need to face him. They can still be saved. "Hide in the barn. Get in the eaves if you need to."

Hélène grabs Charlotte's hand, and they disappear into the thick darkness.

Clara doesn't join them, only squeezes my hand and faces the woods.

The figure draws nearer, and a crack of lightning illuminates him at last, just enough for recognition to sink in.

"Louis?" Clara breathes the name in disbelief.

He stops in front of us, doesn't answer. Only stares down at the wreckage of a man on the ground before us, eyes pointed skyward, unseeing, made visible by the traitor moon peeking out from between storm clouds.

"What have you done?" There is no joke at the corner of his mouth now. No wink at the ready. He presses a fist to his mouth, then looks up at us again. "You killed him?"

I can see fury at the edges of the horror, and I wish again that I'd brought the knife. Will I have to kill another person tonight? Because to save Clara, I'd do it. I didn't think the last one through, just reacted. But now I prepare myself, turn my heart to stone.

"Did you kill Pascal, too?" Louis's hands are fists as he steps over the corpse and toward us.

I never realized how tall he is, how broad shouldered. A wall of a boy, strong and lean. He wasn't on my list of dangerous boys, so I never noticed. God, how could I never have noticed?

"Louis—" Clara reaches a hand forward, gentle, placating. "We—"

He interrupts her. "Where are they? Are they in the house? Have you hurt them, too?"

"What?" I ask. "Who are you talking about?"

He steps toward us, and both Clara and I put up our hands defensively, but he only skirts around us and strides toward the cottage. "Charlotte!" he screams. "Hélène!"

Clara gasps before I put the pieces together. "He knows they're here. He thinks we . . . hurt them?"

Before he reaches the door, a small voice rings through the night, a shadow figure in front of the barn. "Louis!"

He freezes, turns slowly.

A flash of lightning reveals Charlotte, her dress drenched in water and some blood from carrying her father's body. Rain runs off her chin in a steady stream. And on her face—in that brief moment of light—isn't the fear that's skittering across my own skin.

It's hope.

Louis runs to her and throws his arms around her. Hélène appears behind her sister, and he wraps her awkwardly in the same embrace. Then, remembering himself, remembering that he believes we are the villains, he turns, putting himself between us and the girls. "You kidnapped them! Why?"

I almost laugh. Where do I even start? "We didn't."

Before I can say more, he's shouting again. "Don't lie to me. How can you lie when I found them here? When you murdered their father!"

"Enough!" Hélène yells, ducking under his arms and standing between us. Charlotte scrambles after her, the two girls the world's tiniest wall between us and Louis.

"They saved us! He"—she points at her father's corpse—"he killed Pascal, Louis. He *killed* him."

I wish I could see Louis's face clearly in the dark, wish I could see if there's more danger there or less. The silence stretches long in the wake of Hélène's words, and when Louis finally answers, his voice is smaller. "Why?"

"Why do you think?" Hélène says, and I startle. Because the

familiarity of the question means Louis knows them. *Really knows them.* Not just stumbled upon what he thought was a random crime. Hélène's question means she expects he has an answer for why their father would do such a thing.

I look at Clara but can't make out her expression in the dark.

Charlotte is the next to speak. "Come inside." She steps toward Louis and takes his hand. "Come inside, and we'll explain everything."

My stomach does a flip at the idea of inviting this person—only seconds ago a danger to us—inside the house. But he's no less dangerous out here than he is in there. And prolonged time outside is risky because of what else could be out here watching us even now.

Clara moves forward before I do, opens the door, and waves us all through. Louis follows Charlotte; Hélène and I follow behind them.

Inside, the wreckage of the fight is even more brutal than I remember. A chair lies broken in the corner. Blood smears thick where he went down, a trail of it dragging to the doorway where we took him out. Worse, the sheep haven't given it a wide berth, so now bloody hoofprints decorate nearly every inch of the space. It stinks of iron and salt and death.

I open the door again and retch miserably into the night.

Louis sits at the hearth with Charlotte's hand still in his. Clara, apparently having decided he's not a threat, lowers herself to the floor before them and reaches out a hand to pat his knee. I'm still not sure what kind of threat he is or isn't, so I stand a few steps back, my body tensing so hard that a headache has started to beat behind my eyes in time with every other part of my body that's pulsing with pain.

Hélène moves through the space, cleaning up. When Clara tells her not to, she says, "But this is what I know how to do," and we all let her be after that. Because I think we all know what she means. That when you feel helpless, powerless, overwhelmed by a flood of horrible things outside your control, sometimes the body just needs to do *something*. Even if that thing is cleaning up your own father's blood from the floor.

In the light of the room, Louis can't take his eyes off my throat, which I assume must be blooming with the red and purple of the violence done to it. I reach a finger up to touch it, and the skin is hot.

Louis turns to Charlotte, perhaps because he still doesn't trust us. "Tell me what happened."

And she does. She tells him about the fight Pascal and her father had, about following them and seeing him hit his son. Then, worse, seeing him go back for the knives. She closed her eyes after that, thank God. She doesn't give us details, but none of us need them. It's clear what happened, clear the lengths that man would have gone.

Louis goes from looking enormous and threatening to so small that I have a strange impulse to make him tea because it's what Mémé would do.

"How did you get here?" Louis asks, a fat tear tracing down his cheek.

Charlotte tells the rest of the story, and in her mouth, I am a miracle. I found her and I took her, no hesitation. I guess that is how it went, but it didn't feel brave or miraculous. I was only angry, furious even. It felt inevitable. I couldn't send her home with that man. And so Clara and I took her.

Louis's voice grows smaller still, if that's even possible. "Do you know what they were fighting about?"

There's something in the question. It's important to him in a way I can't quite put my finger on.

And it's not Charlotte who answers, but Clara. "If you're trying to turn his death into your fault, *it isn't.*"

His fault? I furrow my throbbing brow. Why would it be his fault that Pascal fought with his father?

Louis looks stripped bare by the words. Hélène scrubs harder behind me. And my fool lamb headbutts my leg. I lower myself painfully to scratch his head.

"You know?" Louis finally says, searching Clara's face, his voice more vulnerable than I've ever heard it.

She nods. "Pascal told me."

He told her what? I look between them, not understanding.

Louis drops his head, crying in earnest now, releasing some dam of emotion he's been holding back.

Clara's arms are around him then, Charlotte gripping his hand still.

"Pascal really cared about you," Clara says. "He said he was going to tell you he was in love with you. I hope he got the chance to?"

Understanding knocks its way past my headache. This is the reason Clara looks at Louis the way she does. She's not in love with him; *she knows that someone else is.* Knows they've been keeping it a secret. Some of the distance between Louis and me evaporates with the knowledge, with the ability to see him as he is.

Louis cries harder now, and I feel the tears coming for me again. The unfairness of it, the loss he's been living with in secret. I thought Pascal was just someone on his periphery, but he is so much more. Everything snaps into focus. Why he would put himself at risk to come after the girls here. Why he was crying the other day. Why the girls know him. Love him, even. The flashes of something other than humor on his normally unbothered face. The reason that no matter how many girls in the village throw themselves at his feet, he never did more than shamelessly flirt.

I hope he got the chance to. Clara's words hold so much weight. Hope shivers in my own chest alongside the grief and surprise.

"He did tell me. The night before . . . it happened. I wanted to run off together, but he said he had to bring the girls. He wouldn't leave them behind. He didn't say why. I didn't know. I promise, I didn't know." Louis looks pleadingly at Charlotte, then Hélène, who has paused her cleaning to watch, her eyes shiny with tears.

The tension in my body—the fear of Louis—vanishes entirely then, replaced with that familiar rage, the rage of the things happening to us that we cannot change. No, worse than that: the things that *are done to us.* Pascal's death didn't just happen. It was done. It was covered up. Louis is one of us—not hurter but hurt.

And even though the man outside is dead, the world that

made him isn't. The priest who wouldn't believe Hélène when she told him the truth about her father. The crowd that let that man pull her away. Even the outsiders who've come here to save us but are slowly robbing us of what little we have instead.

Louis goes on, his eyes on me this time. "Did he do that to you? Did their papa attack you?"

I nod, wondering again how bad it must look. Part of me wishes I had a mirror here; part of me is glad that I don't.

"It's my fault." He looks to the ceiling, agony etched across every line on his face. "I sent him here. I'm so sorry. Oh my God. He could have killed you all. I was such a fool."

"You sent him?" Clara asks, soft.

"I saw Joséphine going into the forest—and I can smell a plot from a mile away. You know who I spend my time with. I knew something was happening, and I followed her. If nothing else, I thought I'd witness some romantic rendezvous that I could tease someone about."

"Why were you out on your own in the storm?" I ask. "I thought you were in jail after your prank on the d'Ennevals."

He takes a deep breath, uses the heels of his hands to dry his eyes. "We made so much fuss that they got irritated enough to let us out. Besides, our jailer was old Monsieur Perrin, and he doesn't think those outsiders are gods like some of the rest of them. He was tired and didn't much care what we'd done. So he let us out. And I had the bright idea of putting some cow poo in their big old stupid cage trap to make it look like they caught something and it magically got away."

He laughs, but his heart isn't in it. "The others went home, and I went to the cage, and that's when I saw Joséphine. And I followed you here and looked through the window . . . and I saw Charlotte. I didn't know what to do, so I went to tell him. I told him where you were." He looks like he might vomit.

"Then why weren't you with him when he came?" Clara asks.

"He sent me home. He said he'd come out here when the storm stopped. But he thought maybe I was like the rest—seeing a ghost. And I thought, hell, maybe I was. Maybe I wanted so badly not to have failed Pascal that I made it up."

He takes a deep breath, goes on. "I started to go home. But then I saw him leaving the house. It kept bothering me, all the way home, that he said he was going when the storm let up but he went as soon as he thought I was gone. I didn't know why, but it felt *wrong*. Something felt very wrong about the whole situation. I got home, and then I realized I needed to come back here. I don't know, in case of the beast. In case something was wrong.

"But I should have made that decision faster. Maybe I could have kept that"—he motions to my throat—"from happening."

"Or maybe you would have misinterpreted the situation and helped him kill me," I say dryly.

"Joséphine!" Clara gasps.

"What? He said so himself." I hold an arm out in his direction. "He thought we'd done something. I'm not saying it to be cruel. I'm saying it so he'll stop blaming himself. We can't know what would have happened if we did things differently. All we can do is change something next time."

The thunder growls—in warning or agreement—and I stand. My intention is to help Hélène, who is throwing all her emotion into scrubbing blood from floorboards. It'll never come out; the wood is too old. It sucks the blood up like a thirsty beast.

Instead of stepping toward Hélène as I intend, though, I go cross-eyed, the room waving around me like the world has been upended. I throw out my hands and catch myself as I fall heavily onto my knees.

"Joséphine, mon Dieu!" Clara and Louis exclaim in unison, both rushing to lift me from the floor and deposit me at the edge of the hearth.

"Stay put," Clara orders. This is something she knows how to deal with, and even through my dizziness, I can see the way her body straightens with purpose. "Charlotte, we need to build up the fire. Hélène, can you bring me the pot? Louis—please fill it with rainwater."

Around me, everyone springs into action, and before I know it, tea is being coaxed down my ragged throat and Clara has a poultice of leaves pressed gently against my neck. I'm propped up beside the dancing fire under wool blankets. And Clara is teasing splinters from my face with her fingernails. I can't decide if the throbbing in my throat or the burn of the splinter removal hurts worse, but I try not to flinch.

"We need a story," Clara says as she works, glancing at me and then over my head at Louis, now perched on the other side of the hearth with Charlotte—exhausted—asleep in his arms and Hélène, hands still red from all the scrubbing, leaning half-asleep on his shoulder.

"A story?" Louis echoes, his voice soft.

"We all need to explain where we were during the storm. I assume you have a soldier in your house, too? Ours will ask."

Louis makes a thoughtful noise, smiles wryly. "Mine knows asking my whereabouts won't get him a straight answer. I've got the whole village trained not to expect much from me."

I almost laugh. Who knew our prankster was so self-aware?

"We'll need to explain Jo's injuries, too." Clara peels another splinter from my cheek, and my eyes sting with tears.

"The good news is that nobody is coming out in this weather to look for us. So as long as one of us is back as soon as the storm breaks, Walter won't raise the alarm. At least I think not," I whisper-rasp.

"That's all I'm going to be able to get with my nails," Clara apologizes, releasing my cheek from its ongoing torture. "I think you're right. If Louis's soldier won't care and ours won't do anything until the storm breaks, we have until then to figure out what to say about your injuries, how to move the body away from here, and what we tell Walter about where we were all night."

The old spark sneaks back into Louis's face for the first time since he got here. He winks. "We could always scandalize everyone by telling them you two were with me all night."

I can feel my eyes roll extravagantly, but Clara laughs.

"And I came out of it looking like this?" I raise a painful eyebrow. "What a lover you must be."

A surprised laugh escapes Louis, and a less surprised one comes from Clara. Hélène's fully asleep now and chooses that moment to start snoring, which makes the joke even funnier.

"I mean, you are in your stay." Louis shrugs slightly with the shoulder that isn't supporting Hélène.

I ignore the comment, realize that it never even occurred

to me with everything that was going on to care that Louis was seeing me in undergarments. "I mean, maybe you are a good alibi for Clara, if she can stand the scandal." I pause, wondering if I actually want to admit my own folly but eventually deciding I don't care anymore. "I thought you two had something going on. Maybe others picked up on some warmth between you."

Clara looks scandalized, but Louis just grins from ear to ear. "Clara, my love, our affair is revealed at last!"

Clara narrows her eyes. "You are not my type in the same way that I am not yours."

I pause on that revelation, and Louis also seems speechless. Does Clara mean what I think she means?

Clara looks between us with a smile creasing her eyes. "Joséphine and I are in this together, *forever*. She's the one I'd run away with and the only one I'd stay for. That's all I need."

Forever.

And ever.

Amen.

Tears rise to my eyes. We've talked like that for years. Promising no matter what, it would be us against the world. But I suppose I never knew that she meant it as much as I did, that it was truth etched in the deepest part of her the way it's in the deepest part of me, too.

In the way that Louis and Pascal belonged to each other, do Clara and I belong to each other, too? It would have never occurred to me to call it being in love, but perhaps that's only because the way people talk about that kind of love never feels familiar to me. It is all frantic, panicked, urgent, stomach-churning stuff. And my love for Clara isn't butterflies or wind-storms. It's the ground I find my feet on. It's the air I breathe. As essential and predictable and reliable as all that.

I weave my fingers through hers, suddenly warm all over. "I love you, too."

She leans across the space between us to kiss me on the cheek but thinks better of it at the last moment and aims for my hairline instead, her lips gentle against that small patch of unharmed skin.

"Bleaa." The fool lamb decides he's feeling left out and squeezes between Clara and me to settle on my lap.

"Jealous, eh?" I chuck him under the chin with a finger.

"We still need a story." Clara directs us back to the problem at hand. "Where could we say we were?"

"We could say we got caught in the storm and sheltered in a cave," I offer.

"Or took shelter in old Madeline's barn," Louis suggests. "She's on the other edge of the village, and her barn's rather large. Unless she checked on the sheep during the storm, which seems unlikely with all this"—he motions to the rain still pelt-ing the window coverings—"it's plausible you could have been there."

"How do you know about Madeline's barn?" I side-eye Louis. He grins but doesn't answer.

"Feels risky," I say. But then again, everything feels risky.

"I think the cave thing leaves the least room for contradic-tion," Clara muses. "But there's still the question of your injuries."

Hélène is awake now and has been following the past few

threads of conversation. Her suggestion is a sharp-edged thing in a soft tone. "If someone hurt you, you probably wouldn't tell people. The most realistic thing to do is make up stupid stories."

We all pause, taking in her words.

Is that what they were doing before . . . making up stupid stories to cover up what their father was? For the first time since we came back inside, my thoughts leave the cottage and stumble back across the clearing. My mind flashes me scenes from the past few hours. The pressure in my head when his hand was on my throat. The feeling of wood against my cheek. His hand off my throat and my hand going for his. The blood. The light leaving his eyes. I picture him out there, a tumble of cold limbs growing colder, blood flooding away.

Everyone is quiet as Hélène goes on, her eyes not quite meeting ours as she plays with the edge of her now-drying dress. "Hide the bruises that you can. When people ask, say you fell down or something. It doesn't even matter if it is a good lie. Nobody here cares."

Those last words stab at me.

"We cared," I remind her, reaching my hand out to touch hers. Clara and Louis have the same idea, and all our hands meet for a moment on Hélène's. In this together. All connected before we even knew it.

27

I TRY TO SLEEP, MY GOOD CHEEK PROPPED ON CLARA'S LAP, but I only float in and out of nightmares. I killed a man. It isn't until everything is quiet and done that the realization sinks deep into my marrow. It's one of those moments in life that has a distinct *before* and *after.*

Before, I was afraid of what he'd do to me. But is after better? After, my mind just replays what I did to him. Over and over and over again. The knife goes in. The life goes out.

I tense, and Clara runs a hand through my hair. I half sleep, and the nightmare of the past hours tangles up with my usual nightmare. Fingertips throbbing with cold as I carve my way outside this house, but instead of dragging my limp body to Clara's, I stumble over the corpse of the man I killed. I scream without making a noise.

When I jolt out of another half nightmare, the roar of rain

has become a soft patter on the window coverings, and sunrise must be here because through the rain there are shafts of pinkish light streaming in.

I lift myself, aching, to a sitting position, waking Clara by accident as I breathe harder with the painful effort. Beside us, Louis has slid down to the floor, and both Hélène and Charlotte are fast asleep, curled up on either side of him. The fire has burned down to just lukewarm coals behind us all. The sheep snuggle in a cluster near the door. Only Clara and I are awake, and seeing her pushes the nightmare, the pain, to the back of my mind. I killed a man, yes. But Clara is here and safe—we all are. Or as safe as we can be with the beast stalking the woods. That's what matters about last night.

I would kill that man again to save her. Even if it means nightmares every night for the rest of my life. I hold to that truth like an anchor.

"I didn't know you felt that way." I squeeze the words from a throat that somehow hurts even more than when I started to drift in and out of sleep.

"What?" She blinks, confused.

I face her and take her hands in mine. "What you said before. About me and you being like Louis and Pascal."

Her eyebrows quirk in surprise. "I thought you knew. I thought that's what we both meant. Forever and ever, amen."

I exhale a tiny laugh. "It was what I meant. I feel the same. But I guess we just never said it like this before. This . . . clearly. I feel . . ." I run my thumbs along the soft skin of the top of her hands, holding her gaze. "I feel relieved. Happy. I think I was carrying this tiny doubt, and I didn't even know it. But now it's one thing I don't have to carry anymore."

Clara smiles, flitting her gaze to our hands, and I can't help but think how pretty her eyelashes are, dark and curled over deep-brown eyes. When her eyes meet mine again, they have tears in them. She reaches up to brush a fingertip featherlight at the angry skin of my throat. "When he hurt you, I felt it in my own body."

My own tears rise up to match hers, and I reach across the space to press hers away with my thumbs.

"I was afraid I'd lose you," she whispers.

I close my eyes slowly, then open them again. "I know that feeling."

She tilts her head. "I haven't been attacked like that."

"No, but I was afraid you might leave. Go south without me." It's the first time I've told her that secret fear, and my heart seizes with the admission. Like even though she just said we were always in this together, saying the words out loud might change her mind. I know it's foolish. And yet I cannot help the way my lungs freeze, waiting for her next words.

Her eyebrows rise again, and she puts both hands behind my neck, pulling until our foreheads rest gently against each other. "I wouldn't *ever* leave you behind."

My breath releases in a soft, relieved laugh. "Even when I am a hotheaded fool running toward the sound of gunshots instead of away?"

"*Especially* then. Especially when you need me most."

Tears drip off both our chins and onto our yet-again en-twined fingers.

Long, quiet moments later, I realize the rain has gone from soft patter to almost nothing. I pull gently back from Clara, though it's the last thing I want to do. "It's letting up. We need to move the body and get home before anyone gets the idea to come out and look for us."

Clara nods, raises herself from the floor, and rouses Louis as I pull my now-dry dress over my underclothes.

"We need your help to move the body," she whispers to him. "We need to take it somewhere they can find it and believe it was the beast—somewhere far from here."

He pauses a moment, like he's remembering where he is and what's happened, then gently eases his arms out from under the girls and pushes to his feet.

Outside, the clearing is a collection of intersecting mud puddles with water still flowing fast downhill in impromptu streams. If this far up the hill is such a torrent, parts of the village might be flooded. My stomach turns at the thought. I hope Mémé is all right and that any flooding hasn't reached that far.

I force myself to turn toward the edge of the clearing where we left the body, my chest tight at the thought of seeing it again, even tighter at the thought that we have to move it somewhere. Touch it again. Feel the weight of him. Get it away from us and the girls.

I shudder, force myself to look. I thought it was far to the right of the house, but I don't see anything there. Just mud puddles and dripping branches. I pause, scan the edge of the clearing. It was late, and it was horrible, and maybe I am mis-remembering where we left him.

I scan the trees again, now with my heart inching toward my throat, the hair on the back of my neck rising. It takes a moment for my mind to catch up with what my primal instincts already know. Like the butterflies in blood, the scratches on the barn.

I haven't misremembered anything.

The body is gone.

28

LOUIS IS THE FIRST TO MOVE TOWARD THE FOREST, SCAN-
ning for any sign of the body we left there. As if it got up and
walked a few feet into the trees.

I follow, with Clara's hand in mine.

Before we get there, a strangled sound escapes Louis. Something primal, surprise and terror.

"Don't look," he says, turning toward us and swallowing
hard. "Don't look."

But it's too late. I've already seen.

A shoe. But not just a shoe. A shoe with a foot and a bit of
leg. A shoe *chewed off a corpse.* Part of the man I killed, but not
his whole. I separated soul from body, but something else has
partitioned him further.

The rest of the body has disappeared. Consumed or
dragged away.

Mon Dieu, it could have been us. We were out in this clearing in the rainstorm, served up on a platter. Not even our pikes with us. It could have taken one of us so easily. Was it the blood that invited it to our doorstep—or was it here before I tore out the man's throat, a beast in my own right?

Was it fear that called to it? Sweat and tears and terror scented in the night?

"Get inside," Clara whispers, pulling my hand, her gaze sweeping the trees. "We shouldn't stand here."

"You think it's still hungry?" I try for a joke, but it smashes up against our horror and falls flat.

Clara tugs me back to the house, and we slip inside and close the door again.

"It was right here." Louis presses his knuckles to his lips.

Ah, how close we were to death without knowing it.

Clara and I force ourselves home through the drizzle and the fear, weaving around deep puddles, fighting our way through slimy mud and the tree branches that nudge us backward. Even the sheep seem to know how close the evil thing came, all clustering together as we make our way down the slick trail toward the house, with fewer complaints than usual. The fool lamb keeps close to my heels. No detours into bramblebushes today.

Before we left, Louis proposed the next part of our plan. He'd tell the town that Hélène's grief-stricken papa had gone into the woods to look for the beast and never come back. The third child his last straw. Louis will point them in the wrong direction. Send the search party up into the hills on the other side of the valley. It's a good plan—the only possible plan—but the more lies pile up, the tighter the fear bunches in my chest. We're one wrong move away from everything falling apart. Before we only had to keep suspicion off one disappearance, then two. Now it's unexpectedly three, and when we take Eugénie, four.

So many secrets to keep. So many suspicions to redirect.

"Do you think we can keep getting away with this?" I croak the words into the tense silence as Clara and I pick our way around a puddle.

Clara shivers. "I'm more worried about the beast itself now. It's been at the house too many times."

An edge of guilt intrudes on my fears. The beast was always a threat to us, but it was that first decision to fake Charlotte's death that keeps us trespassing on territory we know the creature has claimed.

"I'm so sorry." The words hurt my throat and my heart.

Clara looks startled. "For what?"

"Always dragging you into danger."

"You didn't drag me anywhere. We're doing this together."

"I know, and I love you for it. But if I hadn't announced that we were faking Charlotte's death after we found her, you wouldn't be in this position—out alone with the sheep half the time, at my house when we know it's not safe, watching a man die. . . ." My voice goes tight on the last words.

She reaches over to tug on a lock of hair that's come free from my head covering, the gesture grounding, fond. "I wanted to help Charlotte, too. Oui, next time I wouldn't mind being in-volved more in the decision-making. What else could we have done, though? We both did what we had to for her. We still are. And maybe"—her eyes go flinty—"what happened today means God or magic or the beast is on our side."

I stop and tilt my head, confused.

"That man killed his child and went back for the knives." Her voice is sharp. "And then you killed him, and some other thing went back for its own knives. Beast or curse or hand of God."

I almost laugh. It's shocking for Clara to be so vindictive. So satisfied with brutality.

Then again, she hates Belle and Lafont for hurting me. How much more must she hate this man who tried to kill me?

I shake my head and start to walk again. "You really surprise me sometimes."

"People always do." She says it with fondness.

We emerge from the forest trail, and the house finally comes into view. The area around the houses is swampy and puddle-dotted, but not flooded—and we breathe simultaneous sighs of relief. A few houses down from ours, a too-near tree must have come down during the storm and now leans against the roof. But the damage looks minimal. The storm must have felt scarier on the hill than here in the village. I hope Mémé wasn't too wor-ried about us.

Clara pushes through the door first, calling Mémé's name, and I watch the sheep file through before slipping off my mud-caked boots and sliding through the door.

Inside, I pause because everything is different. The usually tidy room is patterned with muddy boot prints, and every dish we own is piled on the little table, dirty. Mémé stands near the hearth, her face flashing irritation, then concern. And ranged around the room in various relaxed, sprawling positions are soldiers. Not just Walter. A half dozen of them. We hardly all fit in the room.

"What's going on?" Clara's tone is guarded, uncertain.

"These young men weathered the storm with me," Mémé answers, forcing a smile.

"What happened to your face?" Walter stares, brazen.

"Tree branch in the storm," I mumble, forcing my own smile.

"Looks like you fought off death himself," another soldier adds in a heavy accent of some kind.

"Or she likes it rough," a third chimes in, and they all titter as if that's the funniest joke anyone's ever told.

"Is the storm letting up, then?" Walter asks, moving past me to look out the open window. "We'll need to present ourselves."

The others scramble upward at that, and before Clara or I have time to ask why they were all here in the first place, they've filed out. I almost laugh. They didn't even ask where we'd been. Just like Hélène said, they didn't care at all that my branch story made no sense. A girl with a purple-blue throat and a face full of splinters didn't merit more than a casual question.

"Disgusting, disrespectful little—" Mémé shakes a fist almost comically at the now-closed door. "Look at this place."

"Why were they here?"

"Came with Walter for dinner and then stayed here because *oh là là,* that storm was something to behold." Mémé waves a dismissive hand, then moves across the room to me. "Child, what on God's earth happened to your face? Are you all right?"

Tears spring to my eyes then, my mind flashing me an image I don't even remember from the night before. It's a look of pure rage on his face, the look that meant I was about to die.

I shake my head, pause. I hadn't thought about lying to Mémé, but I realize now that I have to. With her memory problems, there's no guarantee she can keep our secret, no matter how much she wants to, no matter how much she loves us.

"It really was a branch, Mémé. Well, more like the whole forest churning up around me. I'm all right. It looks worse than it is."

Mémé presses her lips together, and I'm not sure she believes me. But even if she doesn't, she doesn't pressure me. I hope she knows I'd tell her if I could.

Clara takes in a sharp breath from the kitchen. "Mémé, when you said those boys came for dinner . . ."

I turn toward her and examine the empty jar she's holding up. It used to be full of olives. On the table in front of her, there are more jars. The small ones we use for summer preserves to keep through winter. The large ones we use for olives. Even the oil jar.

Empty.

My stomach plunges into my feet. Did they—

"They ate us out of house and home." Mémé shakes her head beside me. "There's barely anything left."

Clara makes a choked noise that mirrors exactly how I feel. Summer is turning toward autumn. The storm is the first sign that the bounty of summer has slammed closed like a door. And that means on top of everything else—of beasts and ice and murderous men—we are in danger of starving to death.

The despair of it curdles to rage. How are there so many ways to hurt? Fangs slicing through the air to rip out a throat. Fists balled. Frost and fear and the kind of hunger that leaves you unable to walk, dragging yourself through snowdrifts, certain each inch will be the last one you make.

Men fancy themselves our protectors, but what have they protected us from? Not from the way I watched my brother breathe a last breath, the hours I clawed my way through ice and snow. Not the hunger that scrapes me raw now, leaves parts of me aching that should never ache, the hunger I thought I would stave off just a little by having something when I got home. And certainly not from themselves. Their fists and grabby fingers and the looks they give like they're wolves and we're sheep. They're hungry, and we're dinner.

My throat screams in pain; my heart screams in fury.

I hate them.

I've never put it into words like that before. There were always just the men I didn't have to worry about and could reasonably ignore and the men that I did worry about, whose names I knew. But now they are all one. The men who hurt us and the men who do nothing about it. And all of them thinking they're protecting us, saving us.

It didn't even occur to those soldiers that they were doing us more harm than good.

And it never will occur to them. By winter, they will leave

and go elsewhere and fill their bellies on someone else's stock-piles. Locusts leaving us behind with nothing.

It's not just Charlotte and Hélène and Eugénie who are in danger here. It's us. It's always been us. It's not just them who need to climb on the back of a merchant cart and slip away to the south.

I've been so afraid that Clara would leave that I didn't face the truth that we both need to. We all need to.

Even if the whole world is full of men like ours, even if there are beasts lurking in other forests, hunger knocking on other places' doors—the devil we know *is* going to kill us if we stay here. One way or another. Our only choice is the devil we don't.

I have to get *all of us* out of here.

29

CLARA INSISTS ON PUTTING A POULTICE ON MY NECK AND wrapping it in bandages before I leave for Belle's house and my afternoon duties.

"You're making it more conspicuous," I object, and she laughs one of those high, surprised, despairing laughs that says more than any words could.

"Joséphine, literally nothing could look more conspicuous than your current state."

I hold a finger up to my neck. "It looks that bad?"

She tilts her head and stares up at me through her eyelashes. "Madame, look." She retrieves our old looking glass and holds it up.

It's the first time I've seen it, and it's so *shocking* that all feeling deserts me completely. Bright, shiny purple. Midnight blue. Red like a burn. Even tiny spots of sickly yellow. My neck is a constellation of violence. And my cheek—mon Dieu. It looks like someone ran a dozen little knives along the side of it. The dark shadows of deep splinters are nearly impossible to tell apart from the dark blood of new wounds.

I must have had too much horror today, because all I feel is numbness. Like I'm looking at my own face from a mile away. A year away. A time and place when all of this has healed over.

Clara takes the glass gently from my hands and kisses my forehead. "I'm putting on the poultice now. And a scarf for cover."

I nod, numb, and let her tend to my wounds, my body almost no longer mine. Perhaps that's the end result of everything these men are working toward: making our bodies no longer our own.

With my neck bandaged, Mémé working muddy boot prints out of the floor, and Clara readying the sheep for grazing, I leave. And the first thing I feel in an hour is *regret*. I don't want to leave them. Don't want Mémé to have to stay here alone, on hands and knees, erasing what she can of the carelessness of those soldiers. Don't want to leave Clara to graze the sheep alone—not with how much more present, how much more real, the beast feels now that it disappeared a body just yards away from us last night. I try to tell myself the beast will be satiated. It took a whole man, after all. But still the dread curdles in my stomach. Clara alone in the fields, vulnerable. It's almost too much to bear, and if the soldiers hadn't eaten all our stores, maybe it'd be enough to make me quit the job with Belle.

But Clara starving isn't a better thought than her alone in the fields. So I walk on. Toward the money that might be the only thing standing between us and the weak, disorienting, slow march toward starvation.

I drag my feet heavily through rain-slick cobbled lanes, press my palm to cold, wet stone walls just to keep from feeling like I'll float away. And when I reach the square, I'm surprised to find a muleteer has set up shop, despite the ongoing rain, and a handful of neighbors mill around, inspecting his wares. They all stare a little too long at my face, but when someone gets up the courage to ask, "Dear, what happened to your cheek?" I can somehow tell she doesn't want an answer.

They all accept my "Oh, I fell out of a tree" without any follow-up questions.

Instead, they lower their voices, duck their heads together. "Did you hear that the father is gone now, too?"

"The beast took the whole family."

"Cursed. They must have been cursed. The rumors were true!"

My heart clenches. It's good—them blaming the beast again. And yet . . . there's something sinister in the building panic, the furtive glances, the word *curse.* The same word that started wedging itself into conversations before the whole town turned on our priest.

I try to block them out, and as I approach the muleteer and see his spread, it becomes infinitely easier to do so. My stomach howls with longing at the sight of the wares now laid out: beans, barley, bacon, cheeses. There are trinkets, too, but I only have eyes—or, well, nose—for the food. I have to turn away and compose myself, the sight of the food unstitches me so. A symbol of what we've lost. What I need. The need so great that it pushes out even the gossip, the fear, the sharp-edged memory of plunging my knife into a man's neck.

My hand flies to the purse tied at my waist. The money I've been saving to get Charlotte and Hélène away—

It's no good saving if we all starve in the meantime.

I have no idea if the decision is a good or bad one, but I palm some of my coins and step into the fray, filling my satchel with the things that will soothe our bellies. The things I swear on my life that I will hide from Walter—from the soldiers—at all costs. I can't afford much, but it's enough to dull the edges of this one fear, to buy us time.

As the muleteer weighs my beans and I count out the correct coins, a woman on the edge of the circle gasps. "Is that what I think it is, monsieur?"

I follow her line of sight to the pile of trinkets I'd ignored just a moment ago.

"Oui, madame! Any interest in a likeness? Guaranteed accurate!"

Likeness? I peer at the little figures, each hand carved, intricate. The wood is a swirled and shining thing with a reddish tint. Cherry, maybe, though I'm no wood expert. Each figure stares up at us—long tailed, mohawked, fire-eyed. Oh la vache, they're supposed to be the beast.

"Mon Dieu, of course I don't want one. Bad luck, that is."

A murmur of agreement passes through the cluster of women around me.

"Why would you make these?" I rasp.

"Give the people what they want!" He seems unconcerned at our collective disgust. "This is the first village that hasn't wanted one for their hearths! How better to ward off the evil thing than with a talisman, a likeness?" He holds one up to the group as if he's made a great point.

And I suppose for some he has, because now two women add the little likeness to their selection of beans and barley. Hedging their bets, I suppose.

I pay for my goods and start to turn when he adds, "The southerners go wild for these!" and the words root me in place.

The southerners.

This muleteer has been south. Is he going back that way?

I turn and try to sound casual. "Are you coming from the south, then?"

"Yes, madame! Going up to Saint-Albain, and then I'll pass back through on my way down south again. If anyone needs goods from Saint-Albain, now's the moment to put in your order."

Hope flutters in my chest. I wonder if this man would take us south. Maybe we wouldn't even have to pay him if we helped with the mules, the goods.

"When will you pass back through?" I ask, trying to sound nonchalant.

"'Bout a week, I expect."

I nod, turn again.

"No orders, then?" he calls after me. "Healing tonics for the face? I heard there's a miracle cure for scarring!"

I don't turn, but I can feel everyone's eyes on me now, tracing the wreckage of my neck that peeks around the poultice.

I try to ignore them. Focus on the more important thing I just learned. One week. Can I have the girls ready to leave in one week? How much money can I save by then? I have more questions, but I've drawn enough attention to myself for one day. I force myself to cross the square to Eugénie's door and knock.

30

"OH LA VACHE, WHAT HAPPENED TO YOUR FACE?" IT'S THE
first time I've heard Belle swear, and I almost laugh at the ab-
surdity of it.

"None of your business," I say before I can think better of it.

"Speak like a lady!" Jean caws, but whether he means me or
Belle is anyone's guess.

Today my primary task is cleaning Belle's room, but, as usual,
she stays nearby, watching as I unmake the bed and remake it
with fresh linens, dust the moldings, throw the window open to
air out the room.

"You know you don't have to be here for this," I tell her, taking a dustcloth to the vanity mirror and cringing at the sight of
my bruises peeking above the bandages on my neck, the angry,
swollen red of half my face.

"How do you take your tea?" Jean whistles, high pitched.

"I need to—I have to—" Belle pauses, uncharacteristically not with an answer ready at a moment's notice, and I watch her in the mirror. She blinks a few times, then puts on an imperious look. "I have to watch you. Make sure you do it correctly."

"Hmmph."

Before I can answer with more than a noncommittal noise, Eugénie slips into the room, leaning slyly against the doorframe. "Mes chéries, I have arrived. I'm sorry that I've left you to your boredom without me for so unbearably long."

I smile despite the fact that it hurts my face. "Our savior."

She raises an eyebrow and takes in my face, something knowing flickering across her features, but she doesn't ask. It doesn't feel like an oversight, the way it has with some neighbors, but rather a small act of respect. Of *knowing*. Knowing that something bad happened and that I might not want to share the details with every person who happens by.

She moves deeper into the room and leans against the newly made bed. "Belle, your father wants to see you in the parlor."

"Mon Dieu!" Jean screams.

"Jean, don't be rude," Belle chides. "You know Papa doesn't appreciate that language."

"Mon Dieu! Mon Dieu! Mon Dieu!"

"You can leave him here if you want. I'll watch the little bastard." Eugénie winks.

"Little bastard!" Jean agrees, and I choke on a laugh.

"Oi, you've taught him another swear." Belle presses a hand to her face as if put upon as Eugénie shrugs.

Belle coaxes Jean off her shoulder and onto Eugénie's.

Somehow, he looks more regal on the shoulder of the taller, curvier, spark-eyed Eugénie, a flash of gorgeous red feathers setting off her deep-chestnut hair.

Belle disappears from the room and takes some of my tension with her. Without thinking about it, I let out a long, loud breath.

"I know what you mean." Eugénie winks again. "That girl is the least relaxed person I've ever met. You should try living with her."

I laugh. "I did." I pause. "Ran away."

"LITTLE BASTARD." Jean tries out his new favorite phrase again at a much louder volume.

Eugénie crooks an eyebrow. "Cheeky bird," she says to Jean, then to me, "I'm about two steps behind you."

"Shall I help you make a rope out of bedsheets? I'm an expert."

"Please." Her tone is exaggerated, but something has shifted in it. She pauses, glances with practiced nonchalance at the door before she speaks again. "Your face. Did that happen like I think it did?"

There's something comforting about the boldness of the question, the way it isn't framed to give me an out, space for excuses. I realize then that the way other people ask it makes me feel like they are hoping, hand on the Bible, prayers to the sky, that I say something benign. The question is obligation or curiosity. It feels like they desperately want me to say everything is fine. Both because they need everything to be fine *and* because it absolves them. If I don't ask for help, they don't have to render it.

It's a flash of understanding—the reason the questions have been scratching uncomfortably at my heart. Not because I'm about to be found out, but because the questions themselves come from the same place that my father's leaving did. A desire not to deal with me. It's like all day people have been preabandoning me. By not asking or by asking in a way that is only obligation, not care.

Another flash burns through me. This time: shame. I saw Eugénie's bruises before, and *I never asked.* I was just as uncertain as the neighbors, just as ready to accept that it was nothing.

But Eugénie's question isn't asking for absolution, for a way out of discomfort, for permission to abandon me, or for me to hate myself for never asking her. She's asking for truth.

Surprisingly, I give it. At least in part. "It's exactly what you think it is."

She presses her lips together. "I would murder them all if I could."

Well, that took a turn. I blink at her. "Them—?"

"Any man who hits a woman. I tried, actually. Tried to kill my brother. A year ago, when he broke my arm. Broke my arm and told me if I didn't change, he'd do to me what he did to the old priest."

Dread tightens around my rib cage. "I thought you—" I feel an absolute fool then. I thought she broke her arm falling from the barn roof. That was what people said; it's what I believed.

She smiles a kind of feral smile at the dawning realization on my face. "Everyone believes the lies until they've seen the monster face to face."

"Does he still hurt you?" I don't know why I ask. Why would her brother have stopped? There are no consequences. And didn't I know? She'd hinted at it. I knew. But I suppose I hadn't put all the pieces together. Hadn't known the broken arm was from a man in her house as well as the swollen lip.

She laughs, a brittle, chaotic noise. "Usually only in places that don't show." She shakes her head then. "The irony is how much he hates me flirting with outsiders—not realizing that they are my ticket away from *him*. The more I flirt, the more he hurts me. But the more he hurts me, the more I flirt. By the autumn, I imagine I'll be gone one way or the other—either I'll convince one of these boys to run away with me or my brother will finally do something I can't recover from."

She's so matter of fact. I blink at her a long time before answering. "What if there was another way out?"

"Mon Dieu!" Jean caws.

She tilts her head.

"What if I told you we're leaving, and you could, too?"

She shrugs. "My brother would come after me. My father wouldn't stand for the shame of a runaway. He still thinks he's important, even though we lost our fortune when I was a child. The only way he won't come after me is if I have a man with me."

"There's another way."

Her eyes shine with curiosity.

I lay my proverbial cards on the table. "He wouldn't come after you if he thought you were dead."

31

YES. THE BREATHLESS HOPE OF THE BREATHLESS YES IS ALL I GET before one of Lafont's servants is in the doorway, requesting our presence downstairs.

Eugénie grabs my hand and squeezes, firm and sure and wildly alive. I squeeze back and then follow the retreating servant into the hall, down the stairs, and into the sitting room—where I stop in my tracks.

To my surprise, the priest is here. His eyes narrow when he sees me, but he doesn't deign to say anything to either of us. Across from him on the settees are Lafont, Belle, Eugénie's father—a painfully thin white man with cavernous cheeks and a kind of desperate self-importance—and her brother. I notice, with an awed respect, that Eugénie holds her brother's gaze, defiant, as she enters the room. This is a girl who has decided that no matter what else he takes from her, he won't take her fire.

Eugénie's father motions for her to sit beside him. And Belle—who looks strangely calm even though the priest is across from her—motions to me, whispering, "Keep our drinks refreshed, please."

My cheeks flush. I'm so tired of being her servant. And all the drinks *are* full, so really she's just using me as some sort of status indicator. *Look at me, I have servants!*

Jean flutters to her shoulder and murmurs, "How do you take your tea?" Apparently even the bird realizes now is not the time for a screamy *mon Dieu* or *little bastard.*

I stand by, watching the drinks as instructed, my hands clasped in front of my skirt, as the priest continues something he must have been saying before. "I have more bad news, I'm afraid. Before I left to come here, one of the boys came with a report. The beast has attacked again. They found a foot—just a foot. The head of household of that same cursed family. Three children gone, and now him."

The foot. My heart crashes into the words. *They found the foot?* I'd heard the ladies mention his disappearance, assumed that Louis's rumor had made its rounds. But no—they found the foot. And it was so close to my house. Why didn't we move it? Mon Dieu, *why didn't we move it?*

If they found the foot, have they also found the girls?

Eugénie's brother joins the conversation. "How did they identify it? How do we know it was him?"

"The boot still on . . . and he's missing. The boys who found it went to check on him."

Every part of me is tense as I wait for more. How much do they know? How close have they come?

"Where did they find it?" Thank you, Lafont, for asking the question I desperately need an answer to.

"At his neighbors' back door."

Confusion slips into my heart, and the terror makes room for it. What does it mean? How did the foot get from my house to his? Did the beast come back and take it somehow? Why? I'm not sure if my next thought is better or worse: Did the girls decide to take it away? Complete the frame job we've done on the beast? Remove what was left of the evidence of my own beastly nature? It wasn't the plan. Why would they change the plan?

My mind can't settle on an answer, but one thing is clear: these men still seem to be in the dark about what's really happening in Mende. I'm glad, of course. But I also feel the skittering terror of my unanswered questions, like a nest of spiders hatched in my gut. The lingering horror of thinking we'd been found out. Are we in more danger or less because of the foot? How close did we come to the edge of our safety yet again?

I try to press my heart into submission, back to its usual rhythm. *They were not near the house. They did not find us out. The foot's location change has only helped us, not hurt us.* Yet the tightness in my gut lingers.

The priest goes on, his eyes on Lafont. "That's not the only thing. The flooding, Monsieur Lafont—it's a sign from God. Not to be taken lightly. If God cannot get our attention with the beast, He will do it with a storm."

Lafont leans over his knees, listening. "And what does the sign mean? What does it all mean?"

"Yes, yes, what does it mean?" Eugénie's father echoes.

Eugénie's brother cracks his knuckles, and I watch her shoulders rise slightly with the tension of the sound.

"It means"—the priest pauses for dramatic effect, enjoying the hefty silence, all eyes on him—"that there is a witch among us."

Belle gasps a little, and the rest of the room shifts uncomfortably. I press my fingernails into my palms, feeling the knife's edge of danger here.

When no one speaks, the priest goes on. "I've suspected it for some time. The supposed ghost sightings of the little girl around the village. The evil thing stalking our forests. The way it has targeted one particular family—first the children and now the head of household. It's not only the sin in our hearts that has brought these blights upon us. It is the sin of *a specific heart.*" His eyes bore into me, and I watch the scar on his hand as he waves it direly in front of him.

Is this how he will finally come for me, then? Revisit his vengeance on me for having the audacity to bite him? For having the audacity again to drive him away from whatever his intentions were with Belle? I know in my gut, in my very bones, that all he needs to do is say my name and that will be my ending. Burned or quartered. *Gone* before I could become gone.

I've known it all along, but now the threat's been spoken. It hovers between us in the air.

Witchcraft may have been decriminalized in France a few generations ago, but that doesn't mean it can't be used against someone. Our old priest is proof of that. What happened to him was almost worse than court-ordered burning. It was hours and hours of torture first and then—I imagine—a lingering death.

If the town believes that witchcraft is responsible for the beast, they will take the witch apart piece by piece, bone by bone.

I watch Eugénie's brother clench his fists, picture them smashing into my face over and over. Frankly, a skull sucked dry by the beast is a better way to go.

The priest's dire words hang in the air, interrupted then by two servants bustling into the room with food. Mon Dieu, *the smell*. Despite the danger hanging over us all, the rich, spicy tang in the air steals all my focus, fills my mouth with saliva, makes my hollowed-out stomach call out, my eyes prick with tears. I have a satchel full of food to take home from the muleteer, but I still haven't eaten anything myself since last night. Since before the fight for my life. My body's longing is palpable.

But here I am a servant. No plate appears in front of me, no offer of food. Instead, it is pressed into the hands, onto the plates, of the people seated around the small table. The priest bites into a chicken leg, juice running down his mottled red chin.

The injustice of it scrapes against every part of me. My skin, my heart, my dry, painful throat. The man who touched me, who tried to touch Belle, whose threats of naming a witch still hang over us all, who probably has never felt the way hunger can make you weak and stupid—he's filling his belly while I watch. Why is it that the worst people have their needs so easily met while the rest of us cry and beg and struggle and steal?

Steal.

The word lodges in my mind like the splinters in my face. The word is a realization. A place to hang my rage. This house is full of supplies, and I have the keys. Stealing from here wouldn't even feel like stealing. Nobody in this house would go hungry even if I took and took and took.

Eugénie's father waves a near-empty glass at me, and I take it, slipping out of the room and into the kitchen, where a carafe of watered-down wine sits on a counter marred with chop marks.

Before I can think better of it, before my rage cools and worries climb into the space it leaves behind, I grab a whole jar of preserves from a shelf above the counter and slip it under my skirt and into my pantalets, wedging it between thigh and cloth, tight enough—I hope—to stay put even as I move.

Then I fill Eugénie's father's glass and return to the room. In my chest, fear of discovery flutters lightly, but it's overpowered by something else. Something unexpected. A proud, satisfied, angry sort of power. The same I feel when I see that scar on the priest's hand. In a world where so much is taken from me, I have just taken something back. And it makes me feel twice the size that I normally do.

Even the continuing conversation about a witch in the village and how they need to root her out cannot touch me. Even the priest's narrow-eyed glares.

It's like when I saved myself that winter so long ago—but this time I chose my salvation before it became a necessity. And this time I'm taking so many more of us with me into a better life.

32

THAT EVENING, WE FEAST. I TAKE EVERYTHING DIRECTLY TO Charlotte and Hélène, and Clara meets me there after tucking in the sheep at Mémé's. We slow-cook beans with a scandalous amount of bacon. I produce two rolls that I stole on my way out the door, and we slather them with bacon fat. It's so good I have to force myself to eat slowly. Even the lingering rawness in my throat can't stop me from groaning in pleasure.

"We have one week," I tell the girls in between bites. "The muleteer comes back then, and we offer him whatever money we have, whatever goods we have, to take us with him to the south."

"Us?" Clara's eyebrows flicker upward.

We haven't had a chance to talk, so now I lay out everything I've learned. Not just the soldiers eating us out of house and home, wading through winter stores like they were nothing, which Clara already knows, but the priest's dire warnings about a witch in the village and the way that I know in the deepest parts of myself that this means he can point a finger at anyone and ruin us. The best-case scenario is being driven away; the worst ends with a fire and an endless scream.

When I get to the part about the foot, Hélène solves the mystery. "Louis. Louis took the foot. He said taking it was a better plan than him just saying Papa went into the woods. And he didn't want Charlotte or me to see it. He wanted it away."

The lingering tightness in me at the mystery—at the slight possibility that the beast itself moved the foot—releases, and I almost laugh aloud with the relief. Louis is more clearheaded than I realized. Clara was right that people surprise us all the time. If we let them.

I'm also surprised the girls found a way to get most of the blood out of their dresses. Which will make our journey south less conspicuous—and is a relief I didn't know I needed. My stay was less salvageable, and they've torn it into strips in case we ever need bandages again.

I finish my story about the priest, reach across the remaining food, and say outright the thing that I've been dancing around. "Clara, we can't stay here, either. We can't stay here any more than they can."

Clara bites her lip and looks worried, but only says, "We should go. We need to get back to Mémé before it gets too late."

I nod, gather our things, kiss Hélène and Charlotte on the tops of their heads, and lead the way out of the cabin and into the woods. Around us, the still pools of water from the storm have turned into humming riots of breeding mosquitoes. Other small bugs fling themselves at our faces as we walk. And it's slow going, with the puddles and the still-sucking mud snatching at our boots.

It isn't until we're a few steps in that Clara speaks again.

"I'm worried about you," she whispers. "You can't just steal things like that. What if you were caught?"

I wave away the concern. "I won't be. It's just one more week. I'll take a few more things, and then we'll disappear."

"That's another thing. You just announced that like it was the truth. And I—you didn't even talk to me."

"I'm talking to you now."

"Not really. You're telling me how it is. You didn't even let me help solve the problem. Hélène and Charlotte could set snares for rabbits while they're out foraging around the house. There are other ways to solve our food problems, and I'm sorry to say it, Joséphine, but you seem to have decided that you're the only one who can save us and therefore you make all the decisions."

The words are like a gut punch, and my defensiveness rises like a sudden, whipping wind. "You're the one who wanted me to work there, to be around Belle all the time. Do you know how hard that is? I realized I could feed us after those bastards ate everything. What did you expect me to do? Starve us for another night because I needed to talk to you about it first?"

"It's not just that."

"Then what is it?"

"You just announced that we're leaving. Like it was nothing. Like there's nothing else to talk about. What about Mémé? Is she coming? How will we get her down south? What about the sheep? Are they coming?"

"Mémé's strong. She can make it. So can the sheep."

Clara takes a long, deep breath. "Of course she's strong. But that doesn't mean we get to put her in danger all the time. She's still old, and she still needs a lot of rest. You've seen the toll it takes on her. I literally just asked you this morning to involve me when you make a decision—and you ignored me the first chance you got." The words are bitten off at the end, as if she has more to say, but she forces herself not to. "Look, let's talk about this later. It's getting dark. We need to get home."

"We can walk and talk at the same time," I offer, but Clara's done. I know her well enough not to push it.

"How in the devil do you put this thing on?" Walter complains far too early the next morning, holding up the dress he pilfered from me when the d'Ennevals decided sheep in girl clothes were how they'd lure in the beast.

Apparently, they finally realized that particular strategy wasn't working and have returned Clara's ewe, who is now being showered in head kisses by Clara and fond pats from Mémé. But even though the dress is back in my house right now, it *isn't* returned. Because now the d'Ennevals are certain that the problem with the plan wasn't that it was ridiculous all around, but rather that the beast knows the difference between sheep and humans. So they need humans in dresses.

More specifically: soldiers in dresses.

Even more specifically: Walter in a dress.

He tells us about it in a self-important tone, but he's already frustrated trying to put the thing on. Standing here in his under-things with the dress on one leg and a scowl on his face.

I'm grinning from ear to ear at his inability to do such a simple thing, and Mémé seems to feel the same, her eyes twinkling every time Walter huffs. But Clara's a kinder person than either of us, so she moves to help him.

"Lucky that you're the same size as Joséphine," she says. I doubt if she means it as a joke, but Walter looks so put off that I stifle a chortle behind my hand. All these soldiers see themselves as larger than life. Telling them they're the size of a short, too-skinny shepherdess has to count as an insult.

"Stop laughing," he orders in my direction as Clara adjusts the dress's shoulders and starts fastening the back.

"Look." She redirects his attention to our small looking glass. "You look quite good in it."

He narrows his eyes. "Looking good is not the point. That's something only girls care about. The point is the beast—and the reward. The king raised it, you know. Six thousand livres! The man who kills the beast will be rich beyond imagining."

"And when you get that reward, will you share your bounty? Buy me a new dress?" I can't help myself.

He frowns. "Maybe if you were nicer to me."

Nicer. Nicer than sheltering him, feeding him, giving up sheep and dresses and privacy? The arrogance of his entitlement to our emotions after we've given him everything else is staggering.

"Do you need anything else?" Clara redirects the conversation.

"No." Walter doesn't even thank her. Just scowls at his own reflection in the looking glass and then marches out of the house.

"Marvin needs life to smack him around a bit more," Mémé observes.

"Who's Marvin, Mémé?" Clara lays the looking glass back on the shelf.

Mémé motions after Walter and looks at Clara like she's lost her marbles.

"That's Walter, Mémé." I speak low through my still-sore throat.

"No jokes today, girls. I know Marvin when I see him. He pulled my hair every day of the apple harvest."

We exchange a glance. Clara's look is pained. Another bad day. She hates to leave Mémé on the bad days.

"Mémé, let's get you some company for the morning since Clara and I have to go out. Why don't you go to Amani's?" I help her up from where she's been sitting propped up on the mattress.

Mémé doesn't fight us, and Amani is thrilled to see her, welcoming her with open arms for a bowl of tea. Clara whispers with Amani for a moment, likely letting her know Mémé is having a rough day, and then we leave the two together, both already laughing.

Our plan today, concocted in barest whispers late last night, is to go after Eugénie first thing in the morning. The beast hasn't killed in a couple of days, which makes it feel like this is our window. Our chance to stage Eugénie's death before things change. Before the beast kills again or moves on to another part of the region or is caught by the now-more-colorfully-arrayed soldiers spreading out through the fields and woods around us in their borrowed dresses.

Walter's mention of the higher reward makes it feel more urgent, too, because surely a higher reward will attract more soldiers, push them harder to find the creature. The window of opportunity that opened with the beast's appearance feels already half-shut with the promise of its capture.

I almost laugh at the fact that part of me is on the side of the evil thing, hoping that it won't be caught just yet.

Outside, the sky is dark with the threat of rain, but no rain is falling yet. We weave along an unfamiliar route, Clara leading the way because she thinks she knows where Eugénie likes to take her sheep. We pass another soldier in a simple gray dress lingering on the edge of a field with his eyes on the forest. Then another figure in a dress spots us and lopes toward us.

"Oh là là là là, the loveliest ladies in the village—come to see me?" Louis's familiar playful tone dances across the space between us as the soldier a few paces away scowls at us all—no doubt imagining that our loudness is ruining his chances at attracting the beast and its reward.

Clara quirks a smile as he falls into step beside us.

"I see you've taken up the same tactic as the soldiers?" I motion to his dress—a pretty red thing that brings out the warmest tones in his skin and makes his eyes look even greener.

He grins. "The whole village has. Started as a joke, but"—he leans in conspiratorially—"quite a few of us like it. Results in a very pleasant breeze on one's undercarriage."

"Louis!" Clara gasps. "Are you naked under your skirt?"

Louis throws his hands up to the sky. "Freedom, I say!"

"Where'd you get the dress from?" I ask as Clara turns us down a thin sheep trail through a small slice of wood.

"Stole it from the soldiers' stash." Louis shrugs.

I squint at him. "Won't you get in trouble?"

He winks. "I'm *always* in trouble."

In the distance, thunder growls as we emerge into another clearing, and Clara makes a small noise of pleasure when she sees that she was right. Eugénie and a cluster of poofy sheep are at the far end of the open space.

Louis's voice goes a bit more serious, and I suppose that's the level we're on with him now, after everything. "I wish that I could dress like this more often. It seems cruel that it's only allowed as a trick or a joke."

I nod. I wouldn't mind trying men's trousers myself. And wearing head coverings less often.

When we reach Eugénie, her eyes brighten, and she thrusts out a delicate hand for him to kiss. "Louis, gorgeous as ever."

He curtsies. "*More* gorgeous, I think."

"I didn't know you were friends." Her gaze flits between Louis and me.

"New friends," I say. Then, "Good friends now, I think."

Louis looks quite pleased with that, his eyes crinkling.

"We're here about the conversation you and I had yesterday." I shift away from small talk. "If you could get out right now, no man attached to the bargain, would you?"

"Hell yes," she answers without hesitation.

Clara nods, then glances at me. "Well, then. Now's your chance."

33

"WHAT ABOUT THE SHEEP?" WHEN WE EXPLAIN OUR PLAN, Eugénie's question is exactly the same one I'd ask.

If someone was trying to whisk me away, fake my death, there would still be that one huge problem. I could not, in good conscience, leave my sheep. They depend on us for safety. If a shepherdess disappears, she leaves them vulnerable to all manner of harm. And sheep are everything. Not just the difference between life and death for those we love, but beings that our own hearts get tangled up with along the way.

Which is precisely why taking Eugénie while she's out with her sheep and leaving them behind will leave no room for anyone to question that she was taken by the beast. It's the best thing I can come up with to keep her brother from questioning her disappearance.

Originally, we were going to stage Clara and me finding the

sheep, but I realize now that Louis is the far smarter option. He's not connected to us in anyone's minds, which means her disappearance won't be, either. Another layer of separation between us as we seem to the village and our secrets.

"Louis will stay with them, say he found them wandering." I reach for Eugénie's pike and press it into Louis's hands. "He'll keep them safe."

His expression flashes surprise, but he nods his assent.

The change in Eugénie is instant. Her whole body straightens, chest and jaw jutting a little forward. With her sheep cared for, she has committed fully. I can see it in every line of her as the thunder rumbles closer overhead and a few rogue raindrops pelt us.

And then she makes her commitment even clearer. She reaches for Clara's pike with one hand, grabs a handful of her own hair with the other, and cuts it off. As the rest of us gape, she slices the pike cleanly across her palm, barely even flinching, and presses the blood against the hair. She hands it to a stunned Louis and then turns to her nearest sheep and wipes a bloody handprint down her flank.

"Mon Dieu, Eugénie," Clara whispers. "You didn't have to do all that."

"*Yes, I did.* You don't know my brother. He needs to be *sure.* Surer than sure. That I didn't run. He won't think I'd bleed myself on purpose. He won't think I'd cut my hair. He's knows I'm vain of it. Louis will say he found the clump of hair in a bush or something. It's the only way my family will believe I didn't run."

She steps into the forest then, and I marvel at her. So decisive.

So ready to take an opportunity the moment it appeared. Half her hair is short now and stands on end. Through the leaves, a dusky orange of sunrise makes her glow and there's something saintly or blasphemous about it.

Clara is the first to shake off the spell of her and step into the forest. I follow, saluting Louis with two fingers to the sky as I go. He returns the gesture with his pike hand in a way that seems to mean he's got the sheep thing covered.

And then we're moving, and the rain is falling harder. Through purple-shadowed, storm-rattling tree branches, over the first leaves that have abandoned their trees, our feet pressing them into still-damp ground. Around us, moss is draped thickly over boulders and rivulets of water cascade down in spiderweb patterns. We don't speak; it's too important to listen. For the movement of a beast or a soldier. Lucky that we picked the day when they're all decked out in periwinkle and rose dresses, easier to spot than a navy-blue uniform.

Eugénie's grazing grounds are far from my cottage, and we take the long way, picking through wood and thicket, doing our best to make sure that no one sees us even though the day is dawning now and more and more soldiers will be out and about even in the rain. The paths shift in color as we go from yellow-gray dirt to pink, gritty pebbles to rust-colored paths that thicken and slow our steps as the rain coaxes them yet again from dust to mud.

Our silence, our caution, is why we hear them before they reach us—when we're just a thirty-minute walk away from the cottage. The thunder of hoofbeats, men's boots smacking into mud, distant shouts growing closer so much faster than I wish they would.

Eugénie turns, wide-eyed, and Clara's breath hitches.

It must be Duhamel and his regiment. The d'Ennevals have been obsessed with trickery, but good old boy Duhamel is as he ever was: a knight riding into the fray. Chasing the beast down by patrolling forest and field.

I whip my head around the unfamiliar landscape. To the left, the noise of the men rises toward us through the trees, though the forest is too thick for us to see them yet. To the right, a hill slopes steeply away, toward another part of the gorge, where I rescued my little fool lamb. Ahead is the way to the girls. Behind us, a stretch of forest where no hiding places present themselves.

The men have spotted something. I can hear it in their shouts now. "To the right! Don't let it get away!"

Are they driving the beast directly for us? And should I be more afraid of that or of them seeing us with Eugénie?

"This way." Clara makes the decision for us and practically dives down the hill.

Eugénie follows without hesitation, and I trip after them, already struggling with the steep grade and the mud shifting underfoot.

We slam down the hill on feet and hands and knees, scrambling to get away from the noises that still grow closer. I can hear the words men are shouting distinctly now.

"La bête!"

"It's here!"

"Onward!"

"To triumph!"

"Here!" Eugénie calls, sharp. "Here!"

I slide a few more feet down to her, and Clara stops and scrambles up. The mouth of a small cave gapes at us, just visible behind thornbushes.

Eugénie pulls back the thornbush, ignoring the way it clings to her sleeve, her skin, what's left of her hair. "Go!"

I dive in headfirst, and Clara and Eugénie follow, scraping into the darkness, the dank, all of us pressed together in the small space.

It's inky dark, and the stone and dirt are rough under my hands. It smells like the corner of a barn after a barn cat has given birth. Damp and musty and animal.

Animal.

The thought stops me in my tracks just as Clara sucks in an audible breath, pointing with trembling fingers at the curved end of the little cave.

Three pairs of eyes shine in the darkness.

Three quiet breaths whisper across the space between us.

A lightning flash reveals their shape for the briefest moment. And after everything, *after everything,* I know in my blood and my bones and my very soul that we are about to die. I hope, fleetingly, that Charlotte and Hélène can find a way out without us. And then I wish with every fiber of my being that I could have saved Clara, too.

34

THREE PAIRS OF EYES SHINE. SIX BODIES NOW BREATHE IN THE tiny space. Outside, the shouts grow louder, the horses' hooves pounding like thunder. Real thunder growls in the background. Another flash of lightning sparks light briefly through the cave. The creatures blink in the brightness. But no attack comes.

My frozen heart stutters back to life, my mind stumbling to catch up with what my eyes are starting to make out in the dusky light. What I saw in the flashes.

The forms in front of us are small—each a little larger than a wolf cub. But they are no wolves. They are little light-colored things with short snouts and round ears. This is not an animal we know here. They don't make sense. Don't look like any drawing I've ever seen. But perhaps that's just the dimness of the space, the way I can't quite make out their detail.

Clara's hand slips into mine, and I see the silhouette of Eugénie pressing her hand to her mouth.

"They're cubs." Eugénie is the first to breathe the words.

"Beast cubs," Clara whispers.

All three of us know what that means. These babies are no danger to us. But their mama could be back any moment. And she has already proved her danger. Her power.

I wonder—uselessly—if she was pregnant when she arrived or if there are two of them here. Death at the ends of more than one set of claws and teeth and muscled jaws.

Outside, the sky finally makes good on its thunderous threats, and the sound of sheets of rain pouring down roars into the cave—trickle turned to deluge. At our backs, cold water splashes in, soaking immediately through our dresses.

I turn then, facing the opening behind us. The place where any danger will come from—be it soldiers finding us out or a furious mother. Will she return here to check on her young, or will she race away from this place, leading the soldiers as far as she can? I don't know this animal, so I don't know the answer.

We wait, each of us stretched thin with the tension, staring out into the now-dark morning. The rain makes it hard to hear how close or how far the soldiers are. But I think maybe, just maybe, they are moving away. The shouts are muted, the crash of hoofbeats replaced entirely by a low growl of thunder and a rumble of rain violently pelting the ground.

I shiver as the rain soaks through the front of my dress, too, the fear and the storm stealing the warmth from my limbs. The forest shudders with the torrent, and I don't know where to look, where to watch for the danger when every leaf is dancing, every branch moving.

Clara squeezes my hand in a nervous rhythm. Eugénie holds

a sharp rock in her right hand. It'll be futile if the beast finds us here, but I understand the impulse. It's the same one that kept me dragging my limbs through the snow to Clara.

When the voices have faded and I'm pretty sure what I'm hearing is just rain, no hoofbeats, I shudder out a breath and grab the thorns like Eugénie did on the way in, holding them back for Clara and Eugénie to scramble out.

"Go," I say shakily as I follow. "Run."

We don't look back.

35

WHEN WE CRASH INTO THE HOUSE LIKE A THREE-GIRL STORM, Eugénie lets out an animal noise of surprise. She's staring, disbelieving, at Charlotte and Hélène, who we caught in the middle of some kind of yarn game in front of the hearth.

We didn't tell Eugénie about them before we arrived, and now she releases a half laugh, half scream. "You're alive! God's wounds, you're alive! You gorgeous, kidnapping bastards!" She screams the last part at Clara and me, wrapping the two of us in a very wet, very cold hug. The surprise and nerves and relief manifest as shivers and giggles as the three of us shake out the tension of the last hour.

"Mon Dieu. Mon Dieu. Mon Dieu." Clara whispers the words like a prayer.

Hélène and Charlotte unfreeze from their own surprise and move to help Eugénie out of her soaking dress and settle her in front of the fire. Charlotte reaches up to help Clara, but Clara shakes her head. "We need to go. I don't want anyone noticing that we're gone at the same time as she disappeared."

My stomach sinks, though I agree with Clara. Still, we narrowly missed running into the beast just minutes ago. It could be anywhere out here.

I don't say any of that, though, not wanting to worry the younger girls. Instead, I muss Charlotte's hair affectionately. "Show Eugénie the ropes."

And then before I can think better of our fool plan, we're out the door and marching purposefully through the storm toward the village.

I reach for Clara and weave my fingers through hers. We're alive. We escaped. We're still in danger, but it feels so much lesser here on the sheep trail, moving farther and farther from that cozy den. I'm so grateful for Clara's safety that I could weep and keep on weeping.

"Clara." Her name is sacred in my mouth. "I'm so glad you're all right."

She squeezes my hand. "Me too. I don't know what I would have done. . . ."

Both our breaths are unsteady, shivering things through the rain.

"I'm sorry I stole the food from Belle's place without talking to you. You were right. I was being reckless. I was just . . . so angry. It felt powerful to do it," I confess.

"I know." Clara is, as usual, all grace. But there's also firmness in her next words. "You can't do that again, though. You have to talk to me. We're in this *together*."

I nod. "I know. And I'm sorry. I'm such a wreck."

"Oui, you are. *My* wreck."

"Forever," I agree.

"And ever," she whispers through the storm.

"Amen."

Dry and warm a few hours later, I arrive at Belle's house to a frantic, chaotic mess of human panic.

"Did you hear?" Belle's face is paler than usual. "Eugénie's gone. Louis found her flock wandering on their own and there was—blood and hair." She takes my hands, an uncharacteristic intimacy for her, and hers are ice-cold.

I feel strangely sad for her. Is this the first time Belle has experienced this kind of proximity to terror? She arrived in the village acting like it was a game, but now someone she knows is gone. Eaten, for all she understands. And the confidence in her tone has fallen off a cliff.

I squeeze her hands, soft and cold in mine. "I'm so sorry."

From the sitting room, a masculine voice shouts, "Didn't I tell you to bring my gun? What kind of fool are you?"

Eugénie's brother strides into the entryway, his brows pulled together. I have the sudden, furious urge to bite him. Like I bit the priest. Feel his flesh give way under my teeth. And then I recoil from myself, my mind flashing me images of Charlotte's father's neck, the knife going in and then in again. My stomach turns over as a wave of anger shifts to a wave of fear—not of him, this towering figure who hurt Eugénie—but of myself and what I'm capable of. A wolf in sheep's clothing, the girl who will take an eye for an eye.

"Belle." He inclines his head, then thrusts an arm out at a servant who has scuttled into the room with his musket. He takes it, slips into his boots by the door, and leaves.

"He's going after the beast?" I ask, even though it's not really a question. I just need to ask something, to shove aside the skittering mix of fear and loathing and fury mixed up in my gut.

Belle nods. "Oui. The soldiers are already out. He's going to join them. And we've been asked to help, too."

Now, that's a surprise—and a welcome one, as it lets me shove the unpleasantness down in favor of curiosity. What role do these men have in mind for two slight girls, one a shepherdess and one the daughter of a wealthy, powerful man? Two very different types of people.

I follow Belle into the sitting room, where Jean stands on a pretty pearl-colored platform and bobs his whole body at me. "How do you take your tea, little bastard?"

I choke on a laugh.

"With a side of bullets, I hope." It's the younger d'Enneval, standing as we enter the room and bowing slightly.

I stare at him, not understanding the jest, and he motions to the low table in front of him. Spread out like an assembly line are boxes of square bullets, pieces of iron, and smaller boxes of something gray and pink and gelatinous that looks suspiciously like lard and blood.

"Sit, please." He motions to the settee, where Belle is already settling herself.

I join her, stiff with the knowledge that I've never been asked to sit on the furniture in this house before.

He clears his throat and pulls a parchment from his waistband, holding it out in front of him. "Now, it's clear the beast is able to repel bullets in some way. Our men have gotten close enough times, shot it enough times, to know that a normal bullet won't bring this evil creature down."

Well, that or your men are terrible shots and muskets are hard to control.

"So this recipe has been developed by the best doctors, astrologers, and priests in the king's court. It should make these bullets stronger and capable of breaking through the creature's defenses—be they human- or devil-made."

Belle nods solemnly beside me, and Jean murmurs, "Speak like a lady."

D'Enneval looks down at the paper and reads off the recipe. "Then the hunters should take twelve ounces of human fat from a Christian."

What the—

What?

I can't help but flinch back from those words. Is *that* what's in the boxes? Where did they get it from? How?

He pauses, taking in the expressions on our faces. Mine is very obviously horror and disgust, I'm sure. Belle looks like she was perhaps prepared for this. Her nose only crinkles a little.

He goes on, "Combined with viper's blood . . ."

Oh la vache.

"And distributed in boxes."

My stomach churns, and I try not to look directly at the shivery mass of fat and blood.

"Arm your men with pistols and three square bullets bitten by the teeth of a woman or girl. . . ." He looks up from the paper. "Obviously, that's where you come in."

I try not to grimace.

"Preferably virgins." He looks up again in inquiry, but neither of us speaks.

"Then join the bullets with pieces of iron covered in the fat, plus hunting knives and iron claws, also greased. Patrol three by three in silence in a large triangle."

I glance at Belle, but her face is a mask of politeness and she keeps her gaze on the younger d'Enneval.

"So, then, I shall leave you to it. Please bite each bullet, transfer it to the empty box beside you, and then the servants will assemble and grease them."

The servants. I have a strong suspicion that means me. Belle will provide her teeth, but I will be the one reaching my fingers into human fat and viper's blood.

The man leaves the room, and I realize the house around us has quieted. Anyone else who was preparing to leave has done so—all out looking for Eugénie.

I'm not sure how I feel about it. They barely went after Charlotte. Nor Hélène. But Eugénie—daughter of the richest man in the village, living in the house where Lafont is staying—her absence requires a hunt, men flying bravely into action. Including the very man who hurt her. His face set as if he were her savior. As if he cared.

"Mon Dieu, how do you take your tea?"

Belle lifts her first bullet to salute Jean, echoing the words of the d'Enneval. "With a side of bullets."

I join her, biting my first bullet. It's weird and metallic-tasting, even though I avoid touching it with my tongue.

"Did you hear about the hunt yesterday? They almost caught it." Belle bites again, throws another bullet into the empty box.

I feign surprise. "No. Tell me."

And she does, relating a story that a soldier clearly told her, in which they faced off with the evil thing, shot it over and over again, and it still escaped.

"There's a rumor," she whispers conspiratorially, "that it can transform itself into a girl." She shudders a little then and goes on. "The priest was by this morning. He said it's further proof there's a witch in our midst. The thing could be a shape-shifter, not even a real beast."

I press my lips together to stifle a frustrated sigh, an ominous feeling in my gut.

I can't tell her that I know it's a flesh-and-blood creature, not because I don't believe in the possibility of the supernatural but because I've seen its young. And even if I hadn't, I wouldn't believe simply because it was the priest who said it. And he can say God speaks to him all day long, but he put his hands on me and any God that actually cares about *anything* wouldn't allow that. So he's an impostor and a liar, and his position as a truth teller makes him the most dangerous man in a village full of dangerous men. I bite another bullet, another, another. But it's not the beast I want to kill.

"He would know," Belle goes on. "He's the one who found the last witch here."

My heart stops. "What did you just say?"

"Papa says there was a witch here once before. A cursed plague one year, and the priest was the one who told the men who it was. He's the hero who stopped the plague."

My throat burns, and I might be sick as my mind catches up to what Belle is telling me. She doesn't know the story. Doesn't know what happened to the former priest, the brutality of it. Him burned and bleeding, battered and broken, fleeing—then caught. She doesn't know that not everyone believes he was a witch. And she doesn't know that she's just confirmed what my gut already knew: all the priest has to do is choose a name and that person will be dead.

That he can and will speak those names aloud. It's not theory; it's fact.

It could so easily be my name. It could so easily happen at any time.

Belle believes him a hero for it, but the truth sits heavy in my gut. *He wanted the job.* He wanted our priest's job, and so he served him up to a desperate, violent mob. I am dizzy with the truth, with this new layer of danger.

When I say nothing, Belle whispers her next words. "I don't hate you."

I drop the bullet I'm holding and have to fish it out from under the low table. The change of subject feels strange when my mind has gone so far down a dark path. "What?"

"You said the other day that I hated you. I don't."

"All right . . . ?"

"Mon Dieu," Jean murmurs.

Belle ignores him, tosses another bitten bullet into the box. "I just can tell that *you* hate *me*. So I defend myself."

I pause at that, let another bullet slip from fingers to box, let thoughts of the priest retreat to the back of my mind. *Do I hate Belle?* No. Not really. She's infuriating, certainly. Absolutely clueless about what anyone's life but her own looks like. Selfish. But I don't hate her. I realize—with a start—that it's not even just that she makes me angry. I'm also *scared.* Not scared of her but of what she represents: a time in my life when I was ripped away from the people I love most twice in a row. Ripped and ripped again. And expected to be grateful for it. I'm angry with her, still. I'm scared of her, oui. And despite myself, I somehow care about her, somehow feel that protectiveness rise up to cover her as well as the other girls around me. Complicated as they are, none of those feelings is hate. At least not anymore.

"I don't hate you, either," I answer after a moment. "I did, I think, when your papa first took me away from here. But that wasn't your fault. And I don't hate you now. I really don't."

"I know," she whispers, dropping another bullet. "I knew when you came in when the priest was—doing whatever he was doing."

I set the bullet down.

She bites her lip. "I feel like a fool. He's a priest, a hero even. I shouldn't feel so . . . afraid. And he didn't do anything. Just, I don't know. I wish he wouldn't touch me."

I reach across the space between us and, for the first time in my life, I slip my hand into Belle's and squeeze. "He *shouldn't* be touching you. You're not a fool to feel that." *And he's more dangerous than you realize, Belle.* I don't say the last part out loud.

She meets my gaze and then—another surprise. "I'm sorry I haven't been the nicest to you."

I raise an eyebrow.

"Thank you for being there for me anyway. With the priest that day and also for coming down to that meal we had with him. I know you don't like him, but I wanted you there because I felt safer with you in the room."

The vulnerability of it is staggering. Belle has never been this honest with me. Something about this situation has cracked her open. And now I realize that my feelings about her wanting a servant, wanting to show off, were so very misplaced. I almost laugh. Belle isn't nice to me and I'm not nice to her, but she finds my presence *comforting.* My shoulders relax, a strange fondness nudging my fears about the priest aside.

She takes her hand back, but I impulsively lean over and kiss her cheek. "Belle Lafont, are you saying you love me?"

Her mouth twitches, an almost smile. "Don't get crazy."

"Speak like a lady!" Jean chides.

"You heard the bird." I tilt my head toward him. "No name-calling. You love me and that's that."

She waves a disgruntled hand at me, but I only grin. The priest is more dangerous than I knew, but Belle is perhaps less. And that's not nothing.

36

THE STORM CLOUDS ARE BUILDING AGAIN AS CLARA AND I shuffle the sheep into the cottage. The energy of the place has shifted with Eugénie's arrival. She stands in front of the cooking fire, animated, telling a story. The other girls look enraptured, and Louis, who has also returned to check on us, leans—grinning and again in his dress—against the wall near the door.

The fool lamb reacts to the mirth in the room by running in a circle through the cottage, agitating the other lambs into the race. One careens clumsily into Charlotte, does an accidental flip, and lands in Hélène's lap, causing us all to laugh in surprise and Charlotte to clap.

Outside, the clouds release the storm, rain falling in buckets and lightning flashing bright through the windows. Another storm signaling that summer has dropped to autumn now. We might be stuck here again for the night, but this time we warned

Mémé that we might stay out—lying, with a pang, that Clara wanted to visit Madeline to check on her injuries. And last time Walter didn't care one bit, didn't seem suspicious at all. So some of the worry about getting caught feels looser in my chest.

I sink onto the blankets in front of the fire, where Charlotte, Hélène, and three lambs are settled.

Eugénie continues her story. "So my brother was devout back then—and I mean *devout.* He prayed like sixty times a day to those little saint portraits everyone has over their mantel. We had three: Saint Drogo, Charles de Blois, and Saint Denis, the one who carried his own head up a hill."

I'm surprised she's telling stories about her brother with such joy in her voice. I glance at Clara, but she only smiles slightly at me and keeps her attention trained on Eugénie.

"That was the first time Lafont came to the village and stayed with us overnight. He asked about the little portraits, and I told him my brother had bought them from the peddlers who came through the village. Then my brother interrupted me, as usual, and told Lafont—all pompous-like—who each of the saints were and why they were important. Only . . . he was wrong." Eugénie pauses for dramatic effect. "He was wrong about everything. I already knew he was wrong about Saint Drogo because I asked the priest about it. My brother thought he was the saint of strong men, but he's really the saint of ugly people."

Charlotte giggles aloud at that one, and Louis laughs appreciatively as well.

"But he was wrong about something else, too. And Lafont set him straight. Those portraits *weren't saints at all.* The peddlers go village to village selling little likenesses of French generals, passing them off as various saints. People buy that more readily than generals."

Eugénie's laugh is gorgeous spite and mirth all rolled up together. She leans over to smack a hand against her knee. "My brother—who thought he was the smartest person in the whole world—had been praying ten times a day to some old, dead generals."

Louis slow-claps, and the lambs zoom around the room again, soaking in the energy.

Then Eugénie takes a bow, lowers herself to the edge of the hearth, and addresses Clara and me. "I have an idea." Her eyes spark with it.

"When I was still in the village, I kept hearing all those rumors about Charlotte's ghost being sighted. People are scared. My superstitious brother as much as anyone. What if we scared them a little more?"

Something uncertain flutters in my stomach, but Clara's the one to answer. "Scare them how?"

"Stage some ghostly things around the village. Joséphine has access to my house. She could easily put a little general portrait under my brother's pillow. Stage a haunting!"

"No." The word leaves my lips before I even think it through. "We are leaving in less than a week. This whole thing has been about staying away from any suspicion. That only invites it."

"They already invited their own suspicions by starting up their foolish ghost rumors and saying the beast is a shapeshifting girl," Eugénie argues.

"That's exactly why we shouldn't add sparks to their growing fire. The more scared people are, the more watchful they are. And the less forgiving." My mind flashes me an image: us, found. Surrounded by villagers shocked and angry and convinced that we are the shape-shifting thing, a witch coven hidden in the woods, haunting them.

It wouldn't end well for any of us.

Eugénie opens her mouth to say more, but Clara holds up a pacifying hand. "It's late. We won't decide anything tonight. Let's all have a good think about it."

I throw her an incredulous look. Clara is more cautious than I am; she can't think this is a good idea. But she only shakes her head at me in a way that I know means *later*. And *stop rushing already*.

I acquiesce, and so does Eugénie, who smiles slyly and stands again, commanding the room. "Did I tell you about the time that a nest of spiders *accidentally* ended up in my brother's bed?"

When I wake, the fire has dwindled and the room is nearly dark, and my entire body is alert. Hair stands at attention on the nape of my neck and across my arms. My heart knocks painfully against my ribs, ready to run. My hands and feet are ice.

Something is wrong. My body knows it before my mind, and I grope in the dark for a reason that I've woken so ready to run.

Through the quiet, I hear it then.

A snuffling noise at the door.

That's when I realize the rain has stopped. And what woke me was this: a soft grunting in the night. It sounds gravelly, the grunt—almost like a rockslide given voice.

Charlotte sits up beside me, squeaking in surprise. Hélène, who must have also been awake, reaches for her instinctively. And like that rockslide, each waking startles another sleeping form out of dreams.

"What—" Louis speaks, and we all reach out hands toward him, frantically shushing.

Outside, silence. Then the door rattles, shifting back and forth in its frame. Two inches of wood in between us and the snuffling. Such a fragile thing to keep out so much death.

The noises return. We can hear her huffing around the edges, smell her—that wild, rotting, dangerous smell of a carnivore come too close. Like the wolves, but not quite them. *Worse.* The smell of decay and darkness and doom.

I can hear the priest in my head. *Repent, repent, repent!* Girls caused this and girls it is taking.

Beside me, Clara wraps her hand around her pike, and I reach for mine. Louis stands, quietly, and moves to grab the knife we use for food prep, placing himself alongside the door. I can see his intent clearly: if the creature breaks the door down and rushes in, he imagines himself stabbing it as it flies past.

Clara and I are positioned more like when we face off with a wolf, kneeling slightly in front of the girls and the sheep, our pikes ready to be anchored against the ground and thrust into the chest of a charging animal.

I wonder—faintly—if we somehow invited it here. By going

to its den. We didn't touch the cubs, but I imagine our scent, our fear, our sweat, was everywhere. Can this predator follow that through the woods to us? Or is it simply back to the place where it found a good scratching post to sharpen its claws? The place where one body was laid out for it, an effortless meal?

Has it happened upon us by accident or on purpose?

The door shakes again, and Charlotte presses her face to Hélène's chest, the two of them clinging together for dear life.

A low growl shivers through the door. Can it hear us? Or does it simply know we're here by smell?

If I didn't already know it wasn't a wolf, I'd be sure now. No wolf behaves this way. I wouldn't be afraid of a wolf breaking down our door. But the animal outside is so much bigger. I can tell by the growls, by the way what is probably only a tentative touch is rattling the door on its hinges.

Another growl. Another long moment. Hélène and Charlotte pressed together. Louis tense beside the door, knife in hand. Clara clear-eyed, ready for a fight.

And then, it starts to move away. Or at least I think it does. We all hold our collective breath, the tension in our shoulders, our necks, our faces.

When my hackles retreat, I stand and move to the window, staring out into the starlit clearing. Nothing moves. Nothing shines through the dark. No eyes, nor teeth, nor razor claws.

"I think it's gone." I speak the words slowly, my heart still beating out a too-fast rhythm in my ears. "I think it's gone." If I say it again, it must be true, right?

"And this"—I motion unsteadily toward the door—"is why

we cannot stay here. It's why we join the muleteer and go south."
I mean it as the start to a conversation. I promised Clara we'd
talk things through, and now I mean to do it. Because this—the
beast—is not a thing we can live with.

Well, this and the priest and the village and Eugénie's brother.
The rumors of witchcraft. The soldiers eating all the stores.

I hope the beast has made my point for me, wiped away any
lingering hesitations.

Instead, Clara's face goes stormy. "Are you really bringing
that up now?"

My heart jolts a little in surprise. Wasn't this what she
asked for?

"You said we needed to talk about it." My tone is defensive.

"Yes, you and me when everything is calm. Not when we're
all scared half out of our minds."

"Well, I'm sorry, but I don't think there are any moments
coming where we aren't scared."

"Joséphine." Clara is all exasperation now. "This is exactly
what I was talking about. You aren't asking for a discussion.
You're telling everyone what to do again."

"This *is* me asking."

"Forgive me if I didn't hear the question part."

Louis tries to step in. "Maybe Clara's right and we should
wait until we're all calmer. . . ."

"Who asked you?" My anger sparks higher. Yet again a boy
thinking he gets to have the final word.

"See!" Clara's voice rises. "You can't hear anyone but yourself! Poor Louis is just trying to help!"

That stings. Clara almost never yells. And to hear her say I don't listen to her . . . it's unbearable. The feeling that the person I care most about in the world doesn't think I hear her. It makes me want to crawl out of my own skin.

"Why didn't you say any of this to me before?" I'm crying now. Charlotte tries to take my hand, but I shy away. The idea of being touched makes me feel sick.

"I did! I told you that you were making too many decisions for everyone else. I asked you to let me in—to let me help, to stop making decisions for the group."

"I thought I was." I am small and growing smaller. The shame eats at me, hot, whispering the words I've tried to shove down for ten years: *you are nothing.* Not even your own father could stay for you. *No matter how hard you try, you are not enough.*

My mind flashes me images of that cabin window, Papa disappearing into snow. But worse, it flashes me the *feeling.* The desperate aloneness. The knowledge at nine years old that the only person who would save me was me. That I had done something so terrible—even if I didn't know what it was—that no one would ever love me.

"Joséphine, I need you to stop crying and hear me. I shouldn't have to scream for you to hear me. Just because I'm nice to you when I bring up your bad behavior doesn't mean you get to keep behaving badly!"

I've had enough of this conversation. I'm wrung out, sliced through, drenched in that familiar despair. The one that whispers, *You really are worthless, aren't you?* And worse, *They'll leave you just like Papa did.* And worse still, *You can't stop it.*

You are powerless. Less than powerless. A speck. A breath. Here and then gone, forgotten.

I'm at the door now, pressing my back to it, letting the tears dry on my face.

This time, when I do the foolish thing, it isn't impulse. It's choice. I cannot escape my own skin, my own shame, but I can leave this room.

I open the door, slam it behind me, and walk straight into the trees, not even caring if the monster is still here. If she comes for me now, well, perhaps it's justice. Perhaps my death is overdue.

They're right, after all.

I'm a feral girl flying headfirst into a beast's den, slipping unthinkingly down a cliff after a single lamb. I didn't have a plan. I never do. And I drag everyone with me.

Clara deserves better, and if I cannot be better, then I can at least leave.

37

"JOSÉPHINE, COME BACK HERE!" CLARA'S VOICE IS FIRE AND panic behind me, but I only pick up my pace.

Let me go. Just let me go. I'm so tired of fighting. "Don't follow me!" I scream back into the night.

They were right. I put them all in danger. I made all the decisions without consulting anyone. I am an angry mama ewe—all passion, no direction, headbutting my way into situations that don't require it.

But what hurts my heart the most is that I don't know how to be anything else. I don't know how to love another way. I dug through the ice when I was so little, and I've been digging through anything that has stood in my way ever since. I don't know how to go around, to find another path. I only know how to survive. To save myself.

Now I'm doing the opposite. Just as bullheadedly. This time

marching into danger instead of away. I stride purposefully along the sheep trail, toward home. Through a night where I know the beast was lurking less than an hour ago. Trees drip with collected rain. Wind howls, shrill, through the woods. My feet slip and twist on stones and mud and deep puddles that I don't avoid because I'm too tired to try.

I clutch my pike. If it comes for me, then maybe I can be like Marie-Jeanne, fight the creature off by sheer force of will. Maybe even kill it. End one part of the fear that stalks us all through the night.

Overhead, thunder rumbles again, the storm threatening to return.

I slip into another clearing, and another rumble greets me. This one low in a throat. Not the threat of rain or lightning, but the threat of something flesh and blood. Something more immediate. Alive.

I stop, time slowing. My breath a vapor in the cold. My heart a tight, terrible thing.

I know before I turn what I will see. The source of the thunder, the source of the threat. The evil that's been stalking us all.

Shape-shifter. Predator. Animal. Witch.

Nightmare.

She's standing in my path.

38

THE NIGHTMARE IS FIRE-EYED, KNIFE-TOOTHED, MURDER-minded.

She stares me down, unblinking, and I stare back, rooted in place. I know now how foolish I was to think a pike would make any difference. It's so tiny in my hand in comparison to the muscle-bound creature before me, her fur a rich tan color with a darker stripe from the top of her head down her back, her ears rounded—almost friendly if those golden eyes didn't look so alert, so predatory. Her scent is blood and death, and I understand now why they described her as killing with a single breath.

I can't stop staring at her head. So much larger than that of the largest wolf I've ever seen. Her snout is shorter, jaw heavier. She's a nutcracker, and my skull is a nut. Her teeth are knives. Her eyes pin me in place.

In the distance, behind me, the sheep scream into the night, their voices stretched out in demand. They sound almost human, horrified, dying, even though I know they aren't. That sometimes my sheep just love a good scream because something hasn't gone their way. At least they are safe, back in the cabin. Safe with Clara.

Oh, Clara. I shouldn't have left you. Will your last memory of me be a fight?

The beast's head lowers, back muscles rippling in the starlight. That jaw again, it takes my breath away—unnaturally large, monstrously powerful. I can see why so many heads have been separated from their bodies. *Yours next,* my heart says.

I raise my pike. This flimsy, tiny weapon standing between me and my death. I would do anything now—*anything*—to live. I want to survive. I will try to kill this creature by a thousand tiny cuts if that's what it takes. I would fight with a pike. I would fight with a sharp rock. I'd fight with my fingernails if that was all I had.

I almost laugh, because that's what I've been doing all along. Fingernails through ice. Fingernails in a man's eyes. Now fingernails ready to claw at a beast.

She rumbles again but doesn't attack. Why? Is she satiated by the body she stole from the space around the house? If she doesn't need to kill me for food and she doesn't think I'm a threat, if I stand still long enough, will she leave me be? My skull attached to fight another day. Fingernails intact. She's not like a man, driven by unchecked fury. She's a creature of instinct and need. If she doesn't need to do anything with me, can this end in an uneasy truce?

I clutch the pike tighter. Is it better to freeze? To make myself small and nonthreatening? Or to make myself big and not an easy target? With a bear, I'd do the latter. With a wolf, the same. But then again, she's a mother. Making myself threatening might push things in the wrong direction.

As I stand there trying to decide what will keep me alive, she rumbles again. Thunder in her throat. And everything slows down around me as I watch with horror. She's sinking deeper into her crouch, preparing to pounce. Her lips curl upward, wrinkling her nose and cheeks into a hundred angry lines, revealing fangs the size of a man's fingers—sharp, yellowed things that I can picture puncturing deep into my skin, vampiric.

I raise my pike, also in slow motion. Ready to fight. Not ready to die.

And then, with a crash, I'm not alone.

Louis appears behind me first, still clutching the kitchen knife, still in his dress. Like he's Jeanne d'Arc and King Arthur all rolled into one, here to rip sword from stone, kill the beast with a butcher knife.

Clara is hot on his heels, screaming her fury at the beast—wild-eyed in a way that sparks pride and love behind my fear. At least if I die, I will have seen her like this: avenging angel. Hélène is here, too, holding rocks in both hands. Charlotte behind her, also clutching at sharp stones. Eugénie carrying a heavy branch. And behind them—the real surprise.

My sheep.

The rest of us stand and shout at her, but my sheep have no such desire to hold back.

They charge.

My father may have walked away instead of saving me, but

my sheep do not. They scream their fury as they stampede toward the beast. Fear spikes through me for them alongside the gratitude and awe. But the fear is misplaced. The creature was not expecting this kind of fight and decides it isn't worth it.

With a ripple of muscle so visible under its honey-colored coat, it turns and flees, a long tail with a tuft of hair at the end whipping behind it into the trees.

39

CLARA'S HAND IS IN MINE, DRAGGING ME FORCEFULLY BACK to the cottage. Behind us, Charlotte lifts the fool lamb into her arms and ushers the rest of the sheep along, Hélène nudging the stragglers. Louis brings up the rear, his knife still ready.

When we pile back into the cottage, Clara screams—a guttural release of energy and fear and adrenaline—then turns to me and wraps her arms around me, her face in my neck, which hurts, but I deserve that. "You stupid, stupid, foolish, stupid—"

I laugh through the pain, but not because it's funny. It's my own little release. She's not wrong. I let my shame push me out into the dark, not caring about the consequences until they were standing ready to pounce. *Stupid, stupid, foolish, stupid* pretty much covers it.

Clara pulls back to hold my gaze. "I swear, Joséphine! Sometimes it feels like you *want* to get yourself killed. In a blaze of glory. Like you think you can save everyone by sacrificing yourself."

"You're right." Something slides into place in my mind. Clara has seen me so clearly the whole time. I *do* think surviving means pain and suffering and death. My brother, my mother—dead—and me alive. The lamb off the cliff and me offering myself up, a willing sacrifice. It wasn't until Clara put herself in danger to help me that I cared about the risk. With Charlotte, too. And with all my plans. Hell, even my own sheep had to save me from my foolishness.

She presses a hand hard against my cheek as if she can force me to hear her with the contact. "You think saving means blood and danger and death. But I need you to save me by *staying*. I need you to save me by *letting me help*."

I think I understand now. Every time I plowed ahead and threw myself into danger, Clara was the one left behind to either save me from myself or lose me. Off the edge of a cliff. Into the jaws of a beast. We promised we'd always be together, and here I was constantly challenging the edges of that pact. I hadn't counted death as leaving. Perhaps because I didn't feel my mother and brother left me. They were gone, but not on purpose. And so maybe that always seemed like the right kind of gone.

Oh la vache, I'd been throwing myself at danger and thinking I was being valiant. I've been worried that Clara will leave me like Papa did, but I've been the one always on the verge of disappearing from her life. I've been in such awe of her ability to always save me that I never acknowledged I was forcing her to.

Turning her into the avenging angel, the savior, that maybe she never wanted to be.

Charlotte slips silently to Clara's side and wraps her arms around Clara's waist. Hélène puts a hand on her back. And I lean forward and scoop her into my arms, pressing her head to my heart.

"I'm sorry," I say. And this time I mean it. Not as a way out of the fight. Not as way to smooth out the situation. But as a promise. That I will talk to her about things—and not as if I already know the outcome. That I will try to let people help. More than that: *that I will try to stay.* "I'm so sorry."

When I finally pull back again, I'm ready to prove it. Ready to prove that I can change. "What do you all want to do next? Let's make a plan—together this time."

The grand house is quiet when I arrive the next day, knocking softly and calling bonjour as I slowly push the door open. No one responds, and I hesitate, wondering if that means Belle doesn't need me today. There are so many other things I could be doing. Foraging in the forests to keep us alive until our final escape. Setting snares for rabbits. Figuring out if there's a way to take some of our things when we go.

Because *we will go.* This time all of us agreeing together. Five girls, one Mémé, and Louis, who feels that now Pascal is gone, there's nothing left for him here. That he'd rather help Pascal's sisters than do anything else with his time.

It's funny how we came to the same conclusion. How it wasn't my plan that was really the problem, but my attitude. How in trying to grab onto my power with both fists, wrench it back from the village and the men and the beast that took so much of it, I'd also taken theirs. When everyone had power in the conversation, how much more clearly it came together. Louis promising to get us a cart. Eugénie suggesting we ask the muleteer to lead the way, but not until *after* he's passed through the village. We'll catch up to him on the road, giving him no time to accidentally—or intentionally—give us away.

I call for Belle again in the empty house, a little louder this time, before realizing the silence could be sinister. Not Belle out, but Belle cornered again.

"Bonjour?" I'm louder now.

When no one responds, I slip upstairs and find Belle's room empty, the relief of the quiet space unknotting my muscles. I suppose I really am alone. My mind goes straight to the kitchen. I could steal more food. Last time they didn't even notice.

But Clara would hate it. And after everything, it would feel like a betrayal.

Instead, I go to the sitting room to wait for Belle's return. Above the mantel, three portraits hang on the wall, and the corner of my mouth lifts in the slightest smirk. Are these Eugénie's brother's general-saints? The men he prayed so fervently to for strength and courage and other knightly, masculine attributes?

An idea sparks at the back of mind. Another way of making things just a little more right in the world, giving the girls back just a little more control. I said it was too risky to taunt and haunt Eugénie's brother, but now I'm here alone and it would be so easy to do one little thing to set him on edge. I can see Eugénie's spark-bright eyes so clearly in my mind.

I step to the hearth and reach up for the first portrait, unhooking it from the wall, flipping it upside-down, and rehooking it. I move to the second and do the same. I can't help but laugh a little, imagining him noticing the change and wondering who and what would remind him of his own foolishness by drawing attention to the generals.

As I lift the third from its place, the quiet of the house breaks on four words, spoken by someone who must have been here all along.

"What are you doing?"

I jolt and drop the third picture, glass breaking like a chime as it smashes to the floor at my feet. Mon Dieu. What was I thinking? How am I going to explain this?

I turn to face the speaker. Belle, looking tired, her hair uncharacteristically down, her dress mussed. I have the strange thought that she must have been sleeping in the middle of the afternoon. But she wasn't in her bed.

"I—" I grasp for an explanation, but none occurs to me, so I change the subject instead. "I went looking for you. You weren't in your room."

She looks sheepish. "The men were meeting here earlier, and I didn't want to be . . . bothered. So I hid in Papa's room, and I must have fallen asleep."

Ah. By "the men" she means "the priest." I don't blame her.

When she doesn't ask me again about the pictures, I grab the broom and start to clean up.

"We can blame it on the cat," she offers, and a surprise jolt of gratitude warms me. Are Belle and I . . . friends?

I wink. "Clever cat."

"The cleverest," she agrees.

"Little bastard," Jean calls from his cage in the corner of the room.

Not wrong this time, Jean.

If the village knew what I was up to, they'd agree whole-heartedly.

40

WHEN I REACH THE COTTAGE AFTER WORK, THE ORANGE glow of sunset lights the clearing, making it feel almost dreamlike. If I hadn't faced the beast just minutes from here last night, the place would seem so safe now. Magical, even, despite the threatening rumble of thunder in the distance. The promise of yet another storm. The promise that summer really is well and truly over and that every day we wait, our journey south becomes more perilous.

But I barely have seconds to admire the orange light before I hear someone—or something—crashing through the undergrowth behind me. The noise is frantic, panicked, and my first thought is that the beast is chasing something. Deer or wolf or person. Me. Again.

I whip around, my pike thrust out in front of me, and shock shudders through me at what I see flying toward me along the sheep trail.

Not the beast, but Belle. And not Belle as she normally is. Not Belle like beautiful. Belle like *belladonna*. Bell like the thing that tolls your doom. All disheveled hair and torn skirt and face set in determination, white as bleached bone.

Her breath comes fast, and she folds in half as she reaches me, desperately trying to get enough air. Rich girls aren't used to the kind of running she was just doing.

I watch behind her for a pursuer, my pike still ready, but I see nothing. No honey-colored eyes blinking through the soft sunset light. No muscled back slinking through the low bushes.

She finally gets her voice back, and in between gasps, she says the words that we've been trying to avoid. "They're coming. Joséphine, you have to run."

They're coming.

"Breathe, just breathe. Who's coming?"

The girls must have heard the commotion because the door opens behind me, and Clara's voice joins the conversation. "What happened, Belle?"

"The priest." Belle looks at my face. "He's been trying to prove that you're the witch, the shape-shifter, the beast. He followed you here last night. He knows you have the girls here."

Belle herself doesn't seem surprised to learn this about us, that we've been hiding Charlotte and Hélène and Eugénie—all three no doubt pressed against the door, listening and trying to stay silent.

"And he's coming now?" Clara's voice is strangely calm.

"He's coming with everyone. I overheard him telling Papa about it. He's bringing so many men with him from the village.

He wants you burned." The last words are a whisper, as if by saying them softly she can make them less horrible, less true.

Eugénie must have heard enough to know her secret is unsafe because she flings the cottage door open and joins us in the clearing. Over her shoulder, she calls, "Grab what you can, girls. Bring the sheep. We go now."

Belle's face crumples into tears. Maybe she didn't fully understand what she was running into; maybe she didn't fully believe the priest. But now Eugénie stands before her, draped in a soft sunset glow, half her hair standing on end from her impromptu haircut, her face set. And Belle weeps. "You *are* alive."

"And if we want to stay that way, we go." Eugénie aims the words at Clara and me.

Both of us must be in perfect agreement because we move in unison toward the cottage, Clara grabbing her pike from just inside the door, me motioning for the sheep and the other girls to come out.

"Oh là là là là là, oh la vache."

We're too late. The first man steps into the clearing from around the barn, followed by a second, a third.

Eugénie turns and dashes for the woods in the other direction, and the men don't follow, but neither do we. Me because Charlotte is still in the house behind me and Hélène is only half-out, Clara standing in front of them, protectively, and I can't force my feet to move, can't force my heart to leave them behind. I wish Clara would run, would make the selfish choice for once, save herself instead of standing with the girls, but she stays, too, her face set.

Eugénie disappears into the woods, and a tangle of relief and loss and horror knot together in my chest. Relief because I want so badly for at least one of us to make it out of this and now it looks like Eugénie will. Loss because I don't think the same is true of me. I may be able to persuade them to spare the others. But I am the clear ringleader here, the one in the priest's sights.

The one to burn.

And horror because even as I'm relieved that she could be safe, some small part of me wonders how—after everything—Eugénie could so easily abandon us. And then I hate myself for wondering. Because what else could she do? Maybe she thought if she led, we would follow.

Instead, we hesitated, each waiting for the other to move, and now more men fill into the clearing, blocking any potential escape. I hold up my pike to keep one from grabbing me, and Clara swipes her own pike dangerously in his direction. In the doorway, Hélène holds Charlotte tight, the sheep clustered behind them making irritated noises at all the strangers and the negative energy in the space, no doubt.

My fool lamb pushes through the girls' legs and walks over to headbutt me in the calf, then screams at the men now facing me.

"BLEAAA." I imagine that's sheep-speak for *Go the fuck away*.

I white-knuckle my pike, trying to force my breathing even. I see Eugénie's brother, looking murderous. Two pranksters, smirky and unpredictable as ever. Louis slides into the clearing behind them, and that's some comfort, though I'm not sure what I think he can do. And—

"Belle?" A startled voice rings through the crowd, and she turns toward it.

Lafont stares at his daughter, wide-eyed. "Get away from them. What are you doing out here?"

She sets her jaw, her voice surprisingly clear. "I came to warn them—about him." She points at the priest, who has stepped up beside Lafont, fire in his eyes.

Lafont looks from the priest to his daughter. "Warn them? About . . . ?"

But the priest bats away the question with a careless hand, focusing his gaze and his ire on me, now at the center of a circle that has closed. No escape.

"YOU." He growls the word, grits his teeth on it. Then he turns to address the men around us. "We have found the evil that has been threatening our village. This is *she*. This is *it*. The beast. The witch. Shape-shifter or familiar!"

A rumble ripples through the crowd, and tension builds visibly across necks and arms.

"This girl—" He points a bony finger, and I focus on the scar on that same hand. The scar I gave him. My triumph and perhaps now my undoing. "*This girl is a curse.* She has brought death down on your heads! She turned your girls against you, against us all!" He sweeps his finger to Charlotte and Hélène, Clara, even Belle, who flinches back from it.

I'm surprised at how calm I am. How little my usual fear grips me in a situation where I see no way out. This priest will spin his lies. These brutal men will do their brutal worst. And I will have lost. Because all my power came from secrets, and now the secrets are not secret anymore. There is no ice to carve my fingernails through this time. No cliff to scramble back up. No way for Clara to pull me to safety with a branch.

I suppose that means I'm accepting my fate. I am—for the first time—not fighting.

The priest goes on, bony finger skyward now. "She is"—he pauses for dramatic effect—"a seductress! She tried—unsuccessfully—to seduce *even me!*"

The words knock into my calm and smash it to pieces. Fury rises in its place. "I seduced you?" I scream the words, my first of the confrontation. "That scar on your hand is proof of your own guilt! I bit you when you tried to touch me!"

He laughs, and my skin grows hot with the indignation that sound scrapes across every part of me.

"The lies of an unfaithful woman shall not harm us, men! For a prostitute is a deep pit!" He turns his face to the sky as thunder shudders, closer now. He's quoting scripture. You can tell by the change in his tone, the formality of the language. "Like a bandit, she lies in wait! Her feet go down to death; her steps lay hold of hell."

I tighten my fist on my pike, hold it in front of me.

So I am the villain, then? I am your monster? Then you will find me a terrible monster indeed. If this man is about to burn me, then I will end him on my way into ash.

After all, I've killed a man before.

This time, the images my mind flashes at me don't make me sick or small or scared. They make me *powerful.*

Perhaps it doesn't matter that I didn't want to kill a man.

That it wasn't on purpose. Maybe *I am their villain.* The monster under their bed, the danger lurking in the night. I am the ghost, the witch, the darkness. I took their daughters, their sisters, their support, their comfort. I took their sense of safety.

I—we—took their power.

Power.

I realize it then, my body filling with the satisfaction of it. *We changed everything.*

Even if they kill me now, they know that they are not safe.

That girls have tearing claws and sharpened teeth. Feet that run, hands that steal.

We are the beasts who creep through the night, striking fear like ice into hearts and limbs. We are the monsters with burning eyes, watching their every move. The ghosts who will haunt them even if we're gone.

The beast is the prickle of hair standing straight up on your neck. The certainty that eyes are watching you from the forest as you tend your sheep. And we have slid into the nightmare beside her.

We are the goose bumps. We are the eyes watching.

Watching.

Waiting.

To strike.

41

I SMILE THEN—A FERAL, ANIMAL GRIN. TEETH CLENCHED IN warning, not warmth.

"If I am what you say, you should be more afraid of me than you are." For the first time, perhaps ever, I command all the attention of this group of men—and not because they are the predators, but because *I might be.*

I let their silence hang in between us as lightning arcs through the sky.

"What are you doing?" Clara murmurs just behind me to my left.

I hold my pike out toward the men but turn my face to her. My voice is soft when I ask the question, light enough to keep anyone from overhearing. "I want to do something reckless again. But this time I won't do it without asking you. Will you let me save you this time? Will you run and not turn back?"

"BLEAAA," my lamb screams as if in on the point.

Clara's chin trembles and her eyes are full of tears as she reaches out to grasp the hands of Charlotte and Hélène and then nods, firmly. She will run. She will save them. She will—more important to me than anything else—save herself this time.

"Get ready to run," I whisper.

I turn back to the men, my expression flinty, my knuckles clutched white around my pike.

"You never wondered why the beast doesn't eat sheep?" I lean into their fear now. "Because she is a shepherdess."

The crowd—once ready to mob me—looks uncertain now. I raise my pike and swing it in an arc, following it with my gaze. "If I am what you say I am and you touch me or these girls, do you think I will allow you to go on living?"

The priest starts to speak, but I cut him off, my voice booming, stronger than I ever thought it could be. There's no fear here, only fury. "You said so yourself, sir." I address those words to the priest directly. "*You* said that this beast is God's avenging angel. Not the devil's. *God's* punishment for our sin."

I send up a silent apology to God for the blasphemy, but if God is good, then I hope He doesn't mind it. I smack the pike's dull end against the ground for emphasis and watch a satisfying flinch shudder through the group.

"If I am God's retribution, then God is the one who hid these girls from you. God is the one who judges your actions"—I point my pike at the priest—"and your actions"—I slice through the air to point at Eugénie's brother—"and your lack of action"—I swing the pike around at the rest.

Thunder growls and lightning flashes, the storm closer now.

"If you touch these girls, may God have mercy on your souls."

The priest looks like he's about to explode, his own words turned on him, driving away his speech. The rest of the crowd looks unsettled, their anger replaced by fear and uncertainty. What's true? Am I angel or devil? Am I pure enough to bite your bullets or evil enough to tear out your necks? I can see in their eyes that they do not know.

When someone finally finds his voice, it's not loud, but it is demanding. "If you are what you say you are, prove it."

Of course I cannot. I cannot shape-shift into a creature that I am not. I cannot call it. I cannot show them witchcraft when I am not actually a witch. And so this game will soon be over.

But I motion to the girls behind me. This is the plan. This is the point. I cannot run now, *but they can*.

I bluff my bargain at the man who spoke. "They will go, and I will show you my truth."

Surprisingly, he nods.

Surprisingly, I still have that much power, even in a lie. Even just as the lie is about to fall to pieces.

"Go." I turn and hold Clara's gaze one last time. I try to memorize her, the delicate upward arc of eyelashes, the gentle slope of a nose, the soft curve of lips. Fear, relief, and determination flicker across her face in quick succession.

"Forever and ever, amen." We mouth the words in unison.

Then she's gone. Into the forest with the two girls we decided to save. The circle parts to let them through. Not safe yet, but closer to it with every moment this mob gives me. Every moment I can wring from them.

Louis edges around to help them into the woods, and I am so glad he's here.

They run. I can hear their footfalls, even over a thick rumble of thunder.

Lightning arcs through a deepening blue sky.

I raise my arms, buying time. Tilt my face to the heavens. Feel the first raindrop, cold and stark on my cheek.

If I have one last act, it will be this. Buying as much time as I can.

I scream into the air.

42

THAT IS THE MOMENT EUGÉNIE CRASHES THROUGH THE CIR-
cle, knocking two men to their knees.

In her arms, a writhing, golden tangle of limbs objects to being manhandled, squealing pitifully into the night.

A cub.

Eugénie didn't leave. She didn't run *away.* She ran *to.* The den we found. The babies we stumbled upon. Something catches in my throat at the realization. She came back for me. It's not only Clara who loves me, who is willing to put herself on the line for me. We girls are here for each other. All of us. Clara saved me first and most, but Belle came for me too, and now Eugénie. My father may have left me to claw myself out of danger, but these girls . . . they never have and never would and never will.

Perhaps the knowledge was there before, buried somewhere under the fear. But now I know it so bone-deep, feel the truth in my very soul: I am not alone. I have never been alone.

Around us, men step backward, jostling into each other. Some gasp. Others hold tighter to whatever they brought with them—pikes and rocks and knives and a couple of muskets.

"Mon Dieu!" someone breathes.

"Oh la vache."

"God's wounds." The true blasphemy comes out of the priest's own mouth.

My mind scrambles to catch up with whatever plan Eugénie's hatched. Has she brought it here to trade the real beast for my life? To prove that we are connected to these creatures? Or—

The baby wails, high and mournful. A child's cry for its mother and—at the same time—an unearthly thing. It is us, and it is not us.

The clearing seems to hold its breath. The pikes stand frozen. The angry shouts have retreated into their throats. The blasphemy silenced. And then the silence is ripped to shreds.

My question answers itself with a bone-rattling, bowel-loosening, gut-churning roar. So loud. So *near.*

Eugénie took a baby.

Mama is angry.

Eugénie has brought me the beast.

43

WETNESS SPREADS ACROSS THE TROUSERS OF THE MAN NEAR-
est me. He's pissed himself with the realness of it. The realness
of *her.*

The beast coming for her baby.

Before she even arrives, he runs. Then I smell her—blood
and musk and death. I hear her, not just the roar but the smashing, slamming sound of an animal crashing through forest, no
longer caring if it's heard. This is a defensive strike, not a stalking.

And I see her—all fangs and claws and paws the size of a
man's head. She could tear you apart, and she could crush you,
and it's no wonder people say she can kill with a glance.

She crashes into the circle, tearing through two men who
accidentally stood in her way. Their screams are guttural, elon-
gated. They go on and on as one man tries to press his skin back
onto his side and the other writhes on the ground, blood turning
it to mud.

Lightning sparks through the sky, and the beast flies to her baby where Eugénie has dropped it. She turns to face those who remain, ears flat to her thick, massive head, lips and snout curled menacingly. She screams—roars—her rage.

Everyone else is fleeing, running any direction they can. Their terror is so real it's almost another presence in the clearing.

I knew it before, but I take it in again: this creature is no wolf. She is something *other*. Something foreign. A wildness different from our own.

She doesn't belong here.

Belle's voice from days ago floats back to me in the space after the roar, the paused heartbeat. *"Everyone who's anyone has an exotic pet."*

I am certain now. This is what she was. Just a larger, more terrifying version of Jean the macaw. Someone's trinket, proof of their riches, proof that they are somebody.

Ripped from a world where she fit, dragged across oceans, across spaces so vast I cannot imagine them. Torn from the place where her coat blended into the scenery, her kind found company, her thick shoulders fit between trees.

She growls again, darting forward in fake attack, driving the last lingering men from the circle and into the trees. These men who thought they were brave, who have been bragging about how they'll kill her and become rich.

It's violent, the feeling that rips through me. She didn't deserve this. She was torn from her world, thrust into ours. How could we expect anything but violence in the wake of that? Violence meeting violence. Just like the village men and us.

314

She roars again, and this time her eyes find mine and lock on.

She is just like us. She is violence and fear and fury *created by men.* A mother protecting her cubs. It's no different—me slashing through flesh to take down a man who would hurt my girls, and her devouring us all to defend her babies, feed them, make them safe in this alien place.

She is monster. We are monster.

Another revelation shakes through me. We are the beasts, yes. But in a way I didn't realize before. This is a mother protecting her cubs, an act of fierceness not out of selfishness or evil but love.

Love.

The source of our own villainy. The protective instinct that sent me over a cliff, into a cave, into the dirt where I ripped a dress to shreds and drenched it in blood. Staged a girl's death to save her life. Then another. Then another.

This is a violence forged deep in our hearts, a violence that protects, saves, shields.

The stories about her are wrong. She is not God's wrath. She is not evil. She is not the devil.

She is love. And she is pain. And she is survival.

And what did we expect her to do? She's protecting her own just like we are. We invited our own death to this clearing.

She growls, low in her throat, her muscles bunching. Above us, thunder claps.

The village has fled, and it's only me and Eugénie and the beast and Belle—frozen against a tree at the clearing's edge, too frightened or mesmerized to run.

"Lioness," she whispers barely loud enough to hear. And I know she's naming the beast. Belle who has seen more of the world than I. Belle who has been to the menageries—watched the servals and the macaws, the monkeys and the lions.

Lioness.

"Go," I tell Belle. "Run."

I hold my pike to the beast, and she snarls, her baby whimpering behind her.

Belle doesn't run, though. And I know instinctively that she cannot. Her legs are not listening to her mind. She is pressed against that tree for better or worse now. Her life or death in my hands or the lioness's claws.

The lion cub doesn't have the same problem. It scuttles away into the undergrowth, hides itself from view. I have no idea whether its instincts will lead it back to its den or if it is only hiding, but it is no danger to us. Too small, too clumsy, too young.

My hand tightens around my flimsy pike, and Eugénie moves to my side, a sharp rock raised.

Fleetingly, I wonder how I can fight this creature when I understand her so much. When so much of my heart feels that we are the same, actually.

But I will.

I am.

Because I'm fighting for lives as much as she is. Neither of us will stop. Neither of us will give up until we are cold and gone, only bones and flesh with no breath, no life.

I am going to die here. Or she is.

Her body lowers, streamlined, and I know she is about to

lunge. I brace myself, ready myself to put pike to neck as I did with a knife and a man.

Before I can, though, a scream tears through the clearing. Not of terror, but rage.

Louis crashes onto the scene first, knife in one fist, rock in another. He throws the rock with shocking force. It hits the beast on her side, and she yowls in protest and fury. Hélène is next, her rock finding its mark on the beast's hip. Charlotte—tiny against the hulking shape—finds her stone's mark on the beast's face.

And Clara—Clara! My heart stops to see her. Sad and relieved and, more than anything, scared. Clara was supposed to run this time. Clara was supposed to save herself.

The creature roars again and lunges and, without even knowing where the beast has aimed her fury, Clara is the one I throw myself in front of.

44

THE LIONESS CHOOSES THE PERSON SHE MUST THINK IS THE
biggest threat. The largest body in the group. The one who
holds her gaze.

Louis.

She's on him like a flash, but Louis is smart enough to duck,
and her jaws close around air instead of neck, even as she rakes
her claws down his arm. He cries out but manages to aim his
knife and cause some damage of his own on her left paw. My
pike makes contact, too, with the beast's shoulder.

The massive cat lands heavily, an agitated, pained scream is-
suing from her throat, but she lunges for Louis again, and I can
see why she has a reputation for being bulletproof. This cat is
not a quitter. Blood mars her shoulder and pools where her foot
lands, and yet still she comes.

This time, as Louis's hands go up in self-defense, a rebel yell erupts from Charlotte, who has another rock in hand. She's gotten so close without me even noticing, and instead of throwing the rock, she dives in front of Louis and rams the sharp end of the stone into the lioness's face. She must be aiming for an eye, but in the confusion of movement, the rock goes into the cat's mouth instead.

Unable to stop its momentum, the beast knocks into Charlotte and Louis and the three go tumbling to the ground—the knife skittering from Louis's hand across the dirt now turning slowly back to mud in the light rain.

I thrust my pike into the beast's shoulder again as she falls, and she turns to swipe at me, catching my forearm with her claws. The wound burns, a dizzying, heart-wrenching pain that pulls an involuntary "mon Dieu" from my lips. There's so much blood; my hand is immediately slick with it, the wood of the pike soaking it up. My heart slams against my chest in protest.

On the ground, Charlotte and Louis struggle to untangle themselves from the angry cat. She darts her head for Louis's neck, but once again Charlotte is his defender. A tiny, unexpectedly wild thing.

"You cannot have him!" she screams as she throws her tiny body over his face. "I couldn't save Pascal, but I can save Louis!" The words are desperate and then swallowed by a more guttural sound as the cat makes contact with its teeth against her back.

Then, before any of us can react, Charlotte's shoulder is in the lion's mouth and the beast is dragging her across the clearing to the gap in the trees from which she came.

We scramble after her, Louis struggling to push himself from the ground, Clara the farthest from where the cat has chosen to run. I fight against the black spots dotting my vision, the way the world is starting to sway, as I rush after it. I didn't rescue Charlotte from one beast just to let another take her. I didn't fake her death so that she could really die.

Eugénie gets to her first and throws herself at the cat, smashing heavily into its side and slamming a fist—empty of rocks or pikes—into the back of its skull.

Still, it holds on. Keeps going. Charlotte weeping and screaming, the sound slicing through my very soul.

I reach them next and thrust my pike as hard as I can into the cat's side.

This time, it releases Charlotte, who falls to the ground and curls into a half moon of pain.

Eugénie punches it in the nose as it snarls at me and swipes her, catching her in the hip and throwing her several feet into a tree, where she collapses at the base.

The cat reaches for Charlotte again. God, does this creature never give up? Never stop?

Do you? My inner beast roars.

I thrust my pike again, this time catching her in the chest, and I see Clara's pike slice into view, meeting mine at the beast's breastbone. The cat backs away then, hissing and jumping toward us, then back again. Her lips are curled, her mouth all teeth.

My head swims, and all I can think is that she isn't going to stop. She'll just keep coming. Whether we brought her cub here and made this defendable territory or whether she's just that mad or just that hungry. She's not stopping.

I lean down to the ground, lift Charlotte into my arms—my injured arm screaming at me to stop—and start to slowly back away. Perhaps if I can just make it to the barn, I can close us inside. I have a strong feeling that this enormous, muscle-bound cat will operate like a barn cat. If I run, she will chase. If I back away, perhaps she will decide that the danger has passed. That the best course of action is to find her baby and go.

Clara catches my eye as I take the first step back, keeping the cat in my sights. She seems to understand what I'm doing and pulls a still-dazed Eugénie to her feet. Louis has reached us now and joins them, supporting Eugénie and taking steps back in tandem, all of us together.

One step. A growl.

Two steps. A false charge, and Clara thrusts her pike menacingly forward.

Three steps. I notice in my periphery that Belle has disappeared, and I hope—fleetingly—that she found the courage to close herself in the cottage or the barn. Safer than fleeing by herself through the woods.

Four steps. Anger spikes through me again when I realize that there's a reason I have to worry about Belle. *Lafont abandoned his daughter.* Fled through the woods and left her to fend for herself. It's a gut punch, a reminder of my own father. And the first time in a long time that I've thought perhaps Belle and I really do have some things in common.

Five steps. The swaying feeling worsens, and I stumble.

Sensing weakness, perhaps, the beast roars forward once more, spitting and kicking up mud as she slides across the ground. With Charlotte in my arms, my defenses are lowered. I brace for impact, ready my body to curl around the smaller girl.

But no.

Louis grabs my pike from where it hangs loosely in one hand under Charlotte's bulk and thrusts it with perfect aim, catching the cat once more in the chest.

She faces him, furious, and roars once more. But her body language has shifted now. She's decided we're too much trouble. Like the lightning that flashes so briefly, so suddenly, above us, she turns and runs. To the side of the clearing where her baby disappeared. Then, a pause, and I think I see her lift it in her mouth before she runs again.

I was wrong. It wasn't her or me today. Death was not the only option here. Standing our ground was.

Still, we back toward the cottage until Clara reaches the door and flings it open.

Inside, Belle stands pressed against a wall, her face still the white of bone and tooth. More than half the sheep are here, too, complaining loudly.

Black spots dance in my vision; the blood runs down my arm. I can feel my heartbeat in my neck, my throat, my temples, and as I pass through the door to safety, the spots in my vision expand into one—and suck me down into darkness.

45

IN THE SPACE BETWEEN ASLEEP AND AWAKE, I WATCH EVERY evil possibility unfold. I fall from the cliff two weeks ago, egg-cracked, broken-backed onto the rocks below. I fold under the pressure of Charlotte's father's hand at my throat. I stab him, watch the blood flow freely. And I'm back in the clearing, facing a lioness defending her cub.

I sputter back into reality with a rebel yell, a wild thing hell-bent on survival, half sure I'm still in the fight.

But around me there is no fighting. Just a handful of teen-agers putting each other back together.

Clara has used the bandages we made from my old stay, wrapped them tightly against my forearm to stop the bleeding. By the look on her face, I can tell I've lost more blood than she'd like. I am not all right.

Still, I am aware now, leaned against the wall and feeling the fuzziness in my head retreat. Unfortunately, with that retreat comes pain. Everywhere. A throbbing at my temples. A dryness in my throat. The splinters in my face back to pulsing. My arm hot as coals, the rest of me ice-cold, shivering.

"You came back," I whisper, all of the fear of Clara's return hitting me anew. "You were supposed to run."

She presses a hand to my forehead. "Louis turned back, and Charlotte ran after him, then Hélène. I couldn't leave them."

"We owe you a garden," I murmur.

"What?"

"You said if you didn't have to save everyone all the time, you'd garden and learn to weave and fall asleep in my arms every night. The third thing is the easy one, but we owe you a garden now—and weaving lessons."

Clara laughs, and the sound is the best thing I've heard since this all started.

"Full bellies and warm weather, too. We all owe you." I press my hand shakily to her warm cheek. She's so alive. So gloriously, gratefully alive. And somehow still here with me, despite everything. "Forever and ever, amen." I murmur the words again and hope she can feel the new meaning in them. Not just that I'll be with her, but that I'll do whatever I can to make sure gardens and a full belly and the space to weave instead of heal are hers, too.

Hélène drags blankets over, and they drape them across me. "Why is she shivering so much?"

"It's the blood loss," Clara says, pressing her hand to my forehead.

A few paces away, Belle has unrooted herself enough to

kneel at Eugénie's side. The latter girl is dazed and bruised and cradling her shoulder in an unsettling way. Beside them, Louis gently pulls fabric away from Charlotte's back, washing the place where the lioness's teeth punctured tender skin. He's removed his shirt to use as a washrag and tends her as if she's his own child.

The tenderness in it takes my breath away. It's the tenderness I longed for from my own father, the tenderness Belle—abandoned now—deserved from hers. I'm sorry for every uncharitable thing I've ever thought about Louis.

"You saved me," he whispers to the tiny girl in front of him. "You saved me, ma chérie. Merci."

I'm so focused on the tender moment unfolding before me that it takes me a moment to understand the words when Clara finally speaks. "We have to leave."

"But the muleteer isn't back for days," I say, foolishly, mind still fuzzy.

Clara laughs without humor. "Those men will be back, as soon as they feel brave enough. They'll murder us. We can't stay a minute longer than necessary."

She's right. Claiming to control the beast, to be the beast, to be a witch—it was all just to delay their wrath. But if I am the beast, they want me dead. If I control it, they want me dead. And if I'm liar, they want me dead.

"We don't all have to go," I answer, nodding my chin weakly at Louis and Belle. "Belle is safe no matter what. Her father's position protects her. Louis, too. They don't know he's involved, and besides, he's a boy."

Louis gently replaces Charlotte's dress over the makeshift

dressings he's placed on her wounds. Tears jump to my eyes again, my body and heart so exhausted that every tiny kindness seems insurmountably huge.

"I'm going. Of course I'm going." Louis is definitive.

We all look to Belle, and she licks her lips, fear still written over every feature, all her normal bravado melted away. "Where are you going?"

I share a look with Clara, asking silently: Do we trust her? Can we tell her? But Eugénie has already decided the answer is yes. "South. We're going to my aunt in the south."

Belle takes a deep breath and nods. "I'm not going, but maybe I can help."

"Help how?" Louis asks, Charlotte now in his arms, burying her head in his chest for comfort. Hélène kneels beside them and runs her fingers through her younger sister's hair.

"I can get you a cart."

Cart. Such a small, everyday word—and yet it sparks hope like fire in my chest. It will make us faster, make it possible for those who cannot walk or need a rest.

Louis's eyes spark, too. "I can get us some food."

Eugénie sits upright, straightening, her eyes full of purpose even as one of them is bruising. "And weapons. There are weapons in the shed!"

"Clara's right. We have to go now," I say, because it is the only answer.

We go before they regroup. We go before they make a plan. We go as we have always gone: under the cover of the lioness. We go while they still expect that we are dead at her feet.

46

WE WALK THE SHEEP TRAIL TOGETHER, PIKES AND KNIVES and cooking pots clutched in bloodied, bruised fingers. But the only sounds around us are the light patter of rain, thunder moving away in the distance, twilight bugs singing their croaky mating songs.

I don't know how I know, but I know that the beast will not come for us again. She is not like men, vindictive and scared and convinced we are evil. She is like the rest of the forest—beautiful and dangerous and trying to survive. We scared her away the first time because she didn't want to fight five or six people, a couple dozen angry sheep. And the second time she only fought because we took her cub.

I still understand her, even as she's left me a weak, bloody, battered mess.

She will not come for us now. Not when she can hide away

with her babies, lick her wounds, catch a rabbit for their supper with little fight.

The others still dart their eyes at the forest, but I stare straight ahead. The trees bathed in the deepening blue of twilight, their shapes slowly disappearing into the dark of night. The exact place you might expect to die. The exact place I don't believe I will.

Clara holds me upright, my whole body strangely weak—from the blood loss, she says. My legs feel like they aren't my own, but I order them onward. Everyone else can walk, though Eugénie still clutches her shoulder where Clara and Louis worked together to wrench it back into socket before we left. If I hadn't been so saturated with screams for the past hour, hers would have undone me.

Mémé is lucid when we open the door and tell her to come with us. She doesn't even ask why. Simply looks relieved to see us, kisses me hard on the forehead, gathers what she can carry, and follows.

Because there is no option for her to stay anymore. When they cannot find us, they will look for someone else to blame. And the woman who raised two of us will be at the top of their list.

As we walk, Mémé slips into step beside Belle, somehow knowing without us saying so that the girl isn't coming. "Will you take a message to Amani for me? I need her to know I didn't leave her on purpose."

The second part of our journey is more dangerous. While the rest of us skirt the village on a lesser-used path, the sheep clustered around us like so many dandelions, Belle and Louis disappear into the village and return quickly, quietly. Belle is pushing a cart full of blankets and a musket. The image would have been hilarious to me just two weeks ago. Belle, who has never done a day of labor in her life, pushing a dirty, heavy wooden cart over cobblestones and up little hills. She is more than I expected her to be.

Behind her, Louis appears with another cart, a satchel full of food, skins of water.

Belle hands her cart off to Eugénie, and the two girls embrace.

"When you leave Mende, tell my brother Saint Rita sends her regards." Eugénie raises a cheeky eyebrow.

"What's she the saint of?" Belle asks.

Eugénie grins. "The impossible. He told me once that I'd never be rid of him. That it was impossible. Rita's my patron saint."

Belle turns to me then, her eyes downcast. "Merci."

"Yeah," I whisper.

"And I'm sorry."

I never expected to hear that from her, and even though Belle and I still wouldn't be friends even if she was coming or I was staying, there's something about those words that calms an old, aching wound. That closes out a chapter.

I didn't realize how much I needed them.

"Thank you," I say, and mean it.

And then Belle is turning on her toes and walking fast back into the village, and the rest of us point our faces toward the old dirt road where the muleteer first arrived here coming from the south.

Before we round the corner that will take us out of sight of Mende's pretty stone houses and arching stone bridge, two more familiar faces appear. The pranksters. Louis's cadre.

He grins for the first time in hours, goes to them. They all pound each other on the backs. And then he paints his face with fake worry. "Think you boys can raise hell without me? All our good ideas came from me."

"Shut it! You know I'm the source of the best jokes." Denisot swats Louis playfully on the shoulder.

"Yeah, well, give the soldiers a special kind of hell from me. And"—Louis glances over his shoulder at Eugénie—"Eugénie's brother could use some hell himself. If that man knows a single day of peace, it's too much."

Denisot fake-salutes. "Ah, that asshole? I think we can come up with some ways to make his life pretty miserable."

"I'll miss you," Louis answers, and then the three circle up in a hug and duck their heads so that the tops of them are touching.

"Brothers forever," someone says.

"Brothers forever," the others echo.

Then, like Belle, they turn and go. And we—a gaggle of sheep, two carts, a grandmother, five girls, and a cheeky prankster—turn the corner and leave Mende and all it means for us behind.

EPILOGUE

TWO MONTHS LATER

JEAN-JACQUES COULDN'T BELIEVE HE'D FINALLY MADE IT TO Gévaudan! Finally made it *as a journalist*! The most important story of the age, and it was going to be *his*. The Beast of Gévaudan. Murderous, slavering, evil creature. The first news story that had been making papers not just in France but also in Germany! Britain! Belgium!

Last week, rumor said they'd killed it. This week, he would find out what it was—once and for all.

Jean-Jacques was going to be *famous*.

He paid the muleteer who'd brought him and marched straight to the first door he saw, knocking until a little old lady—her skin almost as white as the cloud of hair escaping from her head covering—answered.

He began without preamble. "They say they killed the beast this last week, madame. Can you tell me what it looked like?"

She paused, taking him in before responding. "It was a girl."

Oh dear. They'd told him the peasants were superstitious, but this really was the height of ridiculousness. *A girl* ravaged the countryside and killed all her fellows?

Jean-Jacques took on a conciliatory tone. "Madame, you are mistaken. There was a *beast* here. Was he a wolf? Did you see him?"

Irritation flickered across her weathered face. "I told you, it was a girl. Now leave me be."

He gave her one of those smiles that felt like a mask on his face, no real emotion under it. Well, he supposed that was what he got for choosing a door at random. Someone here would be reasonable—perhaps just not *everyone.* He'd try another house.

"Thank you for your time." He tipped his hat.

At the next house, an older man—lightly tanned and with a friendly face—answered Jean's knock. "Sir, I'm here to discover what beast has been plaguing your village. Your neighbor seems to think the beast was a girl all along." Jean laughed, hoping it would put the man on his side, loosen his lips.

But the man only looked thoughtful for a moment, then shook his head. "No, not a girl."

Thank God, someone with some sense.

The older man raised his eyebrows. "There was *more than one* girl."

Frustration rose in Jean then. Were all these people fools?

"Sir, you cannot be serious. They killed *an animal* here. I am asking you what it was."

The man shook his head again. "I know nothing about that. But the Beast of Gévaudan—*that I know.* They were our girls."

They were our girls. Something about the phrasing sent a shiver up Jean's spine. This was one of those villages that thought wolves were shape-shifters, then. He'd heard about people like that.

He tried another house. Then another. But the agreement in Mende seemed complete. The beast was a werewolf. The werewolf was a girl. Or five girls. Or ten. The girls controlled the creature, or they were the creature. They killed a man. They killed ten men. They were witches. They were ghosts.

Jean was irritated beyond reckoning. He paid ten whole livres to get here—and for what? Fool peasants! This was supposed to be the story of the century. His big break! His first news story!

What was he supposed to write now?

HISTORICAL ENDNOTE

While this story is fiction and I've taken liberties with the time-lines of real historical events (condensing *a lot* of true events into a much shorter-than-real-life timeline), the one hundred to two hundred brutal attacks attributed to the Beast of Gévaudan are very real.

From 1764 to 1767, the region was plagued by reports of a wolflike animal (with some very non-wolfy characteristics) attacking shepherds and villagers across the wild, impoverished region of Gévaudan. Things eventually got so bad that the beast became one of Europe's first cross-border news stories, with papers in London, Germany, and elsewhere picking up the tales of the ferocious killer. Unsurprisingly, this caught the attention of King Louis XV, who sent out his best hunters (Duhamel and then the d'Ennevals, among others) to lead the search for the dangerous animal and offered staggering amounts of money for its corpse.

In September 1765, the king's gunbearer brought down a very large wolf and strutted back to the capital to show it off to the king. But while the monarchy decided the whole affair was over, the death toll kept rising—until a second animal was killed in June 1767. This animal was not preserved nor definitively identified.

Over the hundreds of years since the terror receded, there have been many theories about what the beast was. Large wolves, packs of wolves, and wolf-dog hybrids are some of the more vanilla theories. Human serial killers training animals to hunt for them (or even dressed as wolves themselves and cannibalizing their fellows) is one of the wildest.

And, of course, no story like this would be complete without supernatural speculation: The beast was a demon. The beast was God's wrath. The beast was a werewolf, a shape-shifter. The beast was the devil himself.

More likely, perhaps, is the explanation of the menageries.

Because that's another true thing in this book: at that time, the richest people in France were *obsessed* with nonnative animals. Lions and tigers and hyenas, oh my. Large menageries imported animals for public beast fights. Other importers brought in monkeys and parrots as pets for the nobility. And it would have been utterly unsurprising for these incautious people to lose a beast or two.

In fact, during the hundred-year period when these imports were particularly popular, there appear to have been *quite a few* strange beasts killing people across France. This particular beast was simply the most prolific and has retained its fame longer than the others.

This is the theory I wanted to explore in this book: a young lion escaped from an incautious noble. Another rich asshole who accidentally killed hundreds for their own fun. The Tiger King, if you will, of the era.

If you're wondering how it's possible that someone wouldn't have identified a lion as a lion, I strongly suggest looking up medieval and early modern drawings of lions—chaotic things that look *nothing* like a real lion. It's also worth noting that the last beast that was killed in Gévaudan, after which the killings seemed to stop, was examined by Duhamel, who proclaimed (loosely translated, emphasis mine): "I believe that you will think, as I do, that this animal is a monster *whose father was a lion;* only God knows what its mother was."

In the end, no one truly knows what the beast was, so we are all free to embrace our theory of choice. If you'd like to learn more about the real history behind the beast, I suggest the book *Beast: Werewolves, Serial Killers, and Man-Eaters: The Mystery of the Monsters of Gévaudan,* by Gustavo Sánchez Romero and S. R. Schwalb. And if you happen to be in France, a visit to the free Le Musée du Gévaudan (Gévaudan Museum) in Mende is never a bad way to while away a few hours.

ACKNOWLEDGMENTS

Since I just made my characters face their fears for several hundred pages, perhaps it's appropriate for me to start my acknowledgments with a fear of my own: I was afraid of being a one-hit wonder. I was afraid that I'd sold one original book (*The Wicked Unseen*—go read it), and I wouldn't be able to sell another. That perhaps my success had been a fluke, a passing fancy, something this oft-fickle industry wouldn't want to duplicate.

This book proved that fear wrong. And for that, I have two people in particular to thank: Paige Terlip, my agent, for her unending support, superfast turnarounds, and even-keeled advice. And my editor, Alison Romig, who believed in me and believed in this story enough to give it its chance. You are both a dream to work with. I hope we have many more books to come.

Of course, it takes more than the three of us to shove my books through the jaws of the monster that is publishing. Special thanks to early readers (Emily Varga, Lani Frank, Anna Sortino, Daniela Petrova, L. C. Milburn, and Chandra Fisher) and late-round readers (Abby, Zoë). To Scream Town for being my safe place. To the No Drama Zone for being *unsafe* for anyone who isn't us. To David De la Rosa—brainstormer extraordinaire and my ride-or-die forever. To the 2k23s for an excellent debut year. To street teamers Emily "Big Booty" Tyler, Lisa Bailey, Anjedah Shamim, and Sky Evans. And to Lindy, who inspired a lot of birb shenanigans.

I'm also deeply grateful for Andrei—who holds my words as if they are my very heart (which they are)—and for Nicola, quintessential Scorpio. Also: Inês, Kerry-Anne, Raele, and Katherine.

The rest of the village that made this book possible: brilliant sensitivity readers Keshav Kant and A (any lingering sensitivity issues are my own and not on them); talented cover artist Jorge Mascarenhas; cover designer Trisha Previte; interior designer Cathy Bobak; publicist Sarah Lawrenson; copy editor Colleen Fellingham; Alison Kolani; managing editor Tamar Schwartz; and production manager C. J. Han.

I'd also like to thank the free museum in Mende, France, and the lovely folks who work there; the pilgrim accommodations that allowed me to book a bed with my little dog while I was hiking through the region for research (especially the ones who served wine with their dinners!); the TikTok sheep farmers who share the lives of their cheeky little fluffballs; and the *Ologies* podcast, which taught me that butterflies drink blood.

Finally, *no thanks* to the patriarchy, the families who should be our safe spaces and aren't, and Uber Eats customer service. May you all get paper cuts in inconvenient places. XOXO.

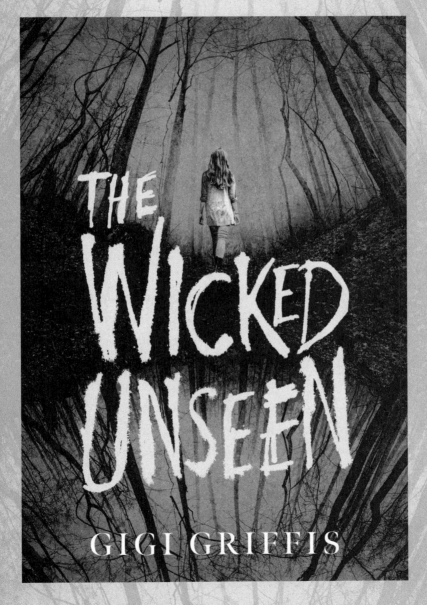

THE WICKED UNSEEN

GIGI GRIFFIS

ABOUT THE AUTHOR

GIGI GRIFFIS writes edgy, feminist historical stories for adults and teens, including *The Wicked Unseen* and *The Empress* (as seen on Netflix). She's a sucker for little-known histories, "unlikable" female characters, and all things Europe. After almost ten years of seminomadic life, she now lives in Portugal with an opinionated Yorkie mix named Luna and a collection of very nerdy books. When she was hiking through Gévaudan, she *just might have seen* the beast crossing her path in the distance. Fortunately, it did not eat her.

GIGIGRIFFIS.COM